GRUFF

ROBERT J. ALVES

Gruff

Book design by Sadie Butterworth-Jones
www.luneviewpublishing.co.uk

Paperback ISBN: 979-8-9873646-2-8
Hardback ISBN: 979-8-9873646-3-5
eBook ISBN: 979-8-9873646-4-2

FOREWORD

Gruff is about an older reclusive character, discarded by his family and community, as he surrenders in despair, accepting that his circumstances are deserved and that he is born for the sole existence of all the ridicule that he continually received.

From this simple beginning, he will be brought to an absolutely amazing adventure, seeking the meaning and purpose of this life from God, His Creator.

The interactions among the characters of this book make for enjoyable reading, and there is a clear message of the purpose and sovereignty of why God created both man and the animal kingdom.

The book clearly defines the gospel of Christ and how God moves in His majestic power over the affairs of His wonderful creation.

We are more like Gruff oftentimes that we would like to admit. *Gruff* has a clear message to all of us and that we are here for a far greater purpose that we oftentimes are not remotely aware of.

Dr. Harley Howard
PhD Ministry
PhD Christian Education

CONTENTS

Revelation 5:13 (KJV)

"And every creature which is in heaven, and on the earth, and under the earth, and such as are in the sea, and all that are in them, heard I saying, Blessing, and honour, and glory, and power, be unto him that sitteth upon the throne, and unto the Lamb for ever and ever."

1. THIS IS HOME

"Why is he so hideous looking? I, I honestly don't think I can face my friends, or the community with this, this, monstrosity!" A female voice echoed through Gruff's tiny ears.

"Why is he so, big? This certainly isn't natural, what did you do?" Came another voice, much lower in tone and harshness.

"I didn't do anything that. . ." the female voice started to say.

"Well, he is NO good to us being a total freak, but. . ." the voice paused, "maybe he will be..."The male voice suddenly got cut off.

"There is no, 'maybe this,' or 'maybe that.' You KNOW what needs to be done!" the female squalled.

"Well, I'm sure that it probably has something to do with the crowd you insist on hanging out with all day," said the male.

"That has NOTHING to do with it!" the female voice whined. "The grass is no greener from this field to that!" the female argued, now stomping her feet. "I tell you this, if YOU don't do something about this, I certainly will!" she continued, yelling at the top of her lungs.

"Don't take that tone with me, woman! He is YOUR responsibility. I suggest you stop strutting around like you are some sort of queen and start stepping up and doing some kid rearing for once!" came the male voice.

"Oh no you don't! If I have to raise this kid, then you are going to be involved, all the way to the top of your blasted neck" the female cursed.

Gruff looked up towards the voices but was not able to see anything. "I'm telling you; I don't want him touching me!" Gruff then felt himself being shoved back and forth between the two adults and hit on the head.

As Gruff began to black out, he felt the female spit on him. "I still say that we just leave him out for Aba. . ."

Gruff shook himself awake. He yawned and then drifted in and out of a light sleep. The sun had just begun its journey from behind the mountains, where it would scratch and climb across the valley and then finally onto the plains.

The peaks of the Granite Mountains stretch their shadow out onto the wilderness and then down into the various valleys, stretching and sprawling their way to the horizon. During the spring and through the summer, the sweet grasses, berries, and flowers of the plains grow and give life to all manner of living things.

Gruff yawned again and stretched as he groggily cracked one eye open while the other was held firmly shut by its lid, attempting to protest yet another morning invasion. He lay silent at first and then softly began to grumble with each moment that the shadows inched higher. He could tell by those shadows that he only had about an hour before the warmth of the sun would reach him. However, he could already feel the dread building in his mind as the community started to wake and move about.

The valley came to life, not slowly like a flower opening over the course of a few hours to drink in the morning mist, but rather with the usual instant commotion, ruckus, and constant yelling of the kids, along with their parents, practically on a daily basis.

Gruff flopped over on his bed and tried to get comfortable for at least a few more minutes, "I'm really, really not in the mood for this today." He held both eyes tightly closed now in hopes this day would, just for once, pass him by.

As the area sprang to life, the adults all stood around in their various circles, flapping their lips about absolutely nothing, their heads just as empty as their words. Even though they thought themselves to be scholarly, their high morals and aptitudes were of no value. The entire community had bad attitudes and terrible habits, yet they all thought themselves far superior to anything else around. Their daily chore was pretending not to notice their offspring's obnoxious behavior but, instead, reward their failures. After all, the kids were just a reflection of who THEY were.

One thing the community absolutely prided themselves on and had in common with each other was that they ALL chose Gruff to be their object of total abuse. After all, if HE was the most disgusting thing in the community, then THEY certainly were not responsible for their actions. It was, and always would be, Gruff's fault.

The valley plains were Gruff's home, but he usually just stayed among the sticker and briar bushes. The mountains would have been his playground, but he rarely, if ever, got a chance to interact with anyone, at least in a positive way. For many years, Gruff longed to be a part of the community, regardless of how they treated him, but he was shut out completely from their lives. The mountains, the hills, and valleys were absolutely beautiful, but this had become a horrid, lonely, life for Gruff.

Gruff started life like he was living it now: rough, abused, and devoid of any pleasantries. The fact was that he was well developed, if not extremely overly developed, with perfect physical condition and intelligence, which certainly did not meet the approval of the family, nor the community, for that matter.

He had some sort of oddity that terrified his family and all who saw him, but this was the norm in the community. Things that just weren't understood, or what they considered normal by their ideals, would be treated as outcasts. As a result, Gruff was constantly told by his parents and the community that he would NEVER be anything more than what he was: disgusting, a freak, a vile stain on their lives and their perfect society. Anyone who saw him did not mince words, and they would tell him openly that he should just accept what they say about him as the cold plain truth. In the end, they all just wished he would get out of their sight or, better yet, go somewhere, ANYWHERE, and die.

No hope, no future, and apparently, no life was what Gruff had going for him, according to the world he knew. He was simply crushed in spirit daily, and because of this, Gruff sat, played, if there was such a word, ate, and slept by himself. Yet, through everything, he never completely lost heart. Gruff often wondered when he would lay in the grass to look up at the starry night IF what he was being told was true. He felt to his very bones that there was simply more to his existence, but what exactly, he wasn't sure.

So, Gruff would lay in his bed looking out at the world, and as he watched, the community and life would just walk over him, on him, and past him.

Gruff got up, stretched again, and then sat down exactly where he had just gotten up from. He yawned and looked across the field to where the family had gathered. He watched them playing and eating and running about their day. Slowly Gruff dropped his head and took another mouthful of the sweet spring grasses that were growing and looked up at the goings-on and chewed slowly while he thought.

You see, Gruff was an absolutely huge, dirty, smelly, woolly mess of a mountain goat! He was easily twice the size of any other goat and three times as strong for that matter. As far as goats go, if there was ever a stink, clod of dirt, or muddy mess it was attached to Gruff.

He had finally come to a dangerous time in his life where he was starting to think and believe that what the community told him was probably true, buying into their lies. And, *if what they say is true,* he thought, *then what really was the point of his trying to do ANYTHING?*

He continued chewing and thinking, *if all he was going to be is a stupid waste of an existence, why bother?* And so, he sat alone in all his glorious filth, listening to the constant barrage of insults and suffering the beatings from everyone that could see him, waiting for a death that would free them all, and himself.

Poor Gruff's heart had started to harden and match the sheer toughness of his filthy hide and his very bones and muscles that were now like the granite mountain he lived on. The years of physical, verbal, and mental abuse had, in turn, built a mountain of a broken hearted, lonely creature.

Gruff finally grew tired of where he was, so he walked slowly back up a small hill and over to a rather large patch of sticker and briar bushes, that he actually liked to sleep in. He grunted and flopped to the ground with a thud, his size then tossing up a huge dust cloud that slowly dissipated.

He lowered his head and placed it on his front legs like a pillow. He then looked down to watch some ants moving along hurriedly. From left to right, and right to left, the little insects moved methodically.

Gruff spent many an hour watching life in general, and there was not much that made it past his eye. He looked down "Yep, just like every day." No ant was where they shouldn't be, and not even one was left out of their frantic dance, quickly moving food back to their home.

"You little things certainly have it easy" said Gruff. "All of you working together, no outcasts," he continued, feeling alone and more than a little sorry for himself. "Must be really nice to have a home and be included."

He blew at some of the ants and scattered them, all of which immediately dashed back into their ranks as if nothing had happened.

Just as Gruff began to get comfortable, he let out a soft drawn-out groan and rolled his eyes as he watched several kids approaching him. *Lovely, just lovely. Here we go again. It would be nice to have one, just ONE, single day to myself,* Gruff thought wearily.

I suppose, though, that any interactions with others can be a good thing, right? He thought, closing his eyes, and pretending to be asleep in hopes they would just leave.

"Come on! He's asleep!" snickered Lucas, one of the older kids and their ringleader.

"Ok, get in line," Lucas said excitedly, and they all ran to line up like obedient little soldiers, bony shoulder to scrawny haunch.

As soon as the group had formed, their tails all stood at attention like little furry flags, waiting for further orders from the self-proclaimed leader. Their excitement and tensions began to build, and they shoved momentarily at each other, jockeying for position.

"Alright boys, move forward slowly," their leader spoke, and all the kids walked forward as they were commanded.

"When we are within ten feet, we go!" They all started to giggle with excitement as they continued their advance towards Gruff, who was more than aware of their approach.

The commander raised up on his tiny rear legs, bleating as loudly as he possibly could, and led the charge crashing into Gruff's side, over and over again, each of the little brats tried to outdo each other in seeing who could smash into Gruff the hardest!

When they were younger it was hardly noticeable, thought Gruff. *But now that their little heads are forming stumpy horns, it starts to hurt after a bit. Though, now it's really still more of just an annoyance.*

Gruff could feel the bruises slowly beginning to form on his side and ribs, and with each blow from the little degenerates, he began to yawn and grow tired of this nonsense. Gruff grimaced just a couple times but, just kept repeating in his mind, *Just endure it for a bit longer and they will lose interest and move on to something else.*

Unfortunately, the kids didn't lose interest, and they all began to jump on top of Gruff and use him as a springboard to kick wildly into the air, shrieking and screaming the vile words that they had learned from hearing the same filthy, disgusting things from the mouths of their parents.

Two of the larger kids, Lucas and Oliver, in an effort to show off to their followers, began to devise a new game and dared each other to play. So, they began to leap from Gruff's back and onto his head, trying with all their might to kick him in the face on their way back to the ground.

The younger kids all shrieked and bleated with excitement, and they all sang while watching the older kids:

Who's the biggest idiot of the band,
His dirt and stink pollute the land?
Why it's Gruff, Gruff, whose head is empty stuff!
He is stupid, stupid, sure enough,
From his filthy hooves to his muddy scruff!
The only thing better, and we don't lie
Would be for him to wander off and die.

The kids all built up their courage, and now Gruff found that he had all five kids jumping, dancing, and singing with the older kids while trying to kick him in the face. Gruff closed his eyes tighter and tighter with each blow until he finally had enough.

Gruff stood up suddenly and towered over the little bratty snots. He looked down at them and calmly said, "Ok kids, I think play time is just about over, and it's time for you to go back to your mothers." He then grunted and snorted at each of them.

Lucas stepped forward again and stuck out his chest, acting boldly to impress his friends. "Why don't you just shut your stupid, blasted, idiotic, no-good face!"

Gruff stared back down at the little brat in disbelief.

Lucas glanced behind himself to make sure he had his little band of miscreants watching, then spoke again. "Hey?! Did I say you could look at me?"

He finally moved close enough to Gruff to be standing under him and looking straight up, barely able to see Gruff's eyes. "Besides, just what are you going to do about it?" Lucas said, now pushing his chest into Gruff's front legs. "I'll tell you what, absolutely nothing! This is all you are ever going to be blasted good for. My mother even said so!" Lucas bleated.

The mouthy little punk then looked back at all his obnoxious friends, who were watching and listening to see how they should respond. He shouted at the small band, "Well? Am I right or what!"

The rest of the gang quickly fell in line and started to chant "Shut up, shut up!" Then, suddenly, ALL of them charged forward and resumed taking turns to see if they could kick Gruff's face and ribs in some form or fashion.

"Lovely, just lovely" Gruff mumbled. He had finally had enough and decided that, since they weren't leaving, it was certainly time for him to find another spot.

Gruff looked around for a better spot and then started walking to another area closer to the brambles where he would normally sleep. He liked that area, as it was a little further away on a small hill and generally hidden from the community, and only he could withstand the thorns and prickers.

As Gruff walked slowly along, the kids surrounded him and continued to antagonize him. They bleated horrible things, shouting and carrying on unfettered. However, Gruff knew that the kids had learned everything they were doing by watching and listening to their parents or, if the parents weren't around, how their community acted.

As Gruff approached his little home of bushes, a random shadow crossed over him, momentarily blocking out the sun, then disappearing just as quickly. Gruff looked into the sky but saw nothing. All the kids also momentarily froze, then immediately went back to their nonsense.

Gruff resumed walking, and once again, the shadow crossed over him. He froze and looked up. This time, though, his eyes caught the fast-moving form of a large golden eagle that had taken a great interest in the kids following along behind and jumping around him.

The eagle soared, rising and falling on the thermal lifts, diving towards Gruff and the kids, hoping that one of them would scatter away from the group. After each dive, the golden eagle would rise again to watch them and wait for its chance to snatch one of the kids for an easy meal.

Gruff spun quickly and looked down at all the kids who, by now, also spotted the eagle. The kids started to whine and shriek. Then, some started to bolt back down the hill. "NO!" shouted Gruff, "NOT THAT WAY!"

Gruff jumped forward and corralled them all back into a group. "Listen to me! Quick! Get into the bushes, lay low, and don't move!"

The kids started to follow Gruff's demands but then froze in terror and started to cry and bleat uncontrollably. "We seriously do NOT have time for this!" shouted Gruff again. Gruff started shoving the kids into the shrubs and briars with his head at first, then resorting to small shoves to push the wailing and shrieking kids into the briars.

As the eagle began its attack, Gruff had to act quickly and forcefully began headbutting the kids, sending them flying into the brambles, one after the other, to hide them. Then, he blocked the kids from the eagle's view with his own body.

The eagle screeched and dove once again at Gruff and the kids. Gruff dug in his hooves and waited until the eagle was close. Then, he raised up and tossed his horns, skirting the eagle's tail feathers. As quickly as the eagle attacked, it changed its mind when it realized just how big Gruff was.

"Well, as mean as this is going to sound, at least all this activity got the kids to hush." He stood there for a moment. "The kids!" Gruff's face squinched when he suddenly remembered the kids he tossed into the bushes. He slowly looked back over his shoulder as he could hear them beginning to sniffle.

He began to retrieve the kids one by one from the shrubbery. They all were now in complete snot wails and cries. "Look, kids, I'm really sorry. I certainly didn't want to shove you like that! I didn't want anyone getting hurt or something much more terrible," Gruff said, trying his best to calm down the sobbing kids.

The smallest of the kids, Remi, stepped towards Gruff. "You saved us, Gruff. Why?" But then Lucas, hoping their parents would come, stepped forward to block him from getting any closer to Gruff.

Lucas then started up again, bleating loudly over and over, "Get away from us!" Lucas managed to bring all the kids back into unison with his antics.

All the kids copied their leader in his buffoonery, flopping on the ground with complete hysterical cries and theatrics to make it look good for their parents, who were indeed on their way to investigate all the commotion.

Gruff looked around at all the kids and began to stammer, "I... I really don't think you understand..." He lowered his head to try and help one of the little brats out of the twisted limbs of the bushes.

No sooner had Gruff looked back up and three of their mothers were standing in front of him. One began yelling at him, "Just what is going on here? You have been nothing but an eyesore and embarrassment to our entire community!"

Lucas then spoke up, between his little snorting sobs, making a grand show for his mother, "Gruff rammed into us, and then he tried to stomp on us before pushing us all into those bushes for no reason!" Lucas continued to wail and flop on the ground inconsolably.

All the mothers then immediately turned to Gruff and glared. Then, Nannie shouted, "How DARE you raise a hoof to my kid?" She continued to bleat her obscenities at Gruff, who was now beginning to back up.

"You just wait until William gets here!" Nannie blustered and then kicked dirt and spat on Gruff.

Gruff looked down at her and began to stammer, "I don't think you really understand what had hap..."

Gruff tried as best as he could to finish a complete sentence, but now all three nannies were bleating, cursing, and carrying on as loudly as they possibly could, drawing even more attention from the community.

"What seems to be going on here?!" came a deep voice. "GET OUT OF MY WAY!" the voice shouted again. "Just why am I always having to come over here and. . .oh, I see." Gruff's father, William, stepped into view, finally having arrived at the commotions.

Nannie backed up and nodded her head in Gruff's direction. "He went and. . ."

William glared at Nannie, and she quickly fell back into the crowd with the other goats, "As if I didn't already know." Gruff held his head low and did not look his father in the eyes.

Nannie quickly bolted forward and bleated, "Do you know what your. . ." William glared angrily at Nannie, and she quickly became silent yet again and turned her head, so she didn't have to face him.

William looked at Nannie. "You shut your blasted blathering mouth and listen to me! I don't want to hear anything coming out of you, and I don't want to hear anything coming out of this creature's mouth either." He turned his head and glared at Gruff, then back to Nannie.

"I have told you before. You have very few responsibilities around here, Nannie." William now stepped forward into where she was standing until she was forced to back up. "Take care of the kids. That's all you need to do. . .and you can't even seem to do that right." William's voice now carried across the entire community as Nannie stood silently, not daring to look him in the eyes.

"You stand around all day flapping your blasted gums and strutting around with your tail in the air with your useless friends..." At this point, all the nannies gasped and looked at each other like they were little innocents, and William had whipped their hindquarters. William glared at them all and continued, "and doing absolutely no kid rearing."

Nannie worked up a moment of bravery. "And I'm telling you, YOU better do something about this if you expect to have any normalcy in THIS community."

William stepped even further into Nannie and pushed her back into her friends. "Do NOT test me, EWE! I KNOW my responsibilities, and it's more than high time YOU learn yours!"

"But, but even you..." Nannie stammered and turned her head to address William's statements but then quickly hushed and lowered her head.

William turned to look back at Nannie and stomped at her. "So, as I was saying, I can certainly see who was at fault and where the failure was and is with Gruff." William quickly turned back to look at Gruff.

William glared at the entire community, "And because of YOUR failures, Nannie, I have to step in yet again."

William stepped forward and approached Gruff. He then spoke in a low, hateful tone, "Boy...now hear me good, we have done this time after time after time, and quite frankly, I'm tired of it, and yet here we are again.

He looked briefly over his shoulder at Nannie, then back to Gruff and whispered frustratingly, "Why don't you just listen to me? Why do you insist on bringing this all on yourself? Why can't you seem to learn?"

Gruff kept his head lowered and spoke, "I understand, Father. Do what you have to."

William's anger boiled when he looked at the crowd that had gathered and started pressing in on him, and he then growled, "You know I am going to have to beat you, and just when you think it's done, I am going to have to beat you again.

"You are going to learn to show a little respect around here, especially to me, and you will learn to stay in your place!" William stamped his hooves and kicked dirt backward, forcing the crowd to back up.

The moment William finished speaking, two of his friends stepped out from behind him. "Ok. Today, gentlemen, we once again need to make a much-needed example. What happens here will be a reminder to the entire community to keep your mouth shut, do as you are told, and not bother us, or you will end up like Gruff!"

William's friends immediately charged Gruff, and each rammed him from opposite sides, initially knocking the wind out of Gruff, who dropped his head in an effort to regain his breath.

William stepped forward to seize the opportunity to look Gruff in the eyes and then proceeded to ram, bash, and kick Gruff repeatedly in the face. Over and over, the other two struck at Gruff's sides while his own father cursed at him and struck at his face.

Gruff stood, not falling to the left or the right, and suffered their blows, accepting their judgment, sentences, and just how little they all truly thought of him. The kids and the nannies all cheered as the viciousness of William and his friends took its toll.

After several minutes, William suddenly spoke up, "All right, that's enough. I think we made our point!" The truth of the matter was that they had grown weary from their savagery and, still unable to cause Gruff to fall, they changed tactics in front of the community and attempted pious mercy.

William finally turned to the crowd that had formed. His tongue fell out of his mouth, and he panted to catch his breath. He quickly collected himself and scorned them. "What are you all looking at?! I am sick and tired of having to come up here and do this!" William bleated loudly, "Over and over and over again, we have to go through this. You ALL would do well to get your noses out of each other's hindquarters and mind your own blasted business!"

He continued stomping at the ground and kicking dust at the community. "You've seen enough, and what happens to those that don't listen!"

Finally, William bleated and screamed at the top of his lungs as the rabble was slow to leave. "Look! I SAID LOOK, at this sad existence of a creature and remember! Now get out of my face and get back to where you belong!"

The gathering slowly started to move off and go back to doing what they were doing before, absolutely nothing. The kids went back to acting like little fools to match the attitudes of the even bigger fools they were now following back down the hill.

Now, William and Gruff stood looking at each other. William looked up at Gruff and his beaten face. "Gruff. . . I," he paused and then tried to speak again, looking into Gruff's eyes. "Gruff, I really am. . ." He then lowered his head slightly, turned, and walked away, leaving Gruff now completely alone, bruised, and bleeding.

2. RANGER KATE BRADIGAN

"*You have a new text message*," the cell phone chirped loudly, then repeated the alarm. Kate looked up briefly from the bathroom sink and leaned around the corner to see her phone blinking feverishly on the bed. Kate let out a long exhale with just enough air left in her lungs to shift the airflow to knock her hair out of her eyes, but not so much as to spit toothpaste on the mirror.

Now, the phone began to ring its allotted number of times before being picked up by voicemail. Once again, Kate glanced around the corner, but this time, she added an eye roll to her current exhalation routine. "*You have a new voicemail message*," the phone changed its tone and alert. No more than 15 seconds later, "*You have a new text message*," began to chirp again.

Finally giving in to the constant barrage of alerts, Kate dropped her toothbrush into the sink and stormed into the bedroom to grab the phone, just catching her pinky toe on the bedpost. Kate let out a loud scream while grabbing her phone and her foot in one fell swoop. Kate lay on the floor clutching her toe with one hand and answering the phone with the other while fighting back the tears.

"WHAT!?" Kate answered sternly.

A voice came across the other end, "You don't have to be so mean. Where have you been?"

Kate was now biting her lip, trying to collect her thoughts. "Mom, I'm a little busy here, and I just talked to you an hour ago! WHAT is now so important?"

There was a momentary silence before Kate's mom spoke up. "Well, nothing really, I guess. I was just seeing what you are up to."

Kate grew more irritated by this point, as her pinky toe was now protesting the phone call as much as she was. "Mom, I'm a little busy here getting packed up. You KNOW this!"

Kate continued, "I can't always respond to your texts and calls on a moment's notice!" Kate paused. "And with where I am going, I cannot guarantee that I will even be able to respond within 24 hours. I'm going to be pretty remote."

"You don't have to sound so angry. Are you mad at me?" Kate's mom now sounded as pathetic as possible. "I guess I will go since you don't seem to have any time to talk to me," she said while full-on snot-sobbing.

"Mom…" Kate barely got the word out before the phone was hung up on the other end. Kate tapped the phone on her forehead and whispered, "Love you mom." Kate glanced at the phone to see if her mom had really hung up and then exhaled in frustration.

Kate got up off the floor, practiced running in place, and did a couple of jumping jacks to coax her wee little one back into unison with the other appendages.

"Well, fortunately, it's not broken!" she said while rocking back and forth from toes to heel. "That would have been a terrible start to the new job."

Kate tossed the phone back onto the bed and started back for the bathroom to finish getting ready for the day. "*You have a new text message*," her phone began to chime again.

"You have GOT to be kidding me!" Kate mumbled through a mouth full of toothpaste and, stomping back into the bedroom, snatched the phone off the bed to look at the screen.

"What did you do to Mom, and why is she now mad at me?" Kate's phone read.

Kate's fingers flew across the digital keyboard. "Well, she has been mad at me for a month, ever since I told her I accepted my new assignment. Just wanted to make sure I shared the love with you.

"So, TAG your IT!" Kate ended with the emoticon featuring a smiley with a tongue sticking out and tossed the phone back onto the bed.

Kate walked back into the bathroom just long enough to rinse her mouth, and her phone again spoke up. "*You have an incoming call.*"

Kate spit the remaining toothpaste into the sink, placed her toothbrush back into the holder, and glanced up into the mirror with a toothy grin to make sure she didn't have any breakfast burrito still stuck in her gums. "*You have an incoming call,*" her phone alert now becoming nearly shrill in her head.

"Some days, it would really be nice to have a different number," Kate mumbled, once again, heading back to the bedroom and looking at the caller ID displaying the name James Bradigan.

"Hey, Dad," she said wearily.

"Hey, Punkin. Your mother made me call, but we just want to make sure that you have everything you need." James paused a moment and then continued, "You know your mom worries about you, even if you weren't headed into the wilderness."

Kate flopped across the bed, looking up at the ceiling with her foot pointed straight up so she could make sure her toe was still attached, and held the phone to her ear with a single finger. "I know, Dad, but of ALL people, you know I've been training for this opportunity for years!"

Kate then dropped her foot back onto the bed. "I'm not ten years old anymore, Dad." She silently chuckled as she toyed with the various stuffed animals scattered about her bed.

The phone grew silent for what seemed like hours, having one of those awkward silence moments. Kate spoke up, "I love you, Dad. Thank you for all you and Mom have done for me." Yet another long silence set in, and Kate could hear her father coughing in an effort to fight back his emotions.

"You be safe, stay vigilant, pray always and often. Always remember, you are never alone. HE will never leave or forsake you." James spoke in broken words from his throat as he fought back the emotional pain that then changed into fighting back tears.

"Please let us know as soon as you get settled in….in Montana of all places!?" James continued, attempting to break the tension. "Montana, could you have chosen a bigger place!?"

Kate was now sobbing like her dad. "Well, there is always Kodiak, Alaska."

"NO!" shouted James into the phone, partly laughing. "Montana will be just fine for you."

"Love you, Dad. I will give you and Mom a call once I get there. Bye." She was now palming the tears off her chin.

Kate lay in silence, still staring up at the ceiling, tapping her cell phone again, this time on her cheek. She closed her eyes and breathed deeply to calm her racing heart. "Ok," she said. "Let's do this!"

She hopped off the bed and stepped towards a crisp letter taped to her mirror. Kate looked at the letter and at herself in the mirror. Clearing her throat, she began to read it aloud.

From United States Department of Agriculture, Chief of the USDA Forest Service

Ranger Kate Bradigan:

Your request has been reviewed and accepted. You will stand detached from your current assignment and are assigned Region 4: Bob Marshall Wilderness Area and Swan Range Mountains, for duty. You will be attached to Spotted Bear and Rock Mountain Ranger District strictly for reporting purposes.

Your assignment will entail working out of the town of Honolulu, Montana, documenting, preserving, and charting new portions of the lands that are being entrusted to the Forest Service's care.

Your duties will be to establish a new ranger presence in the area of Honolulu and the Granite Mountain chain locations. Your services in the area will enable the Forest Service better access to station location, public service, and more effective management and preservation of said trusts.

Welcome to the Continental Divide, Montana!

Kate took another deep breath and looked at the handwritten note from the Regional Park Ranger:

Ranger Bradigan,

You are going to be in very tough, harsh, and exhausting conditions. I'm certainly not going to sugarcoat anything! You will be in areas up in the Granite Mountains by yourself at times and in locations where help may NOT get to you for emergencies right away. Your work will be invaluable in receiving the new land trust, creating a new station, and, of course, working with the residents of the area.

We will talk more once you get here.

Signed,

Regional Park Ranger, Todd McMillan

Kate looked at herself in the mirror again, snapped to attention, placed her campaign hat onto her head, boosting her height to 5'5", and gave a little smile.

"You've come a long way, girl; a very long way," she said while still looking at her uniform. Kate may have been small in stature, but she could go toe-to-toe with ANY other ranger, or civilian for that matter, and still come out victorious.

Kate glanced around the bedroom and focused on her degrees and awards: MS Zoology, MS Wildlife Biology & Conservation, 4th dan Hapkido, and AAS Culinary Arts. She paused for a moment and then laughed out loud.

"Not sure how culinary arts fit into all this, but it's nice to have skills," Kate said, laughing again.

"Ok, looking sharp! Let's get this final meeting done so we can get this show on the road." Kate took another deep breath, held it, then exhaled while heading for the front door.

She took one last look around her apartment. "I'm so glad Dad volunteered to come pack all this up!"

She opened the door to step out into a new adventure, and no sooner had she closed the door than she was immediately confronted. "KATE!" an old, shaky voice shouted.

Kate smiled. "Good morning, Ms. Willison. How are you doing this morning?"

Deborah Willison had to be at least 150 years old, was rather extra plump, and resembled more of a sun-dried apple than a person. But, she was ever so sweet, and if you ever needed anything, she had it, could get it, or would bake it.

"When are you leaving?" Deborah asked, reaching out and touching Kate on her wrist after shifting what looked like a heavy basket four times before deciding which free hand to use.

"I will be headed out in the morning, bright and early." Kate smiled and held Deborah's hand.

"Why in the world do you want to go to..." Deborah paused, shifted the basket to the other hand, thought, and then continued, "Oh yes, why in the world do you want to go to Montana? You are such a tiny thing, and I think a strong wind could knock you over. Besides, you need to stay here so I can make sure you eat!" Deborah said, pinching at Kate's sides.

Kate looked at her and chuckled. "Well, you have certainly made sure I ate!"

She then looked deep into Deborah's eyes, "Ms. Willison, do you ever get the feeling that you were needed somewhere else, but you can't quite figure out exactly where or why?"

"Hmmm," thought Deborah. "You know what, I do, but that's usually just when I need to be looking for a bathroom." Deborah then gave Kate a big smile and a wink that caused them both to burst into laughter.

"I made these for you. Maybe you can take some with you. I don't know how they cook in Montana, but I'm sure it's not as good as this." She then handed Kate a large container filled with muffins, cookies, and various little fruit pies.

"Well, thank you so much! This all looks fantastic, and I do love your cooking." Kate shoved a cookie into her mouth and started sidestepping, finally able to maneuver around Ms. Willison and make it to her car without further interruptions from neighbors and, more importantly, her cell phone.

Kate, grabbing for her keys and balancing the basket with the other hand, shouted back to Deborah, "THANK YOU for everything!" She waved another cookie in the air before finally making it fully into the car and driving off.

Pulling into the station, Kate rolled her eyes. "Ugh, here we go." The station was decorated with banners, balloons, and inflatables. All of which had some form of "Good Luck Kate!" written out in huge pink letters, her most unfavorite color. "I just bet that pectoral, barbaric nincompoop Jaxon had something to do with this! It has his handiwork all over it!"

Kate sat in the parking lot looking at the front of the station as she watched her coworkers drop additional fake props and banners to quickly duck and dash back into the building as if they had been caught by a truancy officer.

She finally turned the engine off, after having contemplated just leaving, and got out of the car. She looked down and wondered which of them used the sidewalk chalk to write the various slogans. "Ooop… yeah, definitely Jaxon's writing."

She looked down and saw the word "COGRANDULATION." Kate let out a small chuckle. "I know he does this just to push my buttons."

Kate snatched streamers off the door entrance and finally made it into the building. After being hit with pink glitter bombs, she stepped into the conference room, where everyone erupted into laughter at seeing Kate covered in glitter. She glared at them all as she walked by, each of them scooting low into their seats, trying to hide, and she finally set the basket of goodies on the table and took a seat.

Slowly, the room filled with the few rangers assigned to the station, all of whom quickly reached into the basket, pulled out whatever favorites Ms. Willison had made for them, and jumped away from Kate.

Of course, the room was loud, and, at times, they were extremely obnoxious, but Kate knew how her size and this chosen profession would be and the type of people she was likely to have to work with.

District Ranger Lloyd Jackson finally walked in, also covered in pink glitter, and sat down, slowly looking over the staff. He scanned each face at the conference table, who by now were all trying their best to stifle their laughter. He continued to look around the room until he came to Kate, who was looking down and answering messages on her cell phone.

Once the room came to some resemblance of order, Lloyd spoke up. "I just want to start off by saying congratulations to Ranger Bradigan on her pending promotion and the new assignment. We are all familiar with that area, the vastness, excitement, and the dangers, and we certainly wish her the best in all her endeavors." Lloyd paused then noticed the basket of treasures on the table.

"Kate, are those from Ms. Willison?" Llyod said leaning forward in his chair.

Kate popped her head up, causing the glitter in her hair to scatter onto the table and whoever was sitting closest. "Yes, sir. She caught me on the way in this morning. It's definitely a full basket this time."

Kate opened the top of the basket and peered in. "She even made you a few of those fruit pies you like." She lifted a small bundle with a tiny ribbon and tag that simply said "Lloyd" on it and set it on the table in front of herself.

Lloyd slapped his coffee mug onto the table, causing everyone to jump. "Excellent, and it's always good to know the team is at least awake!" "Say, Jaxon, how about handing me that fruit pie, would you?" Lloyd said, looking across the table and eyeballing the small bundle.

"Now, as I was saying, Kate will be leaving us and headed to Montana for the chance to open a new station as an Assistant District Ranger and explore more areas of the wilderness up there. We know that Montana is generally thought of as a man's country." Lloyd used his fingers to make air quotes around the words *man's country.* "But I have absolutely no doubt Kate will excel in all she does."

Jaxon stood up to get the pastry for Lloyd. He was a towering man of 6'7" and could certainly have been a television wrestler or maybe better employed at an auto junkyard crushing small Chevies with his biceps. Even though Kate considered him a complete buffoon, he was extremely intelligent. However, he thought very highly of himself and tended to think he was more handsome and dashing than he really was.

Jaxon walked and strutted like a superhero around the table to where the basket and Kate sat and stopped just to the side of her.

Kate was completely unphased by his attempts to peacock and kept looking down, fiddling with her cell phone. She casually swished some glitter off her uniform, making Jaxon wait even longer.

He stood there at first, clearing his throat, and when that didn't have the desired results, he began tapping his boot against one leg of her chair as he rubbed the palms of his hands together, which sounded like two sheets of sandpaper that had turned on each other to fight.

Kate finally looked up, after making Jaxon wait for several minutes, and then back down to her phone, causing Jaxon to grunt impatiently and tap her chair with his boot even more. By this point, the entire conference room was in complete silence, all eyes fixed on them. Lloyd sat calmly, drinking his coffee.

After another minute had passed, she looked up at him and scowled as he towered over her and gave him a very irritated "Can I help you?" She rolled her eyes and head at him, then went back to poking through various text messages.

Jaxon cracked his knuckles one at a time, then leaned forward and took hold of Kate's chair with one arm, bending it backward until its support spring began to protest and Kate was nearly completely flat. "Did you hear what he said, KATE?" Jaxon overemphasized her name and glanced momentarily up at Lloyd, then back to Kate. "Montana is MAN's country!"

Kate calmly slid her cell phone back into her pocket, then glared defiantly at Jaxon. She exhaled slowly. Suddenly, Kate rotated in the chair with some sort of backflip with a twist, grabbed Jaxon by the arm, and proceeded to pin his face to the table.

Kate continued to push and hold down Jaxon's face, which was now being cushioned by the unfortunate fruit pie that was completely smashed from his chin to temple. Kate calmly blew the hair out of her eyes and mockingly said, "Yeah, and I'm looking forward to finally working with some."

The conference room immediately erupted into hysterical boisterous laughter, fist bumps, and high fives that emphasized the unlikely beatdown. Every time Jaxon groaned, Kate hiked his pinned arm and used her free hand to spread the dessert farther and farther from one side of his face to the other.

Lloyd took a sip of his coffee and decided to add another sugar packet, stirring now in rhythm to the grunting at the other end of the table. He took another sip and tapped his spoon lightly on the rim of his cup. He made a few facial grimaces each time Jaxon's face made a complete revolution on the table.

After watching the extremely short skirmish, Llyod finally spoke up. "Whenever you two are done playing around with each other, I would still love to have one of those fruit pies, please, if there are any that aren't stuck on Jaxon's face."

Kate looked up at Llyod while still smashing Jaxon's face around on the table, his arm still firmly jacked behind his back. Jaxon looked up the best he could and nodded his head with as much movement as Kate would allow under the circumstances. She let go of her grip on Jaxon, and he stood up, the pie now dripping and sliding down his face. He turned and faced her once again, towering over her. Jaxon looked down at Kate, and she looked back up at him, daring him to make another move. Then she grinned up at him and said, "You just never learn, do you?"

Jaxon grabbed Kate and lifted her two feet off the floor. As she seemingly disappeared into a massive bear hug, he used the opportunity to make sure the pie was now smeared onto her face and her hair as well. He then spoke into her ear, saying, "You are lucky that you have been learning Hapkido since you were three. Otherwise, this would be playing out quite differently."

Jaxon gave her another hug. "I'm going to miss you. If you need me, you know how to reach me." Kate wrapped her arms around Jaxon and hugged him tight, her feet still dangling off the floor. Jaxon finally set her back down, then moved the hair out of her eyes. "You take care of yourself, little lady. And call mom so she isn't mad at me!"

3. OPEN YOUR EYES

Gruff slowly moved back towards the brambles that he called home and groaned miserably from the savage beatings of his father and his two buddies. The blood dripped slowly from Gruff's nose, only adding to his miserable appearance. He lay on the ground in his spot with his back slightly to the community so he could only see them through the corner of a single unbruised eye.

Laughing and celebrating their self-proclaimed righteousness in beating Gruff, the community returned to their green spring grasses, dancing and praising each other while the kids went back to singing their made-up song at the top of their vile little mouths.

I suppose it could have been worse, and if I really admit it, it's getting less and less painful. I hardly feel anything anymore, thought Gruff, breathing deeply and trying hard to ignore some of the pain that was working to convince him otherwise.

He finally started to relax a bit and began to doze when a raspy voice suddenly cawed out. "So let me ask you this: When do you say enough is enough?"

Gruff looked to his side and, on a lower limb of some trees that grew nearby, he saw a rather large old crow scratching his head, then fluffing some dust from his feathers before finally staring right back at Gruff.

"What are you rambling on about, old timer?" Gruff paused, sighed heavily, and then continued. "It would be best for both of us if you just mind your own business." Gruff shook his head. "You have absolutely no idea what this is all about, much less who and what I am. And to end this conversation, it was certainly what I deserved."

The crow stopped preening, eyed Gruff, fluffed himself again, and then hopped down to the ground to take a better look. "What you deserved? I beg to differ with that statement. So, I ask you again, why did you let them do that to you?"

The crow paused and eyed Gruff. "And before you even try to come up with some lame excuse, you need to know that I watched you, and I saw the entire thing! Matter of fact," the crow paused to scratch under a wing with his beak, "I have watched you off and on since you were born."

Gruff looked up and shifted a bit to try and hide his face from the crow. He then swallowed back his growing anger and spoke as calmly as he could. "If you have watched me for that long, you will already know this is what I am." He then dropped his shoulders. "I cannot do anything right. I am worthless and of no benefit to anyone."

The crow hopped closer and slowly strutted over to Gruff. "No benefit to anyone, you say?" He scoffed, then said, "Um, May I?" now pointing to the top of Gruff's head. Gruff shrugged, and the crow strutted closer before hopping up onto the top of his head and pecking at some insects that had become helplessly stuck in the tangled mess of his fleece.

"No benefit, you say. Yet, Gruff, you just provided me a nice crunchy snack."

Gruff raised his head while the crow was eating. "Great, so I'm just a walking buffet now, and how exactly do you know my name?"

"Yes, I know your name. As I've said, I have watched you since you were born. Besides, it's hard not to hear the lovely songs of such polite kids while they sing and dance." The crow tossed his little head in the direction of the community.

Gruff nodded at the crow, and they both chuckled for a moment.

"So, let me ask you, Gruff, what exactly makes you think you are worthless? Oh, and my name is Zeki, by the way, although that has not always been my name."

"Ok, um, Zeki, try to understand this. I didn't really care to learn the one, and I'm not interested in the other." Gruff tossed his head to try to get Zeki to leave.

Zeki pretended to ignore Gruff and kept on chattering. "Oh, it's a very difficult thing to talk about, as I have to explain who and how I was. There is always pain when you think of the events of the past," Zeki blurted out. "But, since it explains how I came to be called Zeki by the Creator, I would certainly share it with you, and it should be shared!"

He hopped closer to Gruff and poked at him with his feathers. "Even YOU will one day have a story to tell."

"Oh, come on, are you deaf as well as old?" Gruff looked at the crow and then shoved his hoof in the direction of the community. "Besides, if you have watched for years and heard them tell me those things, then you will know and understand they don't talk to me like that because I'm cute and cuddly!

Gruff put his head back down onto his hooves. "This is my home, Zeki. My family, my community; it's all I have ever known, and if I can't believe what THEY say, why believe anyone else? If they ALL say that I'm useless and worthless, then isn't that the truth?" Gruff was growing more and more irritated. "I honestly think that if I were to die right now, that would be the only thing that would benefit them."

Gruff watched Zeki waddling and cocking his head around, taking in the entire conversation. "I'm telling you, Zeki, if I were to die in some grotesque manner and they could all watch, well. . . THAT would be something useful and entertaining; Heck, THEY would finally agree with me for once."

Zeki, taking a moment to choke down a caterpillar, spoke, turning and cocking his head at Gruff. "So, you are saying that the only purpose you serve is to be their source of amusement and that your death would surely be a benefit to them?"

Gruff thought for a moment and said, "Well, yeah, for one thing, it would certainly free them all from the burden of my being around, wouldn't it? It would free them of having to concern themselves with me. They would no longer have to look at me or breathe the same air that I do." Gruff now had turned to look the crow in the face and laid back down.

"Look, when you are finally rid of something that you have considered a major source of anxiety, grief, or even dread, maybe," Gruff, looking up at Zeki, "well, then didn't the thing that died do you a big favor?" Gruff laid his head onto his front legs. "You will no longer have to deal with what it was that was irritating you after all."

"Hmmm," Zeki said with his mouth still full. "Those are some very dark and disturbing thoughts, Gruff. No creature should feel utterly useless, but let me ask you this," now strutting back to Gruff and hopping back on top of his head, "why are you just taking their word for how you are or how you should be? Don't you think that YOU should discover that for yourself?"

Zeki paused, hopped back up on Gruff's head, and looked down at Gruff. "After all, you are not a little kid anymore. You are old enough to go seek the truth for yourself. Or are you content and happy with the constant beatings?" Zeki peered at Gruff.

"Come on, I saw the look in your eyes and on your face just a short while ago. So, don't lie to me!" Zeki paused yet again and began pecking under his other wing.

Gruff tried to look up at Zeki the best he could without going cross-eyed, trying to see this old bird sitting on his head. "So, you are telling me that everyone has been lying to me all this time?"

Zeki hopped onto Gruff's snout and looked him in the eyes. "What I am saying is, don't you think you at least should find the truth for yourself? I'm really surprised that I actually have to suggest that!" Zeki tossed his feathers into the air. "I really think if you looked down deep in your heart, you would already know the answer to this."

Gruff shook his head, but Zeki held on as tightly as he could. "Excuse me? Look, I just..." Gruff paused. "Zeki, I cannot carry on a conversation with you while you are sitting on my face!"

Zeki clicked and cooed with laughter and then hopped back to the ground. Gruff then continued, "I guess I have always felt that things were not quite right, that I shouldn't necessarily believe all they told me."

Gruff swirled his hoof around in the grass as they talked, "I mean look around, there are too many things in creation that work in unison, and the outcasts, well, those are generally the weak, lame." Gruff suddenly looked up. "Oh!"

Gruff looked at Zeki. "I guess I've always known that I was the outcast, but I just really wanted to be a part of the family. It is my family, Zeki."

Zeki walked over to the edge of the hill and looked at the community. He then back at Gruff. "Well, my friend, now you are starting to understand WHY they treat you the way they do. But it certainly doesn't excuse their behavior, family or not! You see, Gruff," Zeki took a couple of hops and then sat down, "your community looks down on anything that is different from them. Something being different honestly terrifies them."

"Terrifies them?" Gruff lifted his head and looked at the community.

"YES, and if it's different, or holds THEM accountable for their actions, well then THAT thing that is different," Zeki pointed his feathers down at the community. "It is the reason and the cause of ALL their problems, all their fears. Whatever is different MUST be struck at, so they can feel safe again in their little self-absorbed cocoons."

"Zeki, can I tell you something? Given everything that I could see from up on my hill, watching and learning from other living things, I always thought that, through all the abuse, all the loneliness, maybe I was set aside for something special." Gruff lifted his head and looked up into the sky, then over to Zeki. "The evidence is there; it FEELS like it's there." Gruff looked back down the small hill to the community below.

"Well, Gruff, NOW we have something to really talk about, don't we?" Zeki waddled around, finally looking up at Gruff and then back to the community. "I am here to tell you, or rather I have been sent to tell you," Zeki poked at Gruff with his feathers, "that YOU do have an immense importance. There is a role that only YOU can fill, just like there is a role that only I can fill."

Zeki continued to waddle around, tossing his wings back and forth while he spoke. "Oh, sure, we can choose to live in misery; we suffer the beatings, all the physical and mental abuse, and finally accept the loneliness we are shackled to… to just die in complete, unfulfilled, emptiness. OR…" Zeki quickly looked up at Gruff, "You can stop feeling sorry for yourself, waiting around to die or for some random change to happen that's going to just make it all better like a magical dream."

"So, you are saying what, exactly?" Gruff raised his brow and turned his head slightly, hoping that what Zeki just said would somehow leak in from one ear and be absorbed by his brain.

Zeki spun and smacked Gruff across the face with his feathers. "I'm saying, you pick yourself up by that big hairy backside and set off. Find

THE TRUTH that's been instilled into every living thing's heart by the Creator!"

Gruff continued looking down at the community as Zeki waddled over to Gruff's front leg and sat down on it like a couch. "Let me tell you something, Gruff," Zeki said, once again pointing a feather right at Gruff's nose. "It doesn't matter if we live, nor does it really matter if we die."

Gruff looked down at Zeki and then back to the community. "I have to say, Zeki, that is certainly a lot of options to choose from. So, then, what matters?"

"You tell me there is a great importance to finding the truth, but living or dying doesn't mean anything." Gruff snorted. "I'm sorry, but that sounds exactly like my current pointless existence. What's the point in trying?"

Zeki looked up at Gruff again. "Now you see, THAT is the very attitude of not only your community but those that lay beyond the mountains, even the human communities!"

Gruff looked down at Zeki, then closed his eyes momentarily to listen.

"I have seen it, Gruff! There is a darkness, a stain over everything, and it is grossly corrupted and corrupts ALL things. Take a good long look back down there at your community." Zeki tossed his primary feather in the direction of Gruff's family.

Gruff and Zeki sat silently, watching together and just hearing the community, all the adults bleating at each other their daily course of vile and hate, and even cursing their kid's existence. The kids, in turn, yelling and cursing their parents and performing the same vile deeds as the adults, acting and becoming great fools of their normal society.

"You see, Gruff," Zeki began speaking again, not turning his gaze from the ruckus below, "see them for what they are or at least what they have become. They are only concerned with themselves. They only care about what they, as individuals, can get out of the situation.

"There is NO community, Gruff. There is disorder, chaos, discord between adults, disharmony in the families, each of them going their own lost way, all have descended into individual wretchedness, blinded by their own self-glorification, which will end in the destruction of themselves." Zeki paused and looked again at Gruff. "And sadly, the destruction of their children." Zeki reached out and touched Gruff's face.

Both sat quietly for a moment, reflecting, then Zeki spoke softly, almost in agony. "And it's not just YOUR community, Gruff. It's how all communities are, or at least how they are quickly becoming."

Gruff closed his eyes and lowered his head as tears began to well up. "What then…what is to be done?"

Zeki turned back to Gruff. "Oh, Gruff, you are such a big-hearted beast! Listen, back to your question; it doesn't matter if we live or if we die. NO! What matters is when we do die, when the last bit of air leaves our lungs, and the last wisp of breath crosses our lips, it was exhaled in truth and faith to what the Creator called us to do! If we are alive, then each moment should not be squandered, like what you see down there." Zeki pointed down to the community. "LIVE each day for the faith and the truth found ONLY in the Creator, who was gracious enough to place that truth deep in your heart!

"Now, open your eyes, Gruff, and look down at them again." Zeki pushed his cheek up against Gruff's and looked at the community with him. "Do their actions reflect even a smidgeon of love, a speck of respect, a tiny morsel of integrity? Is there anything that might reflect the love of OUR Creator?"

Gruff sat, watching the community as great teardrops fell from his eyes, and quietly responded, "No, they show none of that. And, Zeki," Gruff said, now sobbing, "I have shown none of that."

He turned his head to look away from the community and Zeki. "I sat walled off from everything, and, yes, you are right, feeling sorry for myself. I was waiting for something to come along so that I might break free from it, but I was seemingly forever chained to it, regardless, too afraid to actually move."

"Exactly!" chirped Zeki, using his wing to pull at Gruff's face to look at him again. "But now your eyes are starting to open, and you can finally start to see a little more clearly."

"Zeki, there seems to be more pain in the beginning when realizing the truth and starting to see things that you have done or didn't do, and pain in regard to realizing just how bad things really are." Gruff tried to turn his head to the side, but Zeki countered and hopped a couple times to make sure they kept eye contact.

"Just because you begin to trust the Creator doesn't mean you will be freed from pain and troubles. It could get much worse, which is why you have to remember what's important, regardless of what may lay ahead," Zeki said, poking at Gruff's side again.

"This all is just the first of your steps into a brand-new life, my friend." Zeki used his wing to pat Gruff's cheek. "It's a new discovery in understanding the truth and what the Creator may have planned for you, and it's going to be beyond what you could possibly imagine."

Zeki hopped back up to Gruff's head, snatched a few more insects that had become entangled, and started talking with his mouth full

"Gruff, let me tell you something that I have learned over the years from following the Truth and faith." Zeki finally decided to sit down for a moment but atop Gruff's head. "One single, solitary creature, regardless of the size, mind you, that lives in the faith of the Creator CAN make a difference, and in doing so, can change the course of everything." Zeki peered at Gruff. "They just have to willingly choose to accept His Truth, step up, and allow Him to work through them."

"I want that, Zeki. I really do, and I suppose, given all that you have said, it's time for me to step up. No, let me rephrase that. I'm READY to step up!" Gruff looked back down at the community and started to stand.

Zeki jumped from Gruff's head and flew back up to the lower limbs of the trees. "Not so fast, Gruff. It's getting late. Best to bed down here for one more evening, and we can get an early start in the morning before the community all wakes up."

"I will tell you this," Zeki hopped from branch to branch, "your journey may have JUST started here, but it certainly will not end here! We will be leaving this valley, and maybe one day you will be led by the Creator to be back this way."

"Leaving this valley? Will you be coming with me?" Gruff laid his head down, propping it up on his legs so that he could look at Zeki.

"I will come with you for just a little while and tell you all the things that the Creator shared with me, but eventually, you will need to take what you know and learn to start standing on your own." Zeki ruffled himself to get settled.

"You will learn to let the Creator be your head, your guide, your teacher, your everything. When you move forward, it will be because you are in harmony with Him." Zeki ruffled himself again and settled into the branches.

"Do you have a family?" Gruff spoke, almost unsure he should have been asking such a question.

Zeki clicked softly. "Why, yes, I have a family! Though I'm now much, MUCH, older, I still have my beautiful, loving wife with me, and we have had dozens and dozens of children over the years. When crows settle down, it's for life! Why, I am hers, and she is mine, and together we have lived in the faith of the Creator. I will go and join her in just a few months when you are ready to stand on your own." Zeki sighed like he was in a hazy dream.

"I explained to her that I had to come and talk with you and lead you out of here. I told you, Gruff, that I've watched you for several seasons ever since you were born, and I was told that it was time for me to come talk with you." Zeki yawned and closed his eyes.

"Told?" Gruff raised his head and looked up. "Told by who?"

"Yes, that's correct. I was told. I really could not explain it at first. It was just two simple words, which were certainly no small echo in my brain! Why, I thought the entire world could hear them as loud as they seemed." Zeki ruffled himself again.

"Yeah...and?" Gruff chuckled at Zeki, who was now half asleep.

Gruff waited a couple of minutes, then spoke up, "And? What were the words?"

Zeki opened his eyes, started preening for a moment, and then looked back at Gruff with a serious, nearly trembling face. He cawed as loudly as he possibly could, his feathers nearly flying off his body. "GET UP!"

Zeki then settled back down. "Let me tell you this, Gruff. It honestly scared me! It shook every hollow bone in my body." Zeki looked visibly shaken. "I thought for sure that I was dead. I certainly deserve death! And then suddenly, I realized that He, the Creator, had been talking to me for quite a while. I just chose to ignore Him, but those words...those words picked me up and moved me."

He grew quiet and stared at Gruff, his eyes piercing deep into Gruff's soul. "Open your ears, Gruff. Hear me, meditate on my words until they are a part of you, and understand wholly so that you will act without fail, without question."

He continued to stare deep into Gruff's eyes, then he spoke again. "When the Creator speaks, when you hear His voice when you feel His hand lift you," suddenly Zeki cawed, and it echoed across the plain, "YOU DO NOT QUESTION, YOU DO!"

"Gruff," Zeki spoke softly, almost in a whisper, "my life has never been the same. That is when He gave me my new name and told me to watch you." Zeki looked down at Gruff.

"What was your name before? You did mention that earlier when we first met," Gruff mumbled mid-yawn.

"I was called Korvus." Zeki shook as if he were fighting back the chill of the air, becoming momentarily melancholic. "My old name was Korvus." Zeki stared up at the night sky.

"I didn't understand, Gruff!" Zeki started to cry softly. "I didn't understand the Creator until so much later in life. So much wasted time. I was wild, Gruff. I did things that I should not have done. I was a cheat, a thief, a liar, and at times much worse. I had made pacts with the evilest of evil things." Zeki continued to cry softly.

Zeki finally shook his head and refocused. "And then, well, the Creator, He came and put His hand on me and explained everything. He told me that I could put my entire past behind me if I only stepped out on faith and trusted Him from that day on."

Zeki looked up into the night sky. "He wanted to reveal something new to me each day, and with each day, I am renewed in Him. I am stronger, closer, and regardless of my past, I now belong to Him."

"Let me tell you this, Gruff," Zeki once again stared at Gruff, his eyes sparkling like the stars they sat under, "open your ears and listen to me! The Creator will give you the strength of a mountain if it be HIS will." Zeki pointed and then looked off into the mountains and froze as if something was calling out to him, and he was trying to listen to it.

After a couple of minutes, Zeki shook his head to bring himself back to the conversation, swooped down from the tree, and poked his feather into Gruff's nose. "When you find yourself alone, and you will; when things seem the bleakest, and they will be; and when there appears to be no hope; remain faithful to Him. Stay strong in spirit, and KNOW that, regardless of what may happen, you are forever His, and He is yours."

Zeki hopped and returned to his branches, glanced back up at the mountains, and then stared deeply at Gruff. "And nothing, I mean NOTHING, will ever separate you from Him!"

4. KATE'S NEW ADVENTURE

Kate rested her head against the seat belt that had some form of smelly, fuzzy shoulder pad cushion on it and glanced sideways through the car window, trying hard not to fall asleep. Besides, the smell of the furry creature attached to the seatbelt was certainly doing its best to keep her from nodding off.

The Uber driver who picked her up at the regional county executive jet port needed a little discussion… or maybe assistance? Kate thought for a moment. While he certainly was a very handsome fellow, Kate had begun to wonder if his neurons and synapse responses weren't running just a little rough, much like the vehicle she was currently bouncing down the road in.

Kate glanced at the driver, grabbed onto the seat belt, and snickered at the thought of the airfield being called an executive jet port. The tiny turboprop was certainly the biggest thing to fly into this area from Billings, Montana, that wasn't dusting crops but… executives?

Kate turned her attention back to the Uber and gave another quick assessment. This expert driver was certainly doing his best to hit every pothole in what was little more than blacktop in places but really couldn't be considered a road. After all, the dividing lines had long since faded and been replaced with gravel spread out by large dump trucks for miles in hopes that the overwhelming traffic would pack it back into a road.

Kate continued to stare out the window at the vast nothingness of civilization, just God's wilderness passing by at a bumpy 60mph. Suddenly, she thought about the entire situation and laughed out loud.

Uber Pierre Marcus took one hand off the steering wheel and mashed just about every button on the radio to try to get a signal and then glanced casually over to Kate. He spoke in a heavy French accent. "Something funny? I do like a good laugh if you have a joke brewing?"

Kate shook her head to try and force her mind back into reality, finally shoving the fuzzy seatbelt creature down from her face and onto her lap. "Oh, no. Sorry, I think I drifted off for a moment, and something funny came and went from my mind." Kate glanced again at the driver to see if he bought her story.

Pierre shook his head. "Oui, I can understand that. Not a lot up here, and a person can find themselves zoned out. Miles and miles of roads like this and more craters than the moon. Bet those NASA fellas didn't have to contend with this sort of thing when they got up there!"

Kate nodded and rubbed the sleep out of her eyes, but she knew what she was laughing about as the joke came back into her mind. *Why did this Uber cross the road? To hit the other pothole.* She worked to stifle a little snorty giggle, causing Pierre to glance again suspiciously at her.

"So, what in the world brings a tiny little thing like yourself way out to these parts?" Pierre reached forward to turn the static on the radio down. "You aren't exactly the kind of lady that just shows up and gets an Uber into a town that is smaller than the plane she flew in on."

Pierre started to laugh. "I think you have more luggage and gear than there are residents! Good thing I drove the executive vehicle today." Pierre reached his hand out and patted on the cracked dashboard of his apparent pride and joy Dodge Caravan.

Pierre's Caravan, his pride, joy, and executive limo resembled a rusty vehicle used on a golf course to pick up the balls from the driving range, but apart from all its issues, the windows were at least intact and scratch-free.

"Let's see," Kate mulled over just how much information to give Pierre and decided the basics were more than enough. "My name is Ranger Kate Bradigan. I'm headed to Honolulu to begin planning and charting a new station and district up in the Granite Mountains."

"You have GOT to be kidding me?! YOU'RE the new Ranger?!" Pierre's accent suddenly changed from French to backyard Texan. Kate's sudden revelation caused him to yank the steering wheel, but he still earned a bonus round of driving for successfully hitting everything that was at least two feet below road level.

Pierre quickly regained control of the vehicle. "We heard of someone coming from the Land Management Bureau who was going to be involved in bringing all this area into the national parks." Pierre was now waving his arm out the window like one of those crazy air dancers you see at car dealerships to showcase the vehicles on sale. "But had someone said that it was going to be something like you, I would have called them a bloody liar!"

Kate glanced at Pierre. "Something like me?! What exactly is that supposed to mean?" Kate sat rubbing her temples, trying to remain calm. "And, just what exactly happened to your accent?"

Pierre lowered his head into his shoulders and kept his eyes focused on the ruts. "Well, Ms. Kate, my name is just Pete. I change it to Pierre when I board and drive the fine craft you are on right now."

Once again, Pete patted the Dodge Caravan's cracked and peeling dashboard. "I think it makes it more relaxing and pleasurable, no? Sort of like being on the Riviera with a fine glass of wine? It really classes it up!

Kate suffered another jarring bounce and looked at Pierre. "Um… no. It really doesn't class things up, Pete. It makes you sound rather like a pompous, arrogant dillweed." Kate looked back out the passenger window, hoping this would be the end to the painful conversations.

"I didn't mean to disrespect you, Ms. Bradigan," Pete said, trying to regain his composure. "If you would forgive me, you are just the tiniest, prettiest lady to ever come through these parts. I was just assuming you were going to be setting up some sort of shop that sells coffee and donuts."

Kate turned and glared at Pete and then adjusted her countenance. "Well, I thank you for your comments, Pete, and I assure you that I am more than able to tackle this wilderness. And, I have been known to hand out a pastry or two." She chuckled again as she imagined getting a chance to pin Pete's face to the dashboard with a cruller.

"Well, there you go, Ms. Kate. Good to see that you can laugh, and I'm glad I could cheer up your day." Just then, the caravan hit a crater that bounced the vehicle so hard that it was a miracle it didn't break in half.

"Woo hoo!" shouted Pete, grabbing the wheel with both hands as his head hit the roof. "That's a new one!" The van swerved sideways briefly before straightening out again. "See, the issue is all the water running off the snow caps."

Pete pointed out the window at the mountains. "All that flash flood water tends to wash these roads out. Will make sure to let the state road maintenance crew know about this one! After all, we got to keep our small town connected to the rest of Montana." Kate glanced at Pete as he cracked a moronic grin. He said, "We are not a volcanic island, you know!"

Kate looked like she was riding a bull at the rodeo and hung on to the seatbelt with her left hand, her right grabbing at the passenger assist handle. "How far from town are we?" Kate asked before finding herself back in her thoughts. *Yeah, this poor fella is definitely a few sparkplugs short of a proper firing order,* she thought again and burst out laughing.

"Oh, I don't know, maybe another hour or so depending on conditions." Pete glanced at Kate to make sure she was surviving the journey and was pleased that she seemed to be smiling and enjoying the ride.

"It can be bone jarring, but that only adds to the excitement!" Pete enthusiastically piped in. "Fortunately, the road should smooth out just up the ways."

"So, then, do you know the area I will be mapping and setting up our stations in?" Kate was finally able to look down at an aerial map she took from one of her cases that had bounced from the backseat and into her lap.

"What area is that?" Pete casually reached over, took the map, and continued driving, at one point using his knees to steer while he used his hands to smooth out the map the best he could across the steering wheel.

"That area marked Sections 2, 3, and 4." Kate pointed while keeping a better eye on the road than Pete apparently was, as the caravan once again bounced two feet into the air.

"You're going up there?!" Pete came to a complete and sudden stop, the caravan skidding another 30 feet down the road on the loose gravel. The seatbelt creature suddenly rose and stuck to Kate's forehead.

Kate calmly slid the seatbelt creature back down to her lap. "That's what I'm out here for, to survey it, map it, document it, and make it all safe for the humans who can't seem to either read a map or manage to stay on one that's marked with pretty signs." Kate reached over, took her map back, and began to fold it up.

"Well, your superiors must not have bothered to tell you what you have gotten yourself into! I'm quite surprised they didn't just send a man." Pete looked at Kate and then checked over the Caravan to make sure it was still running. "Did you volunteer, or were you voluntold?" Pete looked at Kate, then finally back at the road and started to inch the Caravan forward again.

Kate once again found herself glaring at Pete, but this time, she imagined poking him in the forehead with her pen. Seeing as it was her only one, though, she thought better, took out her journal, and started writing some notes.

"I volunteered. Well, actually, I formally requested it. They have said it's remote wilderness and will be difficult." Kate looked back out the passenger window as the mountain range slowly came closer and closer into view. "I have been trained, schooled, coached, and prepared for this. Something up there is calling to me, and I intend to find out what." Kate glanced at Pete.

Pete peered out the window as he drove and scooted down low so he could look up into the air from under the sun visor. "Nothing up there calling you except the crazies, Kate. You would do yourself a favor by going to another assignment. That area, Section 3, is home to creatures and things that just shouldn't be!"

"What sort of things, for instance?" Kate yawned and closed her eyes.

"Well," said Pete in a whisper over the struggling drone of the engine, acting as if the creatures he was about to speak of could hear him and it was simply forbidden information. "The is a strange little fellow that comes down from those mountains from time to time. He hates everyone and everything, and I think he even hates himself when he has to lower his standards to come into town for supplies."

Pete rubbed his head. "It's not very often, and, ya know, it has been quite a while since we saw him last," he paused and thought.

"Well, for that matter, now that we are talking about it, his girlfriend that he went up there with him…, it's been a LONG time since we have even seen her. The town is wondering if she just up and died somewhere. But, you know, people like that, if they don't want to be found, they just will not be found.

Pete glanced back at Kate. "I will tell you this. That little, scraggly, mouthy oddity of a man needs Jesus!" He nodded at Kate and used his index finger to repeatedly point upwards toward the heavens.

"Then, there is supposedly a giant wolf." Pete quickly glanced out of every window as if to survey for areas of refuge.

Kate opened her eyes. "Excuse me? A giant what?" She then looked over at Pete.

"Yeah, you heard me right, Ms. Kate," Pete said, looking over at her as she quickly pointed at the front window, indicating he needed to pay attention to his driving.

"That crazy little badger of a man," Pete said, shaking his head, "when he wasn't pronouncing curses on the town, the people, or the paint scheme they used on mailboxes, was railing on about seeing a huge black wolf the size of a small Volkswagen!"

Kate pondered for a second, then sat up, took out her small journal, and started jotting down notes again. She then thought out loud, "Hmm… giant animals, and people for that matter, are possible if they have a faulty MSTN gene.

Kate scribbled notes mid-bounce and continued to think out loud. "I've read about it but have only seen it in rare situations…say a bulldog with abnormal muscle growth, a kangaroo, oh…hey, my brother…," Kate snickered. "Even in a bull, but again, it's very rare."

"MS what gene?" Pete glanced again at Kate, then back out the front window.

"Um, the MSTN gene. It's what controls the production of myostatin in the body. If it fails to produce, well, then you get something called myostatin-related muscle hypertrophy." Kate looked up from her notes and back out the window.

"I don't really follow you on this, Ranger Kate. I've had a little bit of schooling, but..." Pete scratched at the side of his head.

"Ok, well, let me see if I can explain it another way." Kate closed the journal and looked at him with an expression on her face that seemed to be silently screaming, "Bless him."

Kate cleared her throat. "Ok, if this little bit of blobby thing doesn't produce enough of this other little bit of blobby thing, then you end up looking like a muscle-bound big blobby thing."

Pete hummed and hawed for a moment. "I see, so you essentially end up looking like someone or something that's all roided out."

"Exactement, Monsieur Pierre," Kate chirped. "That means, 'exactly, Mr. Pierre,'" Kate smirked.

Pete glanced at Kate and smiled stupidly. "I see! So, tell me a little more about yourself. Brothers, sisters...husband?"

Kate rubbed her temple again and looked back out the window. "I grew up in a small town, much like the one I'm headed to now." She looked over at Pete. "The thing is, the town was so small that the school could only field sports for boys. "So, I played basketball and soccer on boy teams for years."

Pete's eyes grew wide. "Well, that will certainly toughen you up! You didn't play football?"

"Football and soccer were during the same time. That means during the same season," Kate said as she wrinkled her nose at Pete. "So, I chose the REAL sport. But your initial statement is truer than you know. Took some pretty hard knocks. But of course, my brother didn't help. He is three feet taller and three times heavier than I am, but I can still put him on the ground." Kate smiled.

"Three feet taller than you!" Pete let go of the steering wheel to use his hands as a ruler to gauge like he was measuring a fish.

Kate nodded. "Yeah, I may be exaggerating a bit. He's 6'7". But his ego is just as big as he is tall, and he eats like a Neanderthal."

She glanced at Pete and patted his shoulder. "Now, as far as a husband… I'm not currently accepting any offers, verbal, written," Kate paused, "or arranged." Kate smirked at Pete.

Kate looked back down at her journal, then back at Pete. "One day, perhaps the Lord will choose to complicate my life with a husband. If it be the Lord's will, then who am I to say no? But I assure you of this, Monsieur Pierre…he will be a Christian, God-fearing man!"

Pete let out a loud laugh, grinning ear to ear, then suddenly grabbed and white-knuckled the steering wheel, navigating the Caravan through yet another crater. "You can't have unequal yolks," Pete shot back.

The Caravan swerved through a pothole slalom before Pete, once again, opened his mouth. "I have to tell you, though, I never understood what eggs had to do with relationships." Pete looked back over to Kate, who was now staring back at him, totally devoid of all possible expression.

"It's 'yokes'…the word is 'yokes,' Monsieur Pierre," Kate spoke with her eyes closed. She finally looked back over to Pete and began to wonder not only how much longer this ride was going to take but also just how much Caravan would be left upon arrival.

After about two hours, they finally arrived in town, well, what there was of it. Kate opened her eyes just in time to see the "*Welcome to Honolulu*" town sign, which was hewn from a large timber and hand-carved.

Kate managed a small snicker mixed with a groan and read out loud, "Population 5000," written on a smaller sign just underneath.

"Eh, no…" Pete coughed into a curled-up hand as if he were trying to mask a huge secret from an opposing team. "Correction, 5001." He then gave Kate a wink.

"So, um, I have to ask. Why Honolulu? It's a rather odd name for the middle-of-nowhere, Montana. You know, essentially being a zillion miles from anything tropical and stuck practically on top of the world," Kate said, twisting her head to watch the sign pass by.

"Oh! Well, you see," Pete said, sticking his hand out the window to wave randomly at people. "One of the founders of this small town thought it would be funny and tossed the name into a hat when they were deciding. You can see which way the luck of the draw went," Pete chuckled. "But, after thinking on this name for quite a while over the past few years, I think I can tell you the real answer to this one." Pete once again waved at everyone like he was on a parade float.

Kate looked over to Pete. "Ok, and why is that?"

Pete slowed down and came to a stop at one of the only three stoplights in the town. "Because…" Pete paused and then looked at Kate. "When it's 40 degrees below zero, and you are freezing your Butte off, you will wish you were in Honolulu." Pete laughed, then laughed even harder when Kate finally blurted out a snort.

"Well, Ms. Kate, it's good to see that you are able to laugh!" Pete sat calmly at the stop light, waiting for it to change. "But you being a small-town girl, don't let this one fool you. It may seem small, but we do have a library, a rather small courthouse, and an albeit small but very capable emergency clinic."

The light turned green, and Pete began to move the Caravan forward once again. "WHY, we even have a discount store with a gas station!" Pete started to laugh again and pointed to the 4-pump arrangement as they cruised by.

"It's not a pay at the pump?" Kate said, laughing.

"No. Pay at the pumps are for people in too much of a rush to get to where they are going. Those kinds of people are not in any mood to get involved with a conversation." Pete waved his arm out the window at some of the locals again.

"Besides, Ms. Kate, we are already where we need to be here in Honolulu, and getting into a rush to go a couple of miles is pointless. Anything beyond a couple is going to take a few hours. So, you may as well slow down, engage in the conversation, make a new friend, and enjoy a nice cup of coffee!"

The Caravan slowed down yet again, and Pete looked at Kate. "You just never know; some people around here, well, they just may surprise you."

Kate eyeballed the town as they slowly moved through. Pete was careful to observe the 15mph posted speed limit, so she didn't miss anything. Kate looked down at some papers. "I'm going to be staying at the Granite Lodge. Do you know the place?"

Kate looked up from the papers for a second, flipped them front to back to see if she had missed anything, and then looked over to Pete. "I will be there for a few months while I get a team assembled, and we start heading out into the mountains."

"Granite Lodge, Granite..." Pete scratched his chin stubble. "Ah, yeah, Granite Lodge...nice little place. It's just on this side of town, maybe a mile or so further out in the country, which makes it nice and secluded," Pete said jokingly.

"Matter of fact, here we are!" Pete brought the Caravan to an even slower crawl, driving up a small path. "This gravel drive leads straight up to the lodge, probably a quarter mile, I guess?" Pete ambled the Caravan up the pathway through large trees that enveloped the driveway like a tunnel; then, finally, around a bend to be confronted by a massive two story log cabin.

The rear of the lodge faced east into the Granite Mountains to catch the morning, while the front balconies could enjoy the sun disappearing into the earth at night.

Kate's mouth hung open. "This seems a little out of place, doesn't it?"

She was now scrambling, trying to take in the entire view from under the front sun visor, spotting, of all things, a couple of large black SUVs that looked like they could be in an action movie.

Kate rubbed her eyes and poked at Pete's arm as they got a little closer to the lodge. "Is that a Bell Helicopter?"

"Ms. Bradigan, the Granite Lodge is certainly a beautiful place. I have brought many people from the executive jet port to stay here." Pete glanced back at Kate and smiled. "Some guests, of course, arrange their own transport to stiff me on the tips and fees just to bypass the experience you just had.

"One thing I hear them all say when they leave here is that the view alone is worth the stay! It has 12 bedrooms. Seven are master suites. There's a chef's kitchen. Why, I even think that there may be a jacuzzi in a few of those rooms, from what I hear," Pete said, now peering out from under the visor like Kate was.

"All this, out in the middle of nowhere. Makes you kind of think that the owner may have a few questionable activities going on," Kate said, finally opening her car door to step out and see the entire homestead.

She looked up at the top floor and rolled her head to the side, "I will tell you this though, I have never stayed in OR even seen such a place like this before, Pete. I certainly hope the owner-operator isn't a jerk or doesn't need a visit from Homeland Security."

Pete walked over and stood beside Kate. "Oh, I've never heard anything negative about the owner. He can be something of a jokester, though. His work is on the straight and narrow. I can tell you that. YOU know, in a small town like this, EVERYONE knows your business."

Kate nodded. "Yes, I know all too well about small-town life and how all the ears that live in it are not just on the corn, so..."

"Well, Ms. Bradigan, it certainly is a beautiful location and home. It is a nice small town, far enough out to not be bothered by the major metropolises of Montana but still within a three-hour drive or so." Pete spoke up while struggling to unload the Caravan of all the bags and equipment that Kate had shoved into the backseats.

"All I can really say is it's absolutely beautiful. Perfect! So, how much do I owe you for the Uber? I don't want to cheat you of your tip and fees?" Kate reached into one of her many bags for her wallet.

"Oh, no need to fret over that. It's all been taken care of by your bureau. Nice little tip, too." Pete carried the luggage up to the front door.

"Now, THAT is fantastic news!" Kate exhaled. "I love it when things work according to plan. Now, just to touch base with the owner-operator of the..." Kate leaned forward to read the small brass plaque on the door. "*Granite Lodge, P. Marcus Owner.*"

Pete opened the front door and proceeded to bring the luggage further into the home, stacking it in the middle of the foyer. "So, Ranger Bradigan, can I make you a cup of coffee? Or may I show you to your room so you can freshen up?"

"Excuse me?" Kate stumbled into the foyer behind Pete.

"You said you are looking for the owner-operator." Pete walked a little further into the room and turned around to face Kate. "I cannot guarantee that I'm not a jerk. So far, I've never been hit or cussed out, and I've never been ratted out to Homeland Security. However, I am indeed a little bit of a jokester.

"Uh, yeah. I need to meet with them to arran..." She paused, looking dumbfounded. "What just happened?" She looked up at Pete and around at the foyer, feeling a little flustered.

"My name is Peter Marcus, and I want to welcome you to the Granite Lodge. This is my home, and therefore, I am also your host."

Kate suddenly dropped the few bags she was carrying onto the floor like they were made of hagfish, her mouth still hanging open.

Pete gave Kate a little wink and a smile, then continued, "Your room, Ms. Bradigan is the first suite at the top of the stairs. I moved a few guests around to make sure that you had the best room of the house."

"That will be just fine Pe...uh Pierre...um." Kate stammered in an effort to complete a sentence.

Pete bowed his head slightly to acknowledge her. "Ms. Bradigan, you have a full ensuite bathroom with a jacuzzi, along with a small bonus room. I will be serving dinner at 6pm and breakfast at 6am. Guests are on their own for lunch; however, if I'm here and available, I may be talked into whipping up a sandwich.

"You may or may not believe this, but I do have a life, after all, away from the lodge, and that's not just running people back and forth from the jetport. It takes a very special guest for me to Uber." Pete smiled at Kate and started to carry the luggage up the stairs with her stumbling around in tow like she had just received a new pair of feet.

"Bu...but I really... I don't understand! I thought you were just the Uber?!" Kate rambled, still trying to comprehend what had just happened, while practically jogging up the stairs behind Pete.

Pete stopped on the stairs and looked back over his shoulder. "Ah! You see, Kate, you never asked what I do. You just assumed that all I do is drive people around all day in an awesome minivan, and I don't have enough brain blobby stuff to comprehend adult conversations."

Pete continued his trek up the stairs. "I do hope that you take the time to put the maps, journals, notes, and your work things away, at least on occasion, to really explore and see the stunning area you are in. Experience it, Kate."

"Well, why, I..., I don't. . . WHY didn't you say anything? Why didn't you stop me from making a complete boob of myself?" Kate asked, still stammering.

"Oh, that is just part of my personality, I suppose," Pete laughed. "I like to watch people and see how they interact with others. I certainly wasn't going to ruin the chance to see how you interact and treat the hired help." Pete laughed as he continued up the stairs.

"Here is your room and your key, Ms. Bradigan." Pete opened the door and then stacked all her luggage in the room.

"If you'd like, meet me back downstairs in the kitchen once you get the room looked over and you have had a chance to freshen up. I will get the kettle on and will answer any other questions you may have." Pete smiled and disappeared back down the stairs, leaving Kate alone, feeling rather embarrassed.

Kate slowly unpacked her luggage and then looked at herself in the mirror. "After that long drive, still looking snappy, Ms. Kate, and that bathtub is DEFINITELY going to be on the list of to-dos this evening!"

Kate finally collected herself and slowly came back down the stairs. Following the aroma of fresh coffee and the sound of voices, she wandered into the equally huge kitchen.

Pete was calmly sitting at the table with three other guests who were dressed in business casual. Pete was reading a large book of some sort and jotting down notes on a small pad, then sticking them into manilla folders.

He looked up when Kate came in, and without saying a word, he immediately closed all his materials, moved them quickly out of the way, and set a place at the table for her.

Pete glided over to the counter with his back to her and took another cup out of the cupboard. "Ranger, would you like sugar and cream… or cream substitute?" Pete snapped his hand towel like it was a whip and began prepping.

Kate sat down at the table, smiled, and nodded at the other three people who seemed to be focused solely on her. She turned to watch Pete, still a little irritated that he seemed to play her for a fool. But then, she decided to let it go, considering what she had thought of him initially.

"Oh, Mr. Marcus, if you have a good, sweet creamer that will work perfectly, and please just call me Kate."

"I can certainly arrange that, and YOU can call me Pete or Peter. After all, we shared a ride into Honolulu together." Pete spun around to glance at Kate and then spun back to the coffee pot. "Coming right up!"

The other three guests erupted in laughter. "OH, Dear Lord! You took the executive vehicle from the jetport?"

They looked at each other, continuing to laugh. "I made that mistake… ONCE," they nearly said in unison.

Kate looked at the huge kitchen: the window that was practically the entire back wall framed out and stretched from the floor to the second story, double ovens, the workspaces, the seating for probably 20 people.

Finally, feeling overwhelmed at the entire spectacle, Kate spoke up, "So what's the deal with you, Peter? How is it you came here and have this absolutely stunning place?" She laughed a little.

Pete raised his head and tilted to the side so she could hear him better. "So, you are asking the old cliche' what's a guy like me doing in a place like this?" He was now feverishly hand-mixing something in a bowl.

"Ok, yeah, quite honestly. Let's have the info," Kate said, propping her head up with a finger and thumb as she leaned forward, softly tapping her spoon on the table with her other hand, waiting for her coffee.

One of the guests interrupted, "Oh, this is a really good story. Amazing how things work out!"

"Well, long story short," Pete said, putting a cup of coffee in front of Kate, "my parents were very well off financially," he paused. "VERY well off, and unfortunately, they were killed in some freak car accident. I have no brothers or sisters, so I embarked on a mission to find out why bad things happen to good people. I'm sure you have heard people ask that question many times.

"During all that soul searching and after several self-destructive moments, I found myself in college, completed my master's in psychology, and finally my doctorate in physical medicine and rehabilitation." Pete went back to stirring his bowl.

Kate choked and accidentally spit out her coffee onto the table, the other guests quickly trying to pat her back to assist. "Wait, so you are a physical medicine doctor, and you are here, and you let me blather on about body chemistry on the drive in?" She raised her eyebrows with her mouth still open.

Pete snapped a towel and tossed it to her, then took another and started cleaning the table. "To be honest about being here, I received a job invite at a local hospital in Honolulu. Well, I should have read the fine print a little better, as I really thought it was in Hawaii. And as for you blathering on, I enjoyed hearing your journaling. Not necessarily the blobby bits, but..."

Pete paused and looked out the window, then turned around to face Kate. "But, you know, the town sounded interesting in the invite, and what harm could it do to at least come and check it out, if anything, for a good laugh.

"So, I got here just in time for the sunrise over the mountains. I got along really well with the emergency doctor, who apparently my father was good friends with, and we prayed on the matter. He helped me realize that we are needed in places like this. This was a chance to really build something from the ground up. Something that my father had started but unfortunately wasn't able to finish.

"I was stupid when I was younger. Never took an interest in what my parents were involved with. When they were out of town on business, I took it upon myself to burn down the town, so to speak, with supposed friends. But then there was the accident, and things went from there. I had no idea that my father had any business involvement or anything else for that matter in this area, much less knowing the emergency doctor.

"One day, out of the blue, I got a job invite from Honolulu and said, why not check it out? I didn't know that my father and Dr. Phillips had arranged all this for an *if something happened to me* sort of situation."

Pete turned to face his guests. "So, this really is the short version, but it all has led me to this small town of Honolulu. Yes, it's a silly name. Yes, it's a small place, but there is just as important work to be done here as in any big city. I plan to finish what my parents started." Pete turned around and went back putting the quick snack together.

The guests all then raised their drinks and toasted loudly to Pete and his parents.

Kate sat quietly, looking dumbfounded, before finally speaking up. "So, no brothers, no sisters...wife?" Kate quickly raised her cup and sipped at her coffee, feeling like a total doofus for that having even come out of her mouth.

Pete paused for a moment and turned to look at Kate. He slowly kept stirring whatever was in his bowl and then cracked a stupid grin, thinking about that very question he had asked her on the car ride.

Pete put down his bowl and then took a sip of coffee. "Mmm...Let me tell you something, Ms. Bradigan" Pete wiped his mouth and set his coffee cup back down. "You now know about my background, but I will say that the Lord has not chosen to complicate my life with a wife. I'm not currently accepting any offers: verbal, written," Pete paused in thought, "or arranged."

He turned back around to finish preparing the snack items and lightly hummed some tune designed to get stuck in your mind for a week. After a couple of minutes, Pete turned around once again, still displaying a stupid grin, along with another large coffee pot in one hand and a few dishes and forks in the other.

Kate finally turned to the other guests. "I'm so sorry. My name is Kate Bradigan. I am the new ranger for this area."

"OH! KATE, YES, quite right!" Pete exclaimed. "Please forgive me for being rude!" Pete spun around to face all his guests. "Kate, may I introduce Montana Governor John Shelton, Congresswoman Beverly Hass, and Congressman Alexander James.

They all rose and shook Kate's hand. "Nice to finally meet you, Kate. We know all about you, and we have no doubt you will do great things here!" Kate was able to partially rise out of her seat, still completely dumbfounded, to shake their hands.

Pete walked over to the table and refilled Kate's coffee cup while balancing an assortment of plates, forks, and treats fresh from the oven. He then set down homemade peach and cherry pies in front of them.

Pete then snapped his towel, divided the desserts, and served the distinguished guests. He looked at Kate and slid a large piece of pie over to her, snapping a cloth napkin and handing that to her as well.

Kate stopped fidgeting with her spoon and picked up the fork, looking down at the pie and nearly bursting out laughing. "You make this yourself, did you?" Kate loaded up her fork with the pie and took a mouthful.

"I most certainly did!" Pete exclaimed proudly, quickly slapping a spoonful of homemade whipped cream from his bowl on top. "What do you think?"

Kate looked back down at the pie and loaded up her fork, taking another mouthful with whipped cream. She then made several nods and yummy sounds with her eyes closed. Finally, she opened her eyes and looked at Pete. "Well, it's certainly not a cruller, but..."

Pete and the other guests all looked confused and then raised their eyebrows. Kate chirped, "But it will certainly do in a fight!" Kate then burst out laughing. "Excuse me, but may I have another slice?"

"Will you all be staying long?" Kate asked, finally able to speak.

Governor Shelton wiped his mouth, "Oh no, we have to get back to matters of the State, so to speak."

The Governor then looked over to Pete. "Believe you me, if I could find more time to stay here, I certainly would. However, I think we have got everything in order and ready to move forward on our business."

Governor Shelton then raised his cup to everyone in the room once again and nodded. "We will all be headed out in the morning and work on getting things finalized."

5. A REALIZATION

Just before sunrise, Gruff and Zeki left the community with no fanfare and under the cover of the early morning darkness. Not a word was spoken. It was as if Gruff had never been there.

Gruff was certain that the community would be thrilled to death with this new development, but in all honesty, that no longer concerned him. He started focusing on the pathways, trails, plains, things that he never had the chance to really look at, much less appreciate.

The two travelers headed up and over several ridges and down into a different valley. Zeki occasionally rode on Gruff's back and, at other times, took to the air to cause problems with other birds along the way.

After a while, they came to a wide-open clearing filled with various flowers in bloom. A small grove of trees grew strong, practically in the middle, and the colors and aromas of the entire area were mind-blowing.

Zeki hopped up to the top of Gruff's horn and snapped his beak at a passing insect. He leaned sideways and took a big look around while making another one of his rather unusual clucking sounds. "I think we could spend quite a while in this spot," Zeki said while peering down at Gruff. "Just look at it!"

"There is certainly enough vegetation for the likes of you," and the "local cuisine appears to be quite enjoyable." Zeki dove off the top of Gruff's head onto the ground and tackled some random, extremely unfortunate critter that happened to be sharing the space with them.

Zeki quickly choked down a beetle, then fluffed himself around on the ground to stir up a small cloud of dust. "How about it, Gruff? This looks like an excellent place to start relaxing and learning for a few months, and it's still fairly close to your community."

Gruff looked around, breathed deep to soak in all the flavors, and looked down at Zeki, who was already waddling around and snapping at other insects. "It does look very nice, but don't you think it's still a little close to my family?"

Zeki continued chasing the insects, snapping his beak at anything that flew or scurried. "I just feel you should initially stay close by, in case they need you for some reason, and until you get your feet under you, so to speak."

Gruff looked up. "Uh, why? With the way they treated me, beat on my body, cursed at me, blamed me for EVERYTHING! And you want me to stay close by?" Zeki snatched up a beetle and crunched loudly while listening.

"I don't owe them a single thing, Zeki. They no longer deserve my loyalty." Gruff spoke with a mouthful of roughage.

"It's not about what they deserve or what you THINK they deserve," Zeki said with his own mouth full of various things.

"Well then, what is it about, huh? Honor me once again with your insight, your wisdom." Gruff belched loudly, in turn causing Zeki to make little clucking sounds that could have certainly passed for laughing while turning to look again up at Gruff.

"Hmm, how do I put this? Well, ok. It's about being who THEY think you are versus the truth of what you COULD be. For example, it would be one thing If you turned your back on them, never to speak to them again. Who would honestly blame you?

"But, if you left to find the Truth and then, in having found it, you NEVER seek to improve yourself in the Creator, if you choose to never go back to at least share the Truth, whether they listen or not, wouldn't that be just proving them, right? That you were nothing more than a worthless, useless, disgusting goat, and you never knew the Truth to begin with? You would essentially still be just as lost as your family but in even worse shape because you would have HEARD the Truth!"

Zeki looked at Gruff. "Let me tell you this: just because you present the Truth, you live it, speak it, offer it, doesn't mean that whomever you present it to is going to accept it.

He scratched his head. "I will say this about you. You are certainly an odd one, Gruff. That's for sure, but you are also the only one of your kind, well of ANY kind, that I have ever seen take and get the beatings that you have. Maybe they are just threatened or scared of you. I mean, come on, you are easily bigger than two or three of them put together." Zeki looked at Gruff. "No, I think they are just afraid of you discovering the Truth and will do whatever they can to prevent it."

"You know that had crossed my mind on many occasions," Gruff grabbed another mouthful of green grass and flowers, "and that certainly explains why they would come at me in groups."

"Yes, and by keeping your mouth shut and letting them beat on you, what did you gain?" Zeki pinched Gruff's muscles jokingly and then hopped back up to the pinnacle of Gruff's horns.

Gruff chuckled, "Why, I have bones of granite, and my skin is like, hmmm...like... well, it's like something tough anyway. It's been a long, long, tiring road, Zeki. If you hadn't come along, I think I may have just finally given up."

Zeki interrupted, "Hey, Gruff, let's go check out that group of trees just a little further out. We can grab some shade and rest. It may be a good spot to call home for a while."

The pair moved on a bit further into the small valley and ended up on the other side, just where a new set of trees had sprung up, separating them from another set of rolling hills that blended and gave way to the beginnings of yet another mountain.

Gruff and Zeki slowly strolled through the flowers and came to rest under a young set of fir and hemlock trees. They quietly dozed, or at least they tried to. "Do you hear that noise?" Gruff said, opening his eyes and looking around.

"You mean that strange humming sound?" Zeki cocked his head to the side to listen a little better. "Oh yeah, I know what that is. You are in for a real treat! Come on, let's go find the hive." Zeki waddled around for a few moments, then hopped further into the small group of trees they were resting under.

"It's over here!" Zeki squawked.

Gruff yawned, grunted, then finally got up and ambled over to the general area that Zeki was eyeballing. "So, what exactly are we looking at?"

"Ok, first off, let's just keep our distance, for now at least. However, what you are looking at is a very fine, very full, and VERY tasty beehive!" Zeki snapped his beak in excitement.

Gruff looked on and then back to Zeki. "So, what exactly do you do with it?"

Zeki hopped up onto the back of Gruff's neck and scratched around, briefly causing Gruff's leg to kick. "Oh yeah, that's the spot!" Gruff tossed his head forward and grunted happily, continuing kick his leg.

Zeki chittered and proceeded to bury himself in Gruff's groomed fleece that he had just fluffed. "Well,' said Zeki, finally addressing Gruff, "everything you see there is VERY tasty!" He tried to scoot his body deeper into the fleece. "Let me tell you! I like a little bit of bee on a piece of comb with just a splash of honey." Zeki made chattering noises with his beak in anticipation.

Gruff sniffed the air in the direction of the beehive and could certainly smell something sweet, almost as if all the flowers of the fields were crammed into one small edible package. "Mmmmm, you know that does smell rather inviting, doesn't it?"

"Don't get too close quite yet, Gruff. We need to talk about the current inhabitants a little more. You have to approach this meal with caution, as those little rascals have teeth in their backsides!" Zeki once again chuckled at his cleverness in explaining things to Gruff.

Gruff squinted once, then squinted again before attempting to turn his head and look at Zeki. "Teeth, you say?"

"Well, honestly," Zeki glanced quickly at Gruff, "it's really just one single long one that can really give you a nasty zing if you don't eat and run really quick. One or two of the flying little flower vampires you can deal with... but an entire swarm?! Well, that's an entirely different situation."

Zeki popped his head up from Gruff's fleece, somewhat resembling a commander steering a tank, and looked down at Gruff. "You know, I was just thinking bears don't seem to be bothered by bees very much, and yes, I know you aren't a bear, but..."

Zeki looked down at Gruff face, then back down the entire length of his body, and continued to think. "But then again, you are as big as some bears that I've seen, AND you have a pretty tough hide, so, hey, kudos! This may very well work out to both our benefits!"

Gruff made little growling noises, causing them both to start laughing. "So, how do they make this comb and the honey it contains?" Gruff looked again at the hive and turned his head slightly.

"Ahh…" Zeki hopped out of his makeshift nest and onto Gruff's snout so he could look him directly into his eyes. "THAT'S where the bee magic of the whole process is! Those little savages flit about all day, going from flower to flower, plant to plant, gathering up the sticky stuff that's way down inside the bloom." Zeki swooped out in the field and snatched up a flower, then flew back and sat on Gruff's snout again.

Zeki cocked his head and peered way down inside the flower the best he could while holding the flower in one talon and balancing on Gruff's face with the other.

"They eat this liquid and store it in a special sack, but it's not their stomach. Once the liquid is in their honey stomach, all sorts of little things get added to it that begin to turn it into honey."

"Added to it from where?" Gruff cocked his head sideways and then said, "Zeki, seriously? I cannot talk with you on my face!"

Zeki laughed and hopped down to the ground. "Well, these little things you can't see are in the bee's body, and when they mix with the liquid, a change, a beautiful, wonderful, tasty change begins!" He clicked his beak again excitedly.

Zeki paused long enough to look at the hive again, then continued, "Well, then the bees fly back to their hive and drop off that collection of goo, and that goo gets eaten by other bees, puked up, and eaten yet again by other bees.

"This entire time, the liquid from the flower gets slowly changed into honey. The bees will then spend a long time buzzing and flapping to dry the honey out so that they can store it in the comb for when they need food." Zeki pointed back to the hive.

"I see. So, then, where does the comb itself come from?" Gruff interrupted.

"Oh, yeah! That's all part of the magic!" Zeki spun around and flung the flower, which in turn bounced off Gruff's nose.

"Get this!" Zeki grabbed Gruff's leg and leaned off it like a light pole. "The bees will all gather around like, hmm… like a huge flock of goats?"

"Ok, a swarming flock of goats with a sharp tooth in their rear-ends. I'm with you so far," Gruff said, eyeballing Zeki suspiciously.

"They will raise the temperature of their bodies, which activates some doohickey on their body, and it turns some of the sweet parts of honey into wax!" Zeki patted Gruff's leg and said, "The Creator is quite brilliant, and this is certainly a great example of His wonderful creation."

Zeki turned around and looked at the hive, then back up at Gruff. "The Creator's existence is evident in all the good things you see around you. I am certainly thankful for all the good things and, believe it or not, the bad that he has brought into my life. He has certainly given me the knowledge on how to explain these things to you."

"Why would you thank Him for bad things that happen?" Gruff finally sat back down, dumping Zeki onto the ground as he sat.

"THAT is a great question! Why would I thank the Creator for bad things that happen in my life…?" Zeki fluffed himself and hopped back up into his nest, making himself comfortable. "Well, for one, it teaches me to rely on the Creator instead of myself." Zeki pondered a moment. "Sometimes, when we get busy doing our own things, the Creator will allow issues to happen that shock us back into remembering to honor and rely on Him." Zeki scratched his head. "I know I learned a long time ago that if I'm left up to my own ways and devices, I will just make matters worse."

Gruff spoke up, "So, you are saying I should be thankful that I was beaten, cursed at, and a million other things that a living thing shouldn't have to endure."

"Well now, certainly those things are terrible, and NO ONE should have to suffer it. I couldn't begin to imagine the pain, physical or emotional! But yes, that's exactly what I'm saying…" Zeki looked out over the trees for a moment.

"Look, Gruff," Zeki peered out from his nest to look him in the eye, "it was through all those beatings, through all the horrible emotional scarring, that you have been prepared on how NOT to treat things!

"You know how NOT to perpetuate the lifestyle they were trying to thrust onto you. It has strengthened you inside and outside for the purposes He knows and has determined for you." Zeki unfolded his wings and gave Gruff a hug.

"Your experiences, Gruff, have brought you into a humble understanding and thankfulness to the Creator who has made all good things…for you." Zeki hopped out of his nest and waddled around on the ground. Then he looked up at Gruff and pointed his feathers at him. "BE the creature that the Creator so longs for you to be in Him… loving, humble, honoring, respectful, meek, with your body now made like granite and your new spirit of strength and courage, by Him and for Him."

Gruff looked down at Zeki and spoke quietly, "I have been alone, looking out on the world, waiting for the day I would have someone to call my friend, and I am thankful for you, Zeki. I am thankful that He sent you to teach me, to set my feet firmly on a new path."

Zeki waddled forward, opened his wings, and gave Gruff's face the biggest hug he possibly could. They sat quietly for a while as Gruff thought and meditated on everything that was said. Then, Gruff finally broke the silence. "SO! Zeki, let's talk about honey."

Zeki shot up. "I have been waiting for you to bring this topic back up! I'm nearly starving, and, might I add, there is an entire buffet swirling around just behind those trees!"

"Well," Gruff said, "let me ask you this first. Do you think I can make honey? In all honesty, from the way you describe the process, it doesn't sound all that difficult." Gruff whispered as they scooched closer to the beehive.

Zeki suddenly burst into hysterical laughter, to the point he started to cough, and tears flowed from his onyx-colored eyes. The more he tried to stifle his laugh, the louder he became. "Oh! You think so, do you?!" Zeki now resembled a little dust cloud that was rolling around on the ground, laughing.

"If you are not going to take this seriously!" Gruff said, stomping his hoof.

Zeki took some deep breaths, finally recovering, and looked at Gruff, trying hard not to go into hysterics again. "Ok, my friend, this is what you need to do. You see all those arnica flowers or the really tall bright yellow mullein flowers? OR even the white yarrow flowers?" Zeki asked, pointing his feathers to each.

Gruff looked as Zeki pointed at each one and nodded. "Yeah, I see them."

"Ok, good! BUT..." Zeki hopped onto Gruff's snout, "You can only choose ONE of them to make honey... a bee never makes a cocktail with his flowers." Zeki jumped back to the ground and strutted over to a comfy spot where he could watch Gruff and avoid hurting himself if he had another fit of laughter.

"Go around to a bunch of those flowers, get a really good wad of them into your mouth, and swallow them down. Then, come back here and sit with me for a while." Zeki fluffed himself again and snickered.

Gruff wandered out from under the trees and back into the open field and started grazing on the arnica flowers, occasionally glancing up at Zeki, who was clearly enjoying the show and pointing at other clumps he wanted Gruff to eat. After wandering around for about forty-five minutes, Gruff strolled back to the shade of the trees and sat back down.

Gruff belched loudly. "So, now what?" He looked down at Zeki while still chewing on a serious mouthful of flowers.

Zeki chuckled, looked out over the field, and waited. "You just keep chewing and bringing that concoction back and forth between those stomachs of yours. I will let you know when things should be about ready." Zeki poked at Gruff's side as if to see how much material he was processing and chuckled yet again.

"If I had one thing to do over…it would be YOU!" shouted William as he slammed Gruff to the ground. "You don't listen! You never seem to do what I have repeatedly asked you to do!

"I'm beginning to think that Nannie is right! You have been an embarrassment, a blot, a freak of nature, and I'm nearly to the point of not even being able to look at you!" William raised his hoof to stomp down on Gruff's young face.

Gruff woke with a jarring shake. Flying to his hooves, he looked around in a panic as if surrounded by an unseen enemy. Zeki, who was comfortably nesting close by, cracked an eye open and then popped his head up suddenly, attempting to assess the situation. Finally, Zeki settled back down and looked at Gruff.

"Are you ok? You about caused me to have a stroke!" Zeki grumbled before shutting his eyes again.

"Yeah…I'm ok. Just shaking off the past. I can't seem to get it out of my mind when I sleep." Gruff stood up, stretched, and let out another loud belch.

"Hmmm," thought Zeki. "Well, your past is no longer in control, my friend. You have freed yourself from that. Unfortunately, it will take time to mend."

"Will I ever forget?" Gruff walked over to Zeki and sat down.

Zeki opened his eyes again and touched Gruff on the nose with his wings. "No, you will never forget, and you may very well have the pain of those memories with you for the rest of your life… But trust me when I say that there is peace. You will feel peace and have a way of dealing with those things from your past in the comfort of the Creator."

Zeki poked on Gruff's stomach. "HEY! I think we have been resting for long enough. If you are going to make some honey, there is no time like the present." Zeki chuckled again at the thought of what was about to happen.

"Ok, now remember, if you are going to make honey, you have to get that concoction out of your stomach and let the enzymes do the work." Zeki took several waddles backward, cocking his head sideways to watch.

"Ok, yeah, I got this!" Gruff heaved and hacked, his backend rising in the air with each forced regurgitation in an effort to bring back up and out what was once chewed. With one last retching sound, a steaming gelatinous pile of something came out of Gruff's mouth and plopped onto the ground. For a few moments, the pair looked on quietly.

Zeki hopped closer to Gruff and slowly strutted over to the disgusting pile that seemed to have a pulsating rhythm, as if it had its own heartbeat, and examined it curiously.

Zeki worked up his courage and strutted all around the blob several times before finally looking back at Gruff. "Ok, yeah, um…I'm going to need just a moment."

Zeki shuttered and involuntarily ruffled. He then looked at the blob and back to Gruff. "Um…I have to say that whatever that is, it's extremely disturbing."

Zeki now stood within a beak's length, cocking his head to the side to give the pile a full examination. Still ruffling his feathers and shaking his head, he turned back to Gruff. "You know," said Zeki in a weak voice, "I have been all over this country. I have seen many things, and I ashamedly admit that I have eaten many things. But I tell you this, Gruff. THAT looks nothing like honey." Zeki tried to keep from vomiting. "And it is quite possibly the most disgusting thing I have ever seen…or witnessed, for that matter, coming out of ANY animal, living OR dead!"

Gruff scowled at Zeki and then stepped forward, sniffed curiously, and poked at the heaping mess with his hoof, causing Zeki to hop backward and spread his wings, ready to bolt at first signs that the pile was alive and about to fight back.

Gruff looked back at Zeki, "Oh, stop! It's not that bad!" Gruff then poked at the blob again. "But, according to your instructions, Zeki, if we are going to make honey, you know what needs to be done…" Gruff then scooped the pile into his mouth and swallowed it down again with one gulp and a quick snap of his head.

Zeki began to caw, hack, and stumble around as if he could faint at what he had just witnessed, just barely able to keep his own lunch down. Gruff turned back to the beehive to observe and said, looking over his back to his friend, "You know that tastes NOTHING like honey. I just realized something. I think only a bee can make honey, Zeki…"

Gruff then belched slightly to bring up a piece of the gelatinous mess from his stomach to chew on for a bit, causing Zeki to pass out, but not before vomiting.

6. GREETINGS FROM HONOLULU

Kate sat quietly in the kitchen by herself. She was awake way before Peter and the other guests staying there. She put the coffee on and stared out the huge window that was still showcasing the mountains in the distance. Even in the dark, she could see their magnificence and hear them ever so softly calling to her.

Kate sat down with her cup, took out her small pocket journal, and began logging her first thoughts of the morning.

It's now been a couple of months staying at the Granite Lodge and getting to know the residents of downtown Honolulu.

Kate stopped writing for a moment and laughed at the imagery of that very statement.

Preparations don't ever seem to show much forward progress, BUT they are still continuing. The Bureau has begun to take hard looks at rental space in an office to work out of on Main Street until the primary station and substation are built; however, they are willing to let me use Granite Lodge IF the owner agrees to the conditions.

Kate once again laughed when she re-read her statement about "Main Street."

Being at the Granite Lodge has certainly been a blessing, especially seeing that Dr. Peter Marcus is allowing us to make use of the HUGE garage as a makeshift office. Although my office space is rather small, I am certainly not going to complain! I still have no idea why the Governor or Congress people were here when I arrived or what Pete has to do with them, but all things will be revealed eventually.
I have the shortwave radios, antennae, and HAM radio communications up and running, along with generator backups for the coming winter season that, from what the locals tell me, will be within the next few months. I'm not sure if they are using a Farmer's Almanac or simply the fact that they will be able to make ice cubes by just leaving the trays on their front stoops.

Kate paused for a moment, sipped from the cup of coffee she had made, and then nibbled on a leftover sandwich that Pete had made for her the prior evening.

I have a meeting with the Regional Supervisor, Todd McMillan, at around 1pm today in the office.

Kate paused and looked out the kitchen window, just able to see the roof of the garage.

I really am looking forward to finally getting started on what I'm out here to do. I can hear the mountains and trees calling to me.

Kate closed her log and shoved it into her pack.

She sat quietly, listening and looking out of the large kitchen window that was now beginning to showcase the golds and yellows of the sunrise as it fought to split the mountain and horizon. Kate took in the morning sun as it began breaking across the peaks, shining down into the valley and filtering into the Granite Lodge kitchen window.

Pete walked into the kitchen, and when he saw Kate, he became nearly frozen in place, only a few lightly spoken words escaping from him, "Absolutely beautiful!"

He watched as the sun highlighted and kissed Kate's cheeks. Her hair became almost alive with the warmth of the rays that were trying their best to comb it. She had become completely enveloped in a golden haze as the occasional fine particle of dust would glisten like a diamond, and for a moment, all of time stood flawlessly still, capturing her in all of that day's creation.

"I'm sorry. Did you say something, Pete?" Kate asked, setting down her coffee and turning around to look at him.

"C'est tout à fait magnifique mademoiselle." Pete coughed and tried to play it off the best he could. "The way the sun comes up from the mountains and fills the kitchen. You don't get the same effect back in town. That window is in the perfect place for the perfect times."

Pete walked over to the counter, poured a large cup of coffee, and turned back to the prep counters to begin making breakfast.

"C'est parfait, Pierre, la création de Dieu." Kate smiled, then looked back out the window.

"I will certainly miss that view, Peter, if the Bureau finally gets a place in order and I get settled in some small shack back in town. I got a text message from them saying that they may have some space coming available in a couple of months." Kate looked back down at her phone and swiped through messages.

Pete's face grimaced, and he was thankful his back was turned. "Well, there is certainly no rush, Kate. I have plenty of room here at the lodge. You are more than welcome to stay here for as long as needed."

Pete quickly tossed in, "I may even give them a discount that they just can't say 'no' to. So, what's on your agenda today?" Pete began placing various breakfast items on the table, and half leaned backward against the counter to eat standing up.

Kate watched Pete eat like he was a lean-to. "Peter, quit being a goof, please. Sit with me." Kate kicked a chair, and Pete happily slid into place, his rear sliding into the chair in unison with his plate on the table.

"I have a meeting with the regional supervisor at 1pm today." Kate looked at her calendar. "I'm pretty sure we are about to kick this whole thing off, and I have also been going over the ranger candidate applications for the Honolulu location. We really should be ready to roll. Everything is just about in place.

"I have my maps," Kate said, patting the table, "my aerials, the topography. I just need the green light to head out." She raised her cup and took a long sip of coffee, quickly glancing at Pete, using her cup to hide the fact that she was staring at him, hoping to catch any hint of sparkle in his eyes.

Kate lowered the cup and poked a fork at some scrambled eggs and toast. "I just need the rest of the team assembled, or at least 5 of them, so I can start getting things scheduled. I can't be out there without some sort of support."

"Oh, well, you know you have my support." Pete wiped his mouth and stood to go finish making breakfast. He went back to the counters and started flinging flour and rolling out dough for fresh biscuits, ending up with more flour on himself than anything else.

Kate chuckled at Pete, who was now resembling a young lad she had read about who was fighting to paint a fence. "There is an area up on this part of the mountain that I need to scope out for our station. We have that as Sector 2," Kate said while taking out the various maps and placing them back on the table so Pete could see where she was referring to.

"I'm guessing that it will take me a solid three hours or more to get up to that location. So, you can see why I now have all that equipment stored up in your garage, umm, ranger office, versus some "*Stow-n-Go*" in downtown Honolulu." Kate let out a laugh.

"What's so funny?" Pete said, looking up from the map while hand mixing the flour in a large bowl.

Kate paused and cocked her head at Pete with one eyebrow raised. "Calling downtown Honolulu DOWNTOWN! You don't think that's even remotely humorous?" Kate asked, still snickering.

"Ahh… yeah, ok. I can see the funny," Pete said, mockingly rolling his eyes at Kate. He looked back down at the map, then turned to walk back to the prep counter. Then, suddenly, he felt the back of his head being hit with a biscuit.

Pete looked back at Kate, who was now also turning to look behind her as if looking to see who in the world could have thrown that. She turned back to face Pete, shook her head, and raised her shoulders and arms in disbelief. "Some people, huh?" He just grinned stupidly and cleaned up her mess.

"Hey, look…I'm not a ranger, botanist, or animalologist…," Pete started to speak, "but look at the map." He walked back over to the table to look at everything.

"An animalologist, Peter? Really? I think the word is zoologist." Kate got up and walked over to the sink, rinsed out her cup, and began to arm herself with another biscuit since the last one obviously didn't seem to have any effect in getting him to react to her in any form.

"No, seriously, take a look at it…" Pete pointed down at the maps. He walked back over to the table, took Kate's chair, sat down, and popped another piece of biscuit into his mouth. Using two flour-covered hands, he attempted to smooth out the map and pointed again. "I would advise you to stay out of what you have labeled as Sector 3."

Kate stepped forward and walked to his side. She put her hand on his shoulder and leaned over so she could look down at the maps. "You have information on that area?" Kate asked, flicking bits of flour off that portion of the map.

"Yeah, that entire area is, well, cursed! This is the area you heard me talking about while we were driving up here from the jet port, remember?" Pete turned to look at Kate, but with her standing so close to him, he nearly stuck his nose in her ear.

Pete quickly turned back to the maps. "There have been people who have gone up there and just never came back, Kate." Pete was now pounding his finger on the map. "There are sheer drop-offs, and you could find yourself staring at the bottom of a canyon at 32 feet per second, per second." He wiped the crumbs off his mouth. "i.e., you and the ground floor meet up pretty fast." Pete turned in his chair so that he could look up at Kate. "That area is where that little scraggly, foulmouthed, whack job comes down from, and you already heard me say what HE claims is up there!"

Pete stood, forcing Kate to back up, and looked down into her eyes. "Why, Ranger Bradigan," he paused, "I say even that little fellow shouldn't be up there, and if we could find him and his wacky girlfriend, we would sure see about bringing them down off the mountain."

Pete turned and looked out the window, then back to Kate. "There are a lot of questions that little fellow needs to answer."

Pete turned again to point out the window towards the mountains but looked into Kate's eyes, "Some places people just need to stay out of for EVERYONE'S safety."

Kate's brow furled, and she looked at Pete's beautiful, wonderful, totally stupid face and paused for a moment before quickly regaining her thoughts. "Oh! Relax, Peter." She then turned her back and walked over to the coffee pot, waving her hand in the air.

"Look, in regard to the entire matter, I have as much chance of running into giant wolves and a little leprechaun on that mountain as the roads leading into this town magically getting filled and paved! Besides," Kate looked at Peter and smiled, "I am MORE than able to protect myself!"

She stood firm and defiant while adding a dash of cream to her newly refilled cup. She then popped out her pinky, sipping her coffee as if she were high-class posh. "If I need to arrest that little scraggly stump of a man, I'm certainly capable of immobilizing, cuffing, and booting his little magical self and his pot of gold all the way down the mountain." Kate walked over to the center counter and then turned to look at Pete. "Besides, it's been a little while since my last confrontation with someone, and I'm due."

Pete chuckled, then turned and walked over to Kate. They stood there, just inches separating them. "Kate, I have no doubt that you can take care of yourself, but. . ." Pete paused and looked at her.

"But what, Peter?" Kate raised the cup between them and took another sip of coffee, her heart fluttering.

Pete waited for Kate to finish and to lower her cup. "But, you do know...?"

Kate opened her eyes wide and raised her eyebrows, shaking her head a couple of times sarcastically. She stood looking at him, daring him, and waited for the punch line.

"Things could still happen that you aren't prepared for..." Suddenly, Pete took a muffin that he had been hiding in his hand, smashed it into her forehead, and dragged it down onto her nose.

Pete grabbed his jacket off one of the chairs and quickly ran out the door before she could react, shouting back to her, "Hope you have a great day, Kate!"

Kate sat at a small desk in a small office, in a small corner of an exceptionally large garage surrounded by communication equipment, chalkboards, cork boards, a couple of computers, and some sort of gizmo that they said was important but couldn't really explain why it was important.

This temporary station that Peter Marcus had built in his garage contained her office, a conference room that was big enough for a water cooler, and another room she was using for storage.

Well, it's not exactly the biggest of offices, she thought, looking around with one hand on her chin supporting her head, *but it works perfectly until the new stations get built, and I have the Granite Lodge right HERE, and let's face it Kate...it really is stunning, but I will not tell Peter that.*

Kate sat tapping a pen on her head and then on her desk calendar. She looked at her watch. "It's about 1pm. Surely THIS office isn't THAT hard to find," she mumbled. "It's in the backyard for..." Kate groaned at what came next. "Well, ok, I will say it, for Pete's sake!" She then laughed hard.

Finally, the regional supervisor showed up, pushing on the side door, then pulling the door before finally figuring out the correct orientation to get it to open. "Good afternoon! I'm Regional Supervisor Todd McMillan. I am so glad to finally meet you, Ranger Bradigan.

McMillian twisted momentarily to fit completely through the doorway. "I have been hearing VERY good things from your past crew, and District Ranger Llyod Jackson is a good man. He knows character, which is probably why he bugged all of creation to make sure you were considered for this new role. No one could shut him up!"

"Nice to finally meet you, Mr. McMillan." Kate stood and reached forward to shake his hand.

Todd was a roly-poly of a man, and with him wearing his ranger forest greens, he rather resembled a rotund garden pea that had escaped from the pod. Or maybe the pod simply could no longer envelop his stature and thus had to release him into the wild? Either way, his handshake was almost firm but still like grasping a piece of undercooked veal.

It was apparent that Todd McMillan no longer seemed to care about his appearance, but he still maintained a serious can-do attitude. Even with all that going on, Todd was a very energetic and likable fellow, sort of like a favorite uncle who always had a pocket full of hard candy and shared stories that could only be told around a campfire when parents weren't around.

"Listen, Kate, it's time we got this ball moving," Todd said as he ambled around the small room, waving his fingers that looked like little cocktail wieners. He then tried a couple of chairs before he found one that he could successfully wedge himself into.

"You have everything you need to at least start making initial trips into Sector 2 to start planning a location for a permanent station."

"THAT is what I have been waiting to hear!" Kate eagerly replied, finally sitting back down and getting comfortable.

"The powers that be want this project started. No more delays and lollygagging. So, we will have to play catchup when it comes to staffing and, well…" Todd took a moment to glance around, "the station comforts, if you will." He shifted in his chair, which creaked and groaned in protest.

"I know you are still going over the applications for your team that I sent you." Todd now looked through some of his notes. "I think there are some solid rangers who will be ideal to help you really build something out here. I would love to see if we can get started with five quality rangers, although there is still one more empty slot. But we can fill that a little later down the road." Todd looked up at Kate to see if she was looking and following along in her packet of information.

"Let's get your review completed so that everything is all official, which brings us to some new information for YOU, Kate." Todd once again looked up at Kate, some perspiration forming in beads across his face.

He snapped a handkerchief out of his jacket pocket to wipe off his forehead, flinging pocket lint that had apparently been hidden since time began out into the open. Lint flew through the air, and a couple of chicklets flew across the room like aged trapeze artists, bouncing on Kate's desk before finally coming to rest in front of her.

Kate looked down at the old gum, and Todd turned a rather interesting shade of red in embarrassment. "Ha! uh…er…" He cleared his throat for a second. "Sorry, Kate, as you may be able to see, I have not had to wear my uniform in quite a while. No telling what is hiding in these pockets." he started tapping on each one.

"But that's not going to be much of an issue in the coming year or so." Todd looked back up at Kate before ensuring each pocket was free of other surprises.

"New information for me, and are you planning on going someplace, sir?" Kate wasn't sure if she should really be watching or finding it entertaining to watch Mr. McMillan's attempts to get his arms across his body to pat down his pockets.

"Well, I've not made it official yet." Todd finally stopped fidgeting, shifted in his chair, and attempted to cross his arms while he spoke. After a few moments of effort, however, he simply settled for holding onto each wrist as they rose up and down on his chest with his breathing.

"If I may ask? Made what official, Mr. McMillan?" Kate picked up her desk calendar and slid the contents that had come to rest upon it into the trash.

"Well, I am going to be retiring very soon, at least trying to. Look at me. I am as wide as I am wise, and I'm getting older." Todd paused and looked at Kate, "And I can only run triathlons instead of Ironman competitions." Todd froze and waited for a response.

"I'm sorry. What was that?" Kate quickly looked up, placing the calendar back and arranging her other fidget items, entirely unsure of what she heard.

Todd let out a boisterous laugh. "Don't try to play it off, Kate. I was just seeing how much you were paying attention! I'm going to be retiring soon." He shifted himself around again. "Now listen, I know that you don't have the time or seniority over other rangers, but over the past few years, you have shown to have the people skills, the technical knowledge, the education. . .heck, Bradigan, you are everything that this new area needs to bring it up to speed and certainly give us a better public image when the lens and attention are turned on."

"Are you saying you...?" Kate sat forward in her chair but was quickly hushed.

"Let me finish, Bradigan, the Governor likes you, the Congress folks like you, heck, I even like you!"

"I really do appreciate that, Mr. McMillan, but do you think I am ready to take on your duties as Regional?"

"Let's not get too far ahead of ourselves, Kate! No… no, there is some hard-charging yes-man, who shakes more hands than an octopus, who has been tagged for my position." Todd squirmed in his chair.

"But what I'm saying is that I'm here not only to get your project rolling, but I have officially been sent to ask that you take the role of District Ranger for THIS new area that's being formed!"

Todd let go of his wrists and tried his best to use the armrests to give himself a little push. "It's, of course, all hush-hush at the moment. The people who need to know will know when it needs knowing."

"There are still a couple of hurdles to cross and congressional approvals, that sort of thing. Stuff that happens WAY above our grade levels, Kate." Todd waved his hand in the air.

"I just assumed it was going to be a part of your current district, and I was going to be an assistant. I knew that the district position hadn't been determined if there was even going to be a position for that," Kate said, trying to get in a word before Todd started in again.

"No, no. The sectors laid out are certainly big enough to have a new district created, especially with the amount of land we are talking about that's being conveyed to our care." Todd shifted again. He leaned forward, then back, repeating the process a few times like he was a giant bellows stoking a fire. "Besides, as I said before, you have made quite an impression with all the government talking heads, and they want to see what you got."

Todd wiped his forehead again. "Then, you take a look at Honolulu." He squirmed forward a little to look out the window. "It's certainly one of the up-and-coming cities of Montana." Todd paused in thought, then gave a little laugh. "Well, interestingly, it's one of the larger towns in Montana, anyway, especially with that Dr. Marcus fellow being here Todd once again attempted glancing out the only window toward the lodge.

"Now," Todd looked at Kate with a more serious face, "with me getting older and looking like a soccer ball on a foosball table, it's hard to carry out my duties and get around in my region. If I'm not getting around in the region, well, then I am not a very good manager, and if I'm not a good manager… Well, then you can't have a functional team, and without a functional team, Kate…" Todd looked her in the face.

"Then, what do you get? You get people hurt, damage, and destruction of lands, resources, and animals that have been entrusted to our care." Todd finally took a breath and a moment to gather his thoughts.

Todd finally put his handkerchief away. "YOU, my dear Ranger Kate Bradigan, are the face and future of conservation and responsibility, AND why a new district is being formed. The powers that be want this to happen, and they want YOU leading it."

"Mr. McMillan, I am honored and quite flattered that you would consider me for such a role!" Kate was now turning the same red shade of embarrassment that Todd displayed earlier. "I certainly will not let you, the department, or my district down!"

"I have NO doubt, Kate! No doubt at all!" Todd wiggled himself forward in an effort to dislodge himself from the chair and stand, but realizing he couldn't, he changed tactics and scooted closer to the desk. He tossed out a baby lamb chop of a hand for a congratulatory shake.

"But you need to understand, this is all hush-hush until the official papers are signed, Congress has approved, and you are appointed." Todd nodded knowingly at Kate. Todd attempted to squirm out of the chair again. "It's honestly all formality at this point, my dear… Yes, I can see why they all like you. You are perfect for these new challenges."

Kate stood and eagerly shook his hand. "Ok, Kate, with that out of the way, let's talk about what needs to get done in the present." Todd gave up and then softly flowed back into the chair.

"Mr. McMillan…" Kate started to speak.

"Please, enough of that," Todd waved a hand in the air, "you call me Todd when it's just us, and if there is ANYTHING you need, you contact me!" He smiled and finally rocked himself free and into a standing position.

"Todd, why don't we head into the Granite Lodge for some coffee and better seating arrangements?" Kate waved her hand like she was showcasing the car that had been hidden behind a stage curtain. "I honestly don't think the owner will mind." Kate smiled at Todd and opened the office door.

7. LIFE UNDERGROUND

Gruff and Zeki slowly moved across the valley at the base of some ridges and slopes that would eventually give rise to more mountains. For now, they stayed just at the base exploring, or rather Gruff explored, while Zeki explained how it all came together for the glory of the Creator.

"It seems like we are an endless distance from the community and where I started." Gruff flopped over and scooped up a mouthful of grass.

"It may seem like it, but funny enough, we are really only, I don't know, twenty, thirty miles as the crow flies." Zeki let out a loud, cawing laugh. "We really don't have to travel far to learn, but if you wanted to, you could probably make the trip back in just a few days if you put hoof to the mountain."

Zeki strutted around, looking for insects, "But we don't look back! At the moment, there is no purpose for you there. OUR directions are forward, my friend, ever forward."

Gruff watched Zeki moving around, snapping at insects and using his feet to turn over rocks and small debris. "When do we stop moving forward?"

Zeki cocked his head at Gruff and chuckled. "We stop moving forward when the last breath crosses our lips… and the Creator comes to restore all that was broken and corrupted." Zeki waddled over to Gruff and then held his snout in his wings.

"Then, and only then, my dear friend, do we get to finally rest in His restored creation and enjoy all that will be given to His faithful." Zeki waddled over to Gruff and wedged himself between his neck and legs. They both dozed in the late summer sun, into the night, and into a new day.

The pair wandered around for a little while, eating and catching some breakfast before settling down once again so that Gruff could listen to Zeki talk about all the wonderful things that he had to share with him.

Finally, they decided to move again and came to a spot that had the most curious of small brown animals. Gruff and Zeki sat quietly, watching. "I think those are marmots, yes, marmots." Zeki turned his head sideways to get a better examination.

"They will build their homes underground," Zeki said, hopping up onto Gruff's head. "They are sort of like you, eating flowers, grasses, that sort of thing."

"Well, it's nice to know that there is an expert, other than myself, on what I am and what I do," a brazenly brown marmot said, standing up on his hind legs and looking at Gruff and Zeki.

"Well, now, of course, I meant no disrespect, my friend. I was just…" Zeki hopped down and started to waddle over to the marmot.

"There is no point in coming off your horse, or whatever that thing is," the marmot said, pointing at Gruff. "I don't expect you to be in my way much longer. I have work to do and NO time to loaf, like you and… whatever that thing is with you." The marmot then bared his little teeth and chittered.

"I was just explaining to my rather large mountain goat friend here about all the things that we encounter and how they all work together."

Zeki changed his waddle into small hops while chasing the insects again, then hopped back onto Gruff's head.

"Mountain goat, you say?!" The marmot paused and looked back at the pair. "Oh, whatever, I don't have time to debate what that thing really is. You say it's a goat, so it's a goat."

"My name is Zeki, and this large beast's name is Gruff." Zeki made his best attempt at formal introductions.

The marmot nodded at the pair. "My name is Stephen." He then immediately went back to digging and clearing out space in his underground bungalow.

A few moments later, he stopped and peered back out of his hole at Zeki. "I thought your kind only made friends with wolves? Seems I remember hearing things about..."

Zeki quickly coughed. "Well, some do that, yes, but I am on a different path..."

Stephen quickly butted in after losing his train of thought, "Well, you know, you two just sitting there watching me certainly doesn't help me get this burrow finished. Wife will be along soon enough, that is, once I entice one, and what will I have to show for it?" Stephen looked up out of his hole again and said, "A nosey old bird and a...a whatever you said that was supposed to be."

Stephen went back to digging and, no more than thirty seconds later, looked back up out of his hole while scooping dirt with his front paws, hiking it like a football out from under his rear end onto the surface.

"I'm sorry. Did you have a question, or what exactly was your question, if I missed it?" Stephen paused, looking up at them both.

Gruff, who was now lying on the ground, raised his head and said, "What exactly are you doing again?" Gruff pushed at the mound of dirt with his hoof, causing some of it to slide back into Stephen's burrow.

Stephen started to squall. "HEY! Watch what you are doing! There is a lot of precision work going on here, and I don't need to keep shoveling out all of this dirt because you can't keep your big hooves off my excavations!"

He emerged from his burrow, chittering angrily to himself, then took a lap around his burrow to assess the damage. Then, he shook his tiny fist at Gruff and Zeki.

"Why don't you scoot back a bit? Yeah, let's do that, shall we?" Stephen scurried over to Gruff and shoved on his hooves in an effort to move him.

Gruff and Zeki looked at each other and then back to Stephen and started laughing at the sight of this small brown ball of fur trying to move Gruff.

"Oh, I see," said Stephen. "You both just think I'm here for your tomfoolery."

"I uh..." Zeki looked at Gruff and then back at Stephen.

"I will have you know that my job is ESPECIALLY important! I must get this..." Stephen paused, looked back at his burrow, then looked up at Gruff. "What was your question again?"

Gruff moved his hooves to placate Stephen's irritation. "I was curious as to what you are digging that hole for."

Stephen walked back toward his burrow so he could see Gruff a little better. After all, there was a LOT of Gruff to be seen when you were that close. "It's not a hole! Why, THIS is the most lavish resort a mammal could have come winter. Besides, I don't have the luxury of being a small mountain with legs." Stephen chittered again.

"My size..." Stephen said, using his arms to try to span his yellow-furred, girthy midsection, "and my incredibly good looks make me a very good dinner guest for any number of predators around here." Stephen continued grandstanding. "I am building this burrow not just to live in but for pure underground predator protection!"

Gruff nodded and started to speak, but then Stephen started to chatter again. "And, of course, one of the most important things, it's got to get us through the winter. We will head into our burrows and sleep until spring. I don't know, maybe about six months."

"Six MONTHS?!" Gruff said suddenly. "You spend six months underground?" Gruff looked at Zeki in disbelief. "Sleeping?!"

Stephen nodded "Couldn't tell you what a snowbank looks like. I'm fine; warm and cozy underground all winter. It's always warmer underground in the winter." Stephen paused mid-thought. "Unless it's summer, and then it's cooler." Stephen's whiskers shook while he laughed. "I know to something as large as you, that may seem like nonsense, but oddly, it's true."

Gruff stood up and stretched. "So, you are saying if I dug down and made a burrow, I would be warm all winter?"

"I'm not saying that at all for you." Stephen wandered around Gruff to take in the massive size. "You are built for winter, my friend. By the time the freezing weather gets here, you will have a TON of fleece on you, and with all the eating you are doing.." Stephen stopped and poked on Gruff's stomach. "You should have a nice girth on you as well that will certainly provide a lot of insulation." Stephen patted his fat little stomach again as his whiskers shook with laughter.

"But I suppose if you dug down just a mere couple of feet and stuck yourself in the hole, you could potentially stay a little warmer." Stephen looked over his shoulder and scratched mercilessly at his rear end. "I know whatever you are laying on in that hole would be mighty thankful." Stephen and Zeki looked at each other with a wink and then laughed while trying to imagine such a thing.

Zeki chimed in while still laughing, "It's all in how the heat moves."

Stephen and Gruff looked up. "What…?" they said in unison.

"Yeah, you heard me right. It's all in how the heat transfers." Zeki looked back and forth to both of them.

"Either of you ever lay on a large flat rock on a cool day, and then when you get up, the rock is still warm where you were laying?" Zeki looked back and forth at them. "Look, some of the warmth of your body gets transferred to the rock, or branches, nest, or grasses that you were laying on or in." Zeki cocked his head from side to side to see if they were following along.

"I'm telling you that if I were to be just under the surface in a shallow hole, build a nest in it, and you were to plop that behemoth body of yours on top, I BET you I could take my feathers off and just bask in the warmth all winter." Zeki paused and cocked his head, yet again, at the blank looks from Stephen and Gruff.

"Ok, let's think another way." Zeki ruffled, then continued. "Sitting on eggs is the same concept, my friends. We perch our rears on our eggs to keep them warm by allowing the heat of our bodies to move into the egg."

Gruff walked around for just a moment to find a nice piece of ground. "Ok, so make a nest, er…make a burrow." He started to dig down with his hooves. He worked, scratched, and scooted the earth as he had seen Stephen do and succeeded in making his burrow just as wide but half as deep as he was tall.

When Gruff was somewhat happy with the results, he looked over to Zeki and Stephen, who were now laughing at the sight. They stopped for a moment and were now watching him intensely. "What do you both think?" Gruff looked quite pleased with his progress.

Zeki cocked his head to the side and feathered his beak, eyeballing the earthworks, "There's no roof."

Stephen finally spoke up after walking around Gruff's burrow. "Yeah, I'm not sure we can call it a burrow since, as your friend pointed out, there is not really a roof." He continued his expert inspection. "Yeah, I think this is just more of a large hole, but I'm willing to give you the benefit of the doubt here. Let me see you get in, and then I will let you know for certain." He scratched at his whiskers and waited for Gruff.

Gruff looked at the pair, who were now shoulder to wing, egging him on. "Yeah, I have to see you in the hole if I'm going to give you an honest opinion." Zeki clicked and waddled around the hole curiously before ending back up with Stephen.

"Ok, I can certainly do that. Just give you a little umm…demonstration." Gruff looked back at his friends, then back over to the burrow and hopped in.

No sooner had Gruff spoken and hopped than his leg caught some of the loose soil, and he tumbled, face first into the burrow, his buttocks now sticking into the sky like a huge hairy tree stump, his face stuck somewhere south of the newly formed Alps.

Stephen and Zeki burst into tears from laughing. The more they looked at Mount Gruff, the more they laughed, holding each other up the best they could. Zeki flew up, in between hysterics, and perched himself atop Gruff's rump.

Zeki, now chortling, said, "I don't think you have quite mastered burrow building."

Gruff drew in a large amount of air and then let out an exceptionally long snort, sending up plumes of dust like a volcano. "I'm discovering that it's not building them that's the problem." He said, his voice a little muffled. "It's the entering…and obviously the exiting that's the problem." Gruff shifted his back legs and was finally able to walk himself into a more appropriate and comfortable position.

"You two could have helped, you know," Gruff said, looking at them from his burrow.

"Oh yeah, 'cause my arms are a formidable force in nature." Stephen bared his little buckteeth and pretended to growl and maul the air with his tiny hands and arms, which, once again, sent Zeki into a laughing fit.

"My, my, how the burrow has changed." Stephen casually walked around Gruff and kicked back a little dirt into his hole.

"I'm so glad that I can return the favor and be a source of amusement to you both." Gruff shifted to get a little more comfortable. "Now, can we all get a little serious here?" But the more Gruff tried to be mad while peering at them from inside his burrow, the more he started laughing with them.

Gruff could not recall any time in his life when he was able to laugh, let alone actually had friends he could laugh with.

"You know…" Gruff snort-laughed, "I do feel a little cooler." He then flopped his chin up on the edge of his burrow and looked out across the land.

8. BROAD IS THE ROAD

The counters and kitchen table were filled with maps and papers. Peter, Todd, and Kate all stood there looking down at them, following each other around and pointing out potential issues, presumed safe areas. Peter was quick to keep the coffee flowing.

Todd looked at Kate and nodded. "Yes, there are some great possibilities in Sector 2 for the permanent foundation and ranger station. Looks like it will take you 3 hours or so to get there like you said, but it seems pretty straightforward.

"Not sure the conditions of those old turn-of-the-century logging roads. . .IF you can even call them roads. They look like they would be just wide enough for a good 4x4 truck or maybe even one of those Kawasaki mules." Todd pointed out toward the yard at some of Peter's vehicles.

"Oh, Kate... er. . . Ranger Bradigan is more than welcome to use any equipment or vehicles that I have here at the lodge, and if I don't have it, I can surely get whatever you need within a few days. The Kawasaki hard cab, I think, would be perfect for her to use initially."

Pete continued circling the maps. "I can see about getting that hauled up to the trailhead, and you could establish a small base camp or auxiliary site, if you will, where we can store fuel and other things that might be needed. Would certainly save you a lot of time and resources.

"Using your personal resources, not to mention everything else you have done to help us get established, is certainly beyond what anyone could ever ask for." Todd looked over at Pete.

"Oh, that's not a problem. Glad to be able AND in a position to lend a hand." Pete raised his cup to them.

Todd turned back to Kate, "Ok, so once you have surveyed that area, I recommend that you make the trip in and out of there a few times over the next month or two to really get familiar with the trails."

Todd looked up from the maps to Kate. "You are going to be pretty remote, and if something were to go wrong, the calvary just isn't going to show up in five minutes." He took a gulp of coffee and shoved a whole donut into his mouth. He then mumbled as best he could while holding the food captive in his gullet, "It's going to be HOURS, possibly LONG hours before anyone can get you."

"Right, I understand that." Kate sipped her coffee and glanced at Pete.

Todd's face turned serious as he looked at Kate. "You keep your radio on, your GPS on, and you call in your location and planned routes before you go!" Todd mumbled while eating yet another donut.

"Also, keep to your planned check-in times." Todd pounded his finger on the table. "If you miss a check-in, we will wait four hours before we begin trying to locate you. For the foreseeable future, Granite Lodge will be your primary contact and will relay your information back to the Spotted Bear and Rock Mountain Ranger stations, your updates." Todd and Pete watched Kate cycling through notes, journal entries, and phone messages.

"This is how it will be, at least until you are fully staffed and truly your own district." Todd looked at Pete. "When you are in the field, Kate, one of your rangers will be out in the garage, er, temporary station, keeping tabs on you." Todd pounded his finger on the table again.

Kate looked up at Todd. "Understood. Look, I'm just excited to get this ball rolling."

Todd looked at Pete. "Dr. Marcus, I cannot begin to tell you how much we appreciate your support and putting us up in your home while this new district is being formed. If it hadn't been for…"

Pete calmly sipped his coffee and nodded to Todd. "Look, I'm just thrilled to be in the right places at the right times and have the resources to assist."

Pete paused and looked at Kate, who was face down in maps and digging around in various packs. "The Lord certainly brings people into your life when you least expect it or when you need them the most."

Pete took another drink of coffee and quickly glanced at Todd, who was now smiling at Pete, then glancing at Kate, who was still face down in notes, and then back to Pete. Todd's smile was so big his face looked like a beachball about to explode.

"So, Kate…" Todd wiped his mouth and put down his napkin. He then picked up and shook the convenience store donut box, attempting to peer into the cellophane window, just in case one was stuck in there, hiding.

Todd's arms were so enveloped in his girth that he could only get the box so close to his face. Finally, he reached a level of frustrated disappointment and dropped the box. "BRADIGAN?!"

"Huh? Oh yes, sir, GPS, every four hours. Got it. Spotted Trout…Rocky Bear, check." Kate nodded knowingly and started shoving the maps and loose equipment into her backpack.

Todd looked at Pete as they both raised their eyebrows at each other and gave each other a little laugh.

"Kate, tomorrow morning I will get you up to the trailhead where you would probably want to establish the substation that I talked about just a bit ago on that map." Peter wagged one of his fingers at her packs.

"Oh, that sounds grand, Pete. Thanks," Kate said, reaching out and giving his shoulder a squeeze while she put away her maps and journals.

Kate took a drink of her coffee while looking out the window at the mountains. "I figure that my first venture out, I will get up to the area two or three hours further up that looks promising for the permanent station. Will look it all over and do some surveys of the area.

"Then, of course, further and further ventures with each trip out. Pete, if you wouldn't mind meeting back at the substation the following morning, say around 9am?" Kate finally looked back at Pete and Todd for nearly the first time since they walked into the kitchen.

"That shouldn't be an issue," said Pete while moving on to stack some dishes. "I am not seeing any new patients for a couple days and have some work to do around here."

Pete finally got a moment to turn and take another sip of coffee. "Kate, I also have access to a temporary shipping container office that I can get transported up the mountain to act as your substation. The temp office will take a few days, but for your next several trips, you will at least have a spot to recoup. And we can get a vehicle up there, so you aren't reliant on someone coming to get you." Peter now walked over to stand beside Kate.

"Oh, Pete, that would be wonderful!" Kate reached out again and touched his shoulder. "Not to sound ungrateful, but, umm. . .do you have anything other than the Caravan I might be able to use?"

Pete acted shocked. "Uh, excuse me? The Caravan has feelings, Kate. Don't stomp on them!" He started picked up her various packs and equipment and headed for the front door. Kate squinted, wrinkled her nose, and stuck out her tongue.

"And, just for that one, little Ms. Snotty Britches, we will take Mr. Pibbs." Pete tossed his head and snout into the air and strutted to the door as if he was modeling the latest in fashion wares and was headed out onto the runway to greet the piranhas of the industry.

His walk would have been perfectly executed, except he stumbled twice on some loose rope and rigging hanging off Kate's backpack. This only caused him to raise his nose even higher to the sky after recovering, his strut becoming even more pronounced.

Kate got up from the table, sipped down the last of her coffee, and followed along behind Pete to watch. She became quite amused and finally began laughing. "You are seriously going to throw out a hip with that walk, genius."

Pete finally got to the opposite side of the Granite Lodge with Kate in tow. He stopped at an old barn. "Ms., please wait here for your carriage." He then placed all her gear and packs onto the ground and bowed several times for permission to leave her presence while disappearing into the barn's obscure side door.

Kate heard him trip and fall over something in the barn, which only caused her to laugh even more. Then, the most obnoxious sound of a loud vehicle muffler came to life. Small pebbles shook and rose from the ground, as did seemingly the barn itself.

With each rev of the engine, dust flew out the back of the barn. Finally, the front doors slid open, and some large beast began to slowly emerge and came to a full stop next to Kate. The rumbling of the engine finally settled down but still caused her body to vibrate in resonance. The back of the vehicle held on to a seemingly equally huge ATV with extra gas canisters and equipment.

Pete stopped, opened an old creaky door, and stepped out of the vehicle. He walked around to Kate and began placing her equipment into the bed. Kate's eyes were as big as dinner plates. "What in the world is that thing?"

she asked, practically running up to the passenger side window and having to stand on her tiptoes to peer in.

"I didn't realize rust was a primary color," Kate smirked.

"Ahh... Mlle Bradigan, puis-je vous présenter M. Pibbs" Pierre, bowed and opened the door for Kate to take a better look. "And for your information, that's not rust. It's. . .patina."

"Ok, so THIS is Mr. Pibbs." Kate quickly scooted around Pete, grabbed the door, and hopped into the passenger side like she was first in line for a new roller coaster, then gave the seat a couple of bounces.

"But I do have to ask," Kate said, turning to look at Pete, "Why all the old vehicles?"

Pete closed the passenger door, which was just as creaky as the other. "Take a look at where we are. Winter is brutal, and the one other season we have from time to time is just as bad.

"Vehicles do not last long up here, with the exception of Mr. Pibbs. He is coated head to toe in Rhino Liner." Pete's grin approached the pride threshold. Pete gave Mr. Pibb's fender a pat. "Saw them coat a truck once in a TV show.

"If the Caravan falls apart, I've not really lost much. But could you imagine driving some way overly priced vehicle up here? You need practicality, and if you are going up into those mountains, then you need a big V8, a serious 4x4, and a proven off-road record. And, this old 1948 Dodge Power Wagon may not look like much, but it is perfect for all that." Pete smiled like a lunatic.

"Mr. Pibbs has had a few modifications that will certainly ensure you get to where you are going, regardless of the circumstances or conditions." Pete stood on the front winch, looking at Kate back through the windscreen.

"Well, why didn't you pick me up from the airport in this, then?" Kate asked while looking over the interior and pushing the buttons on a radio that actually still had an 8-track player in it. Kate gushed, "It's wonderful! Oh, this is SO my kind of vehicle!"

Pete laughed. "Mr. Pibbs was my father's. He installed the sound system. I didn't really appreciate this vehicle until the day I got up to Honolulu. But, to answer your question, I didn't want to be a showoff by picking you up in this! Besides, the ride in this can be a little bumpy." Pete winked at Kate and then patted the hood, causing mud and dust to fly up, as he walked back around to the driver's side and hopped in.

"It's going to take us a little while to get up to the site." Pete revved the engine a little, dropped the stick into second gear, and headed out and up the road.

Mr. Pibbs bumped, jarred, and somehow still effortlessly glided across the almost long-forgotten logging and homestead roads. After a few hours, Kate and Pete arrived at the base of the large mountain range, and a longer trail led further up into the trees, disappearing into the low drifting clouds. Mr. Pibbs finally came to a slow, squeaking halt. Pete and Kate sat silently for a couple of minutes to allow their brain to slosh back down into position. Then, Pete turned the engine off.

"Well, here we are, Ranger Bradigan." Pete clambered down out of the Dodge and breathed in the cool air. Kate jumped out eagerly and took in the full view of the mountains. She breathed in deep, then exhaled in short bursts.

"Granite Mountain is absolutely beautiful!" Kate was enraptured with the pure, unmolested wilderness that led into points unknown.

Pete started to unload gear and dropped the ramps to unload the ATV, but then stopped to quietly watch Kate as the mountain mist began to collect in her hair and take in the smiles that would come and go from her face as she looked with excitement out on creation.

Pete smiled and whispered to himself, "Lord, surely from the beginning of time, You created this mountain just for her, just for this moment. Thank you for allowing me to be a small part of it. Protect her, guide her, and keep her safe."

Kate finally came back to reality, after being completely gob smacked, and walked to the back of the Dodge and touched Pete on his arm. "You say something, Pete?"

Pete shook his head as if he had dozed off. Kate laughed, "You were a million miles away, Pete. Where did you go?"

"Oh, uh, it's hard not to get caught up in all this. It can certainly cast a spell on you. . .the beauty of it all." Pete coughed to mask his embarrassment and quickly looked back to getting the gear unloaded.

"Ok, Kate, this is actually the site I think would make a great substation with your primary further up that trail or vice versa." Pete untethered the ATV and backed it down off some fold-out ramps.

"Course, you can see that until I get my guys up here with the temporary building, you are going to be roughing it. This ATV should get you up to an old homestead further up the mountain and, of course, back down again." Pete checked the fuel in the ATV, then took a 5-gallon canister and connected it to the machine.

"I will plan on being back in a couple of days to collect you. Hit me up on your satellite phone." Pete finished getting the remainder of her gear mounted to the ATV.

Kate clambered aboard the ATV and started it. "I cannot tell you how much I appreciate you and all you have done for the Department, Pete, and. . ." She paused and looked up at Pete, then she reached out and touched his hand, "and how much you have done for me." She smiled and quickly pulled his hand off the throttle and sped up the trail.

The pathway was easily wide enough for the ATV, but the tree roots were certainly trying to regain their right of way and dominance. At times, Kate had to come to a complete stop to clear the path with a small chainsaw, and at other times had to use an axe.

She continued to press on the long-forgotten trails, which sometimes seemed to go straight up the mountain. Often, she thought that if she sneezed exactly right, she'd have a very long drop over the edge to the canyon below.

Kate was tired, dirty, and sweaty, but she continued to push on, amusing herself by making sure to document the flora and fauna she came into contact with, at least when she and her trusty mount weren't hugging the mountain to prevent a sudden and unexpected greeting with sea level.

Kate glanced down at her watch and mumbled to herself while taking a drink of water, "Great, if I don't make it to this supposed homestead soon, I'm going to have to sleep standing up."

Finally, Kate came to a clearing of sorts that was free of trees, and she could just make out where the cabin once stood at least 100 years prior. She parked the ATV in the center of the clearing, turned it off, and quietly sat looking and listening to the area. She then jumped off the ATV and walked toward the remnants of the cabin.

Kate walked up to what would have been the front entrance and looked at what was left of hand cut logs, now overgrown with moss. The wraparound porch and roof long since having decayed and nearly vanished.

Just down a small hill, she could make out where a couple of barns stood, and they were really in no better condition than the cabin, if you could really still call it a cabin.

"This all reminds me of an old forgotten homestead way back up in the Pacific Northwest, Washington," Kate said to herself. "Hmm… up in Methow Valley, wasn't it?"

Kate took out her notepad and started walking off what she could make of a perimeter based on the few remaining fence posts. "Hmm, the homestead must have been about two acres in size at least." She once again found herself pausing to document and watch the various wildflowers moving in the wind.

She then ventured back up to the cabin and stood in what must have been the living room. She looked over at the old stone fireplace, now in shambles, having given itself over to time and the elements.

Kate stood silently, looking around, and then walked over to what was left of the fireplace. She poked around at the ground with her hiking pole. In her rummaging, she managed to turn over the remains of a wooden plank, which defied reason that it should have survived when nothing else of the cabin did.

Kate picked up the plank and stepped closer to the fireplace to look at the stone mantle. She looked back down at the wooden plank and wiped off the dirt and moss. Then, she began tracing her finger through the grooves and digging out the ages from the face of the piece of wood. Kate read the wooden plank aloud: "JOSHUA 24:15."

She brushed off what was left of the fireplace mantle, placed the plaque on top, and anchored it with some stones. "Yes indeed, I will serve the Lord."

Over the next several months, Kate made the trip up to the main site, preparing paths, documenting everything she encountered, and getting everything ready for the new rangers that would soon join her team.

It was also nice that she could come and go when she wanted since Pete had now loaned her the use of Mr. Pibbs. She was now able to drive the old Dodge much further up the homestead trails since Pete had some crew up there to assist with clearing and getting ready for the main site.

Kate pumped the gas and revved the engine, causing Mr. Pibbs to scramble up the narrow trail. The late summer was roaring through Honolulu, although it felt more like fall weather overnight. "I need to make at least two or three more trips up here before winter completely shuts me down till spring," she said to herself.

Kate looked out the driver-side window and down into the valley. "Yeah, we definitely need to widen this trail just a bit. This isn't some Bolivian road, and we certainly don't need to go over the edge." Kate patted on the dashboard as if encouraging a faithful pet.

She laughed and then said, "Oh, and on a side note, Mr. Pibbs, I want you to know and understand, I promise with all my heart...you are NEVER going back to Pete!"

She continued giggling for a moment, then yelled loudly and hit the gas, fishtailing around a few of the winding bends. "Oh yeah! You are definitely mine now. YOU AND ME, MR. PIBBS!"

As the days progressed, Kate was finally able to get Mr. Pibbs all the way up the mountain and to the main station. There was a lot of work done by her new crew, and Pete could be credited for a lot that had been achieved. That was for certain!

Kate sat quietly, thinking about everything Pete had done and how she would catch him looking at her, how his eyes could catch the entire light of the universe. She took a breath, held it, then proceeded into a long exhale. "HEY! OH no, you don't! There's too much to be done to go and get all complicated!"

She puffed up her cheeks, blew out the air slowly, and finally shook her head. She looked up, releasing her grip on the steering wheel. "Nope, not looking, not asking, and certainly not taking applications or arrangements!" Kate popped the door of the Dodge open and slid out.

The ranger station site was looking really good. Well, the grounds were anyway. Surveyed, staked, and the build should begin in the coming spring. Kate had cleared out most of the old homestead and was using that has a makeshift camping site, even using the partially functioning chimney for a small campfire to stay warm by at night.

Kate sat down by the fire and took out her journal.

It's happened again, right now as a matter of fact.

She paused and stared at the smoke and then twisted her head to see if she could tell exactly where it was coming from. She looked back down at her journal and started writing again.

I'm hearing what sounds like shouting and screaming from a distance. I'm guessing it could be 10-15 miles away, easy. With the way sounds bounce around up here, it could be even further.

She paused and listened again.

I'm almost certain that its coming from Sector 3, but we have not gone into that area yet and there are no. . .

Kate paused again, listening to the moans and groans that floated across the mountain.

> *There are no really documented cases of people up in that area. Well, nothing but hearsay, anyway.*

She closed her journal and her eyes in an attempt to concentrate. Her eyes snapped open as she yelled in frustration, "Blast it all! That noise could have come from anywhere, or any creature for that matter!"

Kate again closed her eyes and concentrated on the sound. "Heck, the sound is bouncing and echoing all over the mountain and canyon, but it is definitely coming from Sector 3." Kate looked down and pointed the flashlight on her map.

She tapped her pen on her leg, then opened her journal again before saying to herself, "Well, it's certainly my duty to document and investigate." She tilted her head to the side. "All quiet, like every other time. It certainly doesn't make much sense. I will log it in with Spotted Bear Station and make it all official.

"I have at least one…MAYBE two…more trips back here before winter arrives. I will come up the mountain early, and if I hear it, well, then we investigate Sector 3 permission or no permission!"

9. GRUFF FIRST CONTACT

Gruff gave Zeki a hug. "I'm going to miss you, Zeki. You have shown me so much and helped me understand. I really don't know if I can go on further without you." Gruff lowered his head.

"Nonsense, my dear friend!" Zeki latched onto Gruff's face. "You have been prepared as much as I can do these past eight or was it nine months." Zeki cocked his head in thought.

"Either way, our time together has been spectacular, and we have had many a laugh. You have your destiny waiting for you, and I have mine. And we definitely don't want to make my wife come looking for me!" Zeki burst into a chuckle to hide his tears.

"Zeki, you have talked about the great corruption. What was it?" Gruff looked up into the mountain.

Zeki stopped laughing and grew quiet. "You are looking for one final lesson, Gruff?" Zeki waddled around and patted Gruff's huge leg.

"The corruption happened a long, long time ago, thousands of years. What happened has been passed down from generation to generation from the very beginning, back when even THESE mountains were new." Zeki opened his wings, attempting to bring in the horizons to show Gruff the vastness.

"The Creator made everything you see, and He holds it all together with His very Word. He made the humans to take care of it all, from the littlest plant to the largest animal. ALL of it was put under human authority. Man walked with the Creator, and we walked with man."

Gruff looked down at Zeki and walked a few steps. "So, what happened?"

"Humans decided to rebel against the Creator, dismiss His love, His caring, His Great Authority. They turned from everything He had given for their own selfishness and desires." Zeki looked at Gruff and then again back out into the mountain.

"Because of what they did, ALL of creation has become corrupted, a stain that will never be removed until the Creator returns again." Zeki waddled back over to where Gruff was now standing and held on to his leg again.

Gruff looked down. "You said 'again?' He was here after His creation?"

"Yes. The Creator came in the form of a human but was still the Creator, and He offered a way for man to once again walk with Him." Zeki hopped and jumped onto Gruff's back.

"Then what?" Gruff said as he slowly began walking again toward the mountain.

"Well, this part may hit a little close to home for you, Gruff. The Creator looked like a human, but because He was the Creator, some people were terrified of him, treated him as an outcast, afraid that he would upset their wretched and vile way of life that they so enjoyed and became accustomed to." Zeki looked down at Gruff.

"Being treated as an outcast does hit very close to home, Zeki." Gruff stopped walking and looked up into the mountains.

Zeki took in a deep breath. "Because of their fear, they stuck him to a tree in the most horrible of ways and sat there watching him, waiting for him to die. They murdered him, Gruff."

Zeki cried softly. "I had chosen to ignore this for a long time, to dismiss it, but this truth has been passed down from my family, my family's family, and then some. They were there to see it. They even sat on one of the trees that had another human stuck to it."

"The Creator is dead?" Gruff stopped in his tracks.

Zeki jumped off Gruff's back and hopped several times to get ahead of him, then turned around. "Oh! Don't be silly, boy! You can't kill the Creator! The Creator was, is, and will ever be!"

Gruff looked down at Zeki, cocking his head for clarification.

Zeki then continued, "He was working His plans to eventually fix the great corruption, the stain. This was the thing that HAD to happen to bring things back into order for when He would return. There had to be a payment for what the humans had originally done, for their disobedience to Him."

Zeki grew quiet, then said, "His own blood was and is the payment..."

Gruff started walking again, and Zeki continued, "So they murdered the Creator in human form, but that is not where this ends, by no means!"

Zeki closed his eyes as if trying to remember. "Let me tell you, Gruff! He popped up out of the grave a few days later! Caused quite a stir!"

"He told humans that he would be coming back soon, and He would redeem those that are faithful, that have believed in and on Him." Zeki opened his eyes to look at Gruff.

"But that was to redeem humans, Zeki. How does that bring us into the picture?" Gruff stopped walking again and waited.

"Ahh, you see, when the Creator returns to redeem humans, He is also going to restore ALL of creation to what it was. ALL of creation will no longer be under the corrupted stain!"

"Animals do not need to be told there is a Creator, Gruff. It's already instilled into what we know. But, just like humans," Zeki looked up into the mountain, "We too are corrupted and stained, each having gone their own way, and we need to remember that the Creator, who has given all, desires that we remain faithful to Him, and we should give Him our everything, regardless of the cost."

"Why do you keep looking into the mountain, Zeki?" Gruff looked up into the mountain as well, finally realizing that he was traveling on a path leading further up.

"There is evil on this mountain, Gruff. I know you can feel it. It's a small, sweet-sounding song that invites and then entraps you to take part in its deeds. It whispers constantly that no one else needs to know. It's just something between you two, a small secret between friends, but it is evil nonetheless."

Zeki looked down at the small trail they were walking on, then back up to the mountains, before looking back at Gruff. Zeki's eyes grew wide. "This is the journey the Creator has called you to be on." He looked once more from the mountain back to Gruff.

"Be vigilant, my dear brother. Be aware and be strong in the Creator. This is an evil you cannot bargain with. This is an evil that you just do not make deals with. Protect your heart and your mind, Gruff!

"Hear me, Gruff! Know this," Zeki paused and looked Gruff long and hard in the eyes, "there are those who have made dealings with this evil in the past, and this evil will always come, come to collect its payment." Zeki looked into the mountain again and then hugged Gruff.

"I'm really going to miss you, Zeki." Gruff was beginning to feel utterly alone again.

"Look, we are both now firmly secured in the faith of the Creator. We are brothers! We are never really alone anymore. Talk with Him as you have with me. I promise you. He will answer you. You just have to be quiet and listen." Zeki looked Gruff in the eyes.

"But what if the only reason I had faith was because I could see you and hear you? I can't see the Creator." Gruff pawed at the ground.

"You have faith in the Creator, not through seeing Him, Gruff, or by seeing me, I am nothing, but through belief, through FAITH, in things that you cannot see; in things you KNOW. It's a leap of faith. It is something the Creator has instilled into you. You feel, you experience in your very spirit to be True, that HE is TRUTH… you either make that jump or dismiss it like so many others have done."

"What happens if you dismiss it?" Gruff turned as he slowly began to walk further into the mountains.

Zeki cawed loudly to disguise the pain he felt as he watched Gruff leaving. "Death, Gruff. There is death in the corruption of creation, condemned by a stain you can never be freed from. But you and I, we will be together again one day, I promise you! Either here on this mountain or later with the Creator. It's going to be glorious!" Zeki bounced and hopped three times off the ground, spreading his wings into the sun and was gone.

Gruff took a deep breath and, without looking back, set off from the flowered fields and the hum of the bees. He crossed a ridge and came across some pathways that led back up into the forest. He traveled until the sun started to disappear, taking time to rest and explore the small trail as he moved along.

As the darkness started to set in, Gruff started hearing strange noises, finally coming upon the source. Just in the wood line, a strange human had started a fire and was singing, or at least attempting to sing.

After watching for several minutes, Gruff stepped out of the wood line and into open view. He was curious about the strange little figure that was now sitting down around his fire, making little carvings out of tree branches and carrying on a very lengthy conversation with himself. It was getting dark, and Gruff really needed to find a safe place to bed down. The strange little man looked up and pointed a stick at Gruff.

"And just what do you want?" the little man said, sounding more than a little agitated, as he looked up from his carvings.

"The whole point of me being out here is to get away from idiot people and, for that matter, idiot animals!" The strange little man scooted his foot across the ground to kick up some dirt and shoved it in Gruff's direction.

Gruff stood and snorted as the little man jumped up and started to whoop, holler, and scream at the top of his lungs. He waved his hands in the air mercilessly and danced around the fire like some sort of senseless, crazed imp.

The little man's antics could have been absolutely terrifying except for his goofy appearance. His clothing flopped about him, clearly big enough for three people his size, and whatever he had in his pockets made noises like small pebbles smacking together with each step he made. This strange spectacle had just two or three lonely teeth that looked like gnarled tree stumps suspended in a gaping hole, and his need to stop and catch his breath from time to time just added to the exhibition.

Gruff stood his ground for a solid ten minutes and watched this little man carry on in some form or fashion, attempting to scare Gruff off from his campsite. The little man finally became totally winded and stopped, dropped his hands to his side in frustration, and then looked again at Gruff. He shrugged his shoulders and, in one final effort, plugged one nostril with his finger and blew slime in Gruff's direction from the other.

"Well..." The little man panted. "I will certainly give you this: you don't scare easily, do you?" The little fellow tossed a hand into the air. "Whatever..." he said before wandering back to sit at the fire. He hopped up onto an old tree stump and then stroked what could have been a beard.

He spent several minutes rubbing his chin and staring at Gruff. Finally, he said, "And, you know, most idiots that come up here would have lit out by now, but you...you certainly don't strike me as being an idiot."

Gruff finally stepped closer to the fire to get a better look at this odd-looking human. *Hopefully, this is not the best prime example of the species,* thought Gruff.

This human was seemingly short compared to Gruff, as he could look him square in the eyes without so much as moving his head, either up or down.

His hair had gone grey, even though he seemed relatively young, and had the look and shape of the twisted gangly briars that Gruff had once lived in. And this man's face appeared well worn as his troubles built deep ravines across his forehead.

But, in all honesty, this man wasn't in any better shape nor any cleaner than Gruff. The man was dressed head to toe in various animal pelts that were supposed to give him the appearance of a real animal, but a quick sniff and Gruff could tell they were anything but.

Gruff continued to eye this human and cocked his head to the side. The beard the man stroked was more in patches and didn't really grow to form anything proper. In fact, there was more hair coming from his ears than what could be found on the tip of his chin.

His lack of a lengthy goatee is certainly going to keep him from impressing a mate. Gruff snorted and chuckled to himself. *Perhaps if he combed it all together, it would almost make a beard.* Overall, Gruff thought the man resembled a ratty, mangy badger. To top off the oddity, dust and debris flew from him each time he moved.

"You're extremely lucky," said the man. "I don't have a taste for goat, nor really the teeth to be chewing on that tough meat of yours."

He got up and reached out to Gruff to pinch his side, but then he thought better and sat back down. "I came out here a few years back with one of my friends to get away from all the stupid people."

The oddity looked back at the stick he was playing with, poked it around in the coals, and then spat on the ground a couple of times before he continued talking. "It doesn't matter if you can understand me or not, as I'm going to talk regardless, and you are going to listen."

The little man spat again. "I tell you; no one wants to help anyone with anything. This whole rotten, stinking world is all in it for themselves. So, I finally got tired of their nonsense and told them, back in their towns and cities, that they all could just kiss my derriere."

The little fellow paused and let out a loud, creepy laugh, clearly having amused himself. He then pointed his stick at Gruff and shook it while he spoke like it was an extension of his bony little finger.

"So, here I am on this mountain. I sit, carving out little wooden totems from these tree branches, an act of penance, I suppose, to whatever powers that be for being up here, for having been a part of humankind," the man said, spitting again.

"I just enjoy not having any responsibilities. Just me and my little tree folk here." The man looked up. "Have to admit, though, their conversations can be a little sappy."

The little man stopped talking and squinted at Gruff to see if he got the joke. Regardless, the man then proceeded to let out a loud, toothless cackle that echoed across the mountain, down the forest, and into the valley.

"My name is Shaw, Felix Shaw, not that you really cared to know that or understood it." He paused and started rummaging around in an exceptionally large backpack that he had by his side. "I think I have something that you just might like."

Shaw continued digging around in his bag. Had it been any bigger, his entire body would have disappeared into its cavity. "AH, yes, here it is!" He exclaimed happily and emerged from the pack.

He got what little rear end he had perched back up on his mossy tree stump. His short little legs dangled from his stump and were no longer able to touch the ground. He held a closed fist out towards Gruff.

Gruff sniffed the air and could tell it was something wonderful, something that his entire body seemed to crave from time to time. Gruff then cautiously walked over to Shaw, nibbled at his hand, and snorted.

"Crikey! You're huge!" exclaimed Shaw as Gruff came within arm's length.

"Yeah, I know your kind. Seen 'em. Dealt with some of 'em a long while back. I don't know a mountain or two back?" said Shaw. "They had the same reaction you do right now."

"I don't have very much, that is, until I travel back into that miserable dank town." Shaw scooted a little closer and whispered, "That stupid little town some half-witted official named…" He thought for a moment, "I don't know, but it was something totally moronic."

Shaw patted Gruff on his back. "But either way, I'm willing to share this little piece with you." He opened his hand and displayed a lovely little piece of pink rock salt.

Gruff stuck his muzzle into Shaw's palm and inhaled the salt into his mouth. He rolled his eyes, savoring the pieces of salt on his tongue. He then stuck them to the roof of his mouth and then let his tongue and the contents it held roll along his gums before reaching the back of his throat, grunting in pure, passionate approval.

Shaw ran his hand along Gruff's face and down his chest and back. "You are certainly huge for a mountain goat. Don't think I have ever seen a goat built as big and as tough as you." Shaw continued his assessments. "I see you have had more than your fair share of scrapes and scruffs based on all those scars on your face.

"AH, and I see you have been messing with something sticky. What do you have all matted and stuck to your beard?" Shaw chuckled while scratching at his own face. Well, at least one of us can grow proper facial hair." Shaw cackled again.

"You are the first thing I have really spoken to in a couple years, 'cept when I first came up here." He paused in thought, then shrugged his shoulders. "Well…then, and with the exception of the few times I go into that cockamamie town. Gets kinda lonely at times, though. Ever since…" Shaw stopped for a moment, lit a cigarette, and took a long drag, his fingers clutching onto it like an upside-down pyramid.

"Well, look, doesn't matter now. I'm here, and you are here," Shaw said while sitting back down and adjusting his fake buckskins. "How about I give you another piece of salt, and you let me get your coat there all trimmed up." Shaw pointed a bony finger.

He once again started feeling Gruff's body. "Hmm, uhm, just what I was thinking. Because let me tell you this: you really look like my cheeks, and I'm not talking about the ones on my face!"

Gruff chuckled to himself briefly at Shaw's comments, being that he was just as filthy. However, given that, Gruff felt that Shaw was harmless, for now, but not really one to be trusted. So, he obliged him temporarily, especially for another snoot full of pink salt.

Shaw cackled loudly and momentarily disappeared again into his backpack. He then slowly emerged from the backpack with a pair of scissors and a large-toothed comb.

He then stood up and, while approaching Gruff, slowly drew a large hunting knife out of its sheath and grinned maniacally, whether he did it just for intimidation, dramatics, or because he may have been just plain crazy.

Shaw once again ran his hand across Gruff's chest and front legs. "Easy there, lusus naturae. I'm not planning to hurt you." He popped a piece of rock salt into Gruff's mouth and started cutting and combing his fleece.

The man growled, sang, cut, and combed. He proceeded to say more curse words and combinations of curse words than Gruff had ever heard, and he had heard just about all of them, which were almost always directed at him!

Gruff thought to himself, *So this is the human version of my father? I thought for sure humans would be different.* Then Gruff remembered Zeki talking about how creation was corrupted and stained. *ALL of creation is stained*?! Gruff meditated on this while Shaw continued to work.

At one point, Gruff thought he heard Shaw cursing even at the very ground he was standing on. "One thing I absolutely cannot deal with," said Shaw while running a comb over Gruff, breaking off a few of the tines in his fleece. "I cannot stand a messy person, much less a messy, filthy beast such as yourself." Gruff looked at him and thought about the irony.

Shaw continued jabbering. "You do have one up on humans, though, fella." He paused to take a knife to a mangled bit of wool, cutting it free in clumps. "One thing you have going for you, lusus, is humans CHOOSE to be nasty and filthy. You don't. So, yeah, you are better than us in those regards." He then spat on the comb and pulled it through his own hair, trying to slick it back.

"Ok, now, let me take a closer look at that chin of yours. What is all over your face? Is that old honey?" Shaw reached out and took Gruff by his beard and plucked several sticky hairs off his face. He sniffed at the hairs a few times and then popped them into his mouth, swishing them back and forth between his gums. "Yeah, that's honey, alright!"

Suddenly, Gruff's ears stood straight up and then pointed forward. What fleece was left on him seemingly stood on end. Gruff's eyes grew wide, and his breathing increased. Gruff's entire stance changed to that of a brick wall.

"Hey, now! What is it? What do you see, fella?" Shaw whispered while putting the comb into his belt and slowly moving his knife into his left hand. He tried hard to focus his eyes, squinting into the dark forest, hoping his eyes would reveal what was hidden.

The life of the entire forest seemed to come to a complete and sudden halt. No noises, not a single cricket chirp. Even the breeze failed to carry any sounds and came to a cold dead stop.

While keeping his eyes on the wood line, Shaw's blood turned cold, and his chin hair bristled. He slowly moved away from Gruff and scooted toward the fire. He paused for a moment, trying to see if whatever was watching them had picked up on his movements. He then slowly squatted down, keeping the knife in his left hand elevated in case he needed to defend himself and reached into the fire to grab what he considered a formidable club but was really not much more than a small stick.

Shaw stood up, grasping the burning club in his right fist, and began pointing like he was pointing a baseball bat at center field. He strained his neck while pointing his chin and squinted in the same direction as the club went in an effort to see while his flaming stick cast its light into the pitch-black forest.

He once again cursed angrily, spit flying from his mouth between each word after his stick didn't have the desired illuminating effect. He paused, glanced at Gruff, and suddenly jumped up and down, letting out huge boisterous groans, followed by wails, screams, various curses, and vile chants. Then, he started to run in large circles around the fire, carrying on like some sort of crazed beast, reenacting a near-complete performance from earlier. After mere moments, his fiery club was reduced to just a smoking piece of twig that was leaving a thin trail of smoke in the air from a glowing ember that was struggling to stay alive.

And, as quickly as the forest had been silenced, it erupted once again in the full surround sound of life. Without missing a beat, Shaw circled one more time around the fire, shrieking because he couldn't leave things half-done. Finally, coming to a halt, he plopped back on the ground next to Gruff.

Shaw tossed his stick back into the fire. "I think we may have just had a visit from Abaddon." He said solemnly, "Abaddon and I seem to have an agreement, but YOU, you do not want to go looking for or running into him! But I tell you what, lusus, you may just want to keep me as a friend." Shaw's grin sent shivers down Gruff's spine.

"Oh yeah! Hey now, let me tell you something about honey," Shaw said, pausing to look Gruff in the eyes. "It will cure, well, just about whatever your malady is, for sure."

Shaw went back to plucking the hairs that had remnants of honey still stuck to them from Gruff's face and popped them into his mouth like toothpicks. "Something about it treats cuts, scrapes, open wounds, all sorts of things."

The little oddity then stood up and went back to cutting and combing. "Biggest issue for me is getting it away from the manufacturer!" Shaw paused again, looked up at Gruff, and let out another one of his mountainous, toothless cackles.

Shaw finally finished his hack job on Gruff and took a step back. "THERE! You look better...well, sort of, at least better than you did before." He took another step back and stroked his facial hairs to admire his skills. "Well, you look more like a silly poodle or one of those cockerdoodlepoo dog mutations that people are always cooing and gushing over." Shaw nodded his head in satisfaction. "But still, much better than you were. Your coat should grow out nice and full come winter."

Shaw continued stroking his chin and looking at his handiwork. "Yeah, you would certainly make a fine blanket."

Shaw started tossing the sheared wool around in the air and making it fall like snow, then quickly gathered it up and shoved it into a bag. "I will wash this up later. I can at least make a pillow for my beautiful face.

Gruff did a full body shake, causing all the loose trimmings to fly into the air, which, of course, Shaw danced around catching and shoving into his bag. Gruff snorted and thought, *Well, I do have to admit it does feel rather nice to be at least a little cleaner and free from some of that stink.*

Gruff walked around to the other side of the fire and lay down, keeping one eye on this little oddity of a man and one eye on the forest. Shaw now sat on the ground with his back up against the large mossy stump he had been sitting on, just staring at Gruff.

Shaw gazed up into the night sky. "Yes, it's been a while since I shared my campfire." He continued looking up into the sky, once again smoking a cigarette and watching the puffs disappear. Both he and Gruff sat there looking up from time to time, trying to catch a glimpse of some stars when the wind gave the trees a chance to recover from their constant dance and they weren't cautiously watching each other.

Shaw drew his gaze back down to Gruff. "Let me tell you something, lusus naturae, something that being out here alone has helped me to fully realize, to fully understand, and if you can understand me, well, maybe it will resonate with you." He looked back up into the air, watching the rising smoke drift and become lost in the night. "THIS is truth, as sure as I'm sitting here looking at you and as sure as we are breathing the same air."

Shaw looked back at Gruff. "In today's societal mentality," Shaw paused and took a long drag on the cigarette, "we can examine just how humans have now supremely evolved into what we are. And, just what have the overwhelming majority evolved into, you ask?" Shaw let the smoke slowly escape his mouth. "Why, a bunch of self-gratifying, egotistical, loudmouth showoffs whose only purpose is to keep up with each other and be forever in a rush for the next big thing and how they are going to obtain it!"

Closing his eyes, Shaw paused and dragged on his cigarette again. "I will tell you this, lusus, their thought process is quite simple, and yet," he dropped his gaze from the stars back down to Gruff, "it's grotesquely eloquent."

Shaw dug around in his top pocket for what was left of another cigarette. This one he only rolled around in his weathered lips before putting it back. He then pulled a generic menthol out of his and lit it. "You see, my friend, " he said as he then gave Gruff a little sly wink, "In this use-and-toss-away world, the self or individual has evolved but certainly not in intelligence. Our desire and need to acquire things have evolved right alongside; however, the things we collect and desire are not what you would think." Shaw palmed his forehead and then ran his hand into his hair and scratched. His eyes got big as he shifted and bent forward, half pointing his finger at Gruff, "its fellow humans, lusus, we desire and collect fellow humans.

"It is not enough just to have a friend, or friends, for that matter. You see, lusus, a friend is important, but being a friend is NOT what makes them important. It's not really the number of friends that helps you get ahead. No." Shaw closed his eyes momentarily and softly laughed before looking at Gruff again. He bent farther forward, and his voice changed to a low, growly whisper, his eyes reflecting the glowing coals of the fire. "The important thing is in which order you will have to eat them."

Gruff quickly raised his head and looked at Shaw with his ears pointed forward, preparing himself to bolt if it came to that. Shaw's smile was nearly pure evil. "OH! Relax, lusus naturae! I'm not talking about literally eating them. Though, I tell you, THAT would certainly be a kinder end for the lot of them." He leaned back against the stump and laughed. "It's all figurative, lusus, my friend, for how we humans like to use up and disregard people for our own purposes. I tell you, we destroy lives, the same as if you had just slapped one of them on a bun, covered them in steak sauce, and ate them."

Looking back up into the sky, Shaw continued, "Let me tell you another truth, lusus. Everyone is capable of murder. It just takes the right set of events to trigger you." He looked back at Gruff. "You just don't truly know yourself until you are face to face with unsurmountable odds, when the only thing you can think of is self-preservation."

Shaw took the old cigarette back out of his pocket, looked at it, then ran It under his nose and smelled it for a few minutes. Again, he rolled it across his lips with his eyes closed, then, like lightning, his eyes shot open, and he looked at Gruff. "And that, my dear lusus naturae, is when you discover who you are and what your truth really is."

10. ABADDON

Abaddon stretched out his massive paws, arched his back, then kicked out each hind leg one at a time to really feel the tension in his muscles pulled until nearly their breaking point. He then closed his eyes and snorted in huge swathes of air from all possible directions.

He liked to think himself older than the mountains that he lived on, but that was only because he had no equal. He was easily twice the size of a normal timber wolf.

He traveled the valleys, the hills, and into the mountains, and there was not so much as a leaf that could fall from the trees that did not pass his knowledge or gaze. He made it his business to try to control the very air that crossed into his territory. As for his territory, well, it ALL belonged to him.

Abaddon didn't bother wasting his time trying to remember his beginning. As far he was concerned, he always was. Therefore, since he didn't have a beginning, he had no reason to think that he had an end or that he was a subject to death.

He traveled alone. No other living thing stood up to his opinion of himself or his perceived importance. So, EVERYTHING was treated as inferior.

Any pain that he may have gone through, whether it was in his mind or actual physical pain, was more than any other living thing could possibly understand. To him, the pain, the suffering, or the lack of suffering was greater than anything else could ever experience. In his mind, this made him more important, stronger, and wiser than everyone else, but in truth, it only made him darker and more twisted than anything else and blackened his spirit.

Abaddon was not typical of timber wolves, or any wolf for that matter. He had absolutely no pack mentality or family bonding, and his hate and rage would strike out at everything around him. On rare occasions, he would grant mercy to whom he chose, but that was just so that he could feel superior. And Abaddon's mercy came with a price, and you could best believe he would eventually collect.

Abaddon came upon a ridge that overlooked a grassy plain with rolling hills. He was just high enough to see to the entire horizon but close enough to earth to see and watch the lives going on, oblivious to his presence.

He laid down and hung his head off a ledge, using his front paws as pillows but staying out of sight of the pesky birds that would screech and warn others about him. He grew tired and bored and flopped over to one side. He then used one of his massive paws to scratch into the hard rocks that formed the ledge. Four long and deep grooves were etched into the stones as he sharpened his claws, indicating that this area belonged to him and him alone.

He continued to laze, and eventually, his huge mouth opened, and his tongue popped out and flopped onto the rock face as he panted, producing a puddle of saliva. He watched, and he waited into the night. He waited until he watched the sunrise. If he had one positive trait, it would be said that Abaddon was very patient. He was in no rush, as everything was under his subjugation.

Some noise and commotion eventually drifted up into his ears, and he turned his gaze back down into the plains. As he watched, his attention became more acute. "Well, now, what in the world do we have going on here?" Abaddon spoke slowly from a deep, raspy voice, his eyes fully focused on the commotion down below.

Abaddon leaned a little more forward over the ledge, and he could see a massive mountain goat, or at least something that resembled a mountain goat, coming out of some briars and attempting to get comfortable.

"How is it that I have missed seeing this one before?" Abaddon shifted. "Hmmm, he is certainly formidable, but I really doubt he is much of a threat or challenge." Abaddon once again got comfortable and watched Gruff with great interest. "I think I will track that one down later just for the fun of it." Abaddon snickered.

"But, once he goes back to whatever bush he came from or whatever it is he calls home, well then, it will be time for me to pay a little visit to this new collection of umm…little friends?" Abaddon produced a raspy chuckle and went back to watching the little kids playing.

A shadow passed over Abaddon, and he quickly glanced up. "Well, this is unfortunate. Seem to have gained the attention of a high-flying loudmouth." Abaddon snarled at the eagle that circled over him and then watched as it headed toward the tasty goats that were just a short distance below the ledge from where he sat.

He went back to watching. "What in the world?! What is that stupid goat doing?!" Abaddon sat up a little more, not believing what he was seeing. Down below, he could see the massive goat getting surrounded and beat on by all the tiny goats. "He does NOTHING!? He has to be a complete muttonhead!" Abaddon went back to watching, still quite unable to believe his own eyes.

"Did I just wake up and find myself on the other side of some crazy mountain?"

Abaddon watched as the eagle dove and hastily flew off when confronted by the large goat. Abaddon watched the collection of goats and how they all came at the bigger one, beating him. "I am just totally speechless…"

"Are you seeing anything interesting?" An old voice spoke up and startled him.

Abaddon exhaled, agitated. "Go away, Korvus, or whatever it is you call yourself. Our business is well past finished, and I'm in no mood for you." Abaddon rolled his eyes and sneered. Unless…" he looked up at Korvus.

"That's not my name anymore, Abaddon, and I owe you nothing, not even my new name. My business is down there with that goat." Zeki began turning to leave.

"You would do well to just fly off and find another charity case for your preaching…Korvus," Abaddon growled. "Take this as a warning, Korvus. You interrupt me again, and I will kill you." Abaddon lazily tossed his paw at Zeki.

Zeki dodged Abaddon's massive paw and hopped a few times to take flight. He soared briefly and then flew down to where the mountain goat was now lying.

Abaddon watched Korvus and the goat talking for a long while and into the evening. "Dang, that feathered freak to the mountain. I don't need that numbskull getting in the way of anything!" He scowled and decided to sleep there to keep an eye on the situation.

Just before the morning came, Abaddon caught movement from Gruff and his apparent new little friend and watched as they came up the hill just to the side of where he was lying and disappeared into the mountains. "I will deal with both of them later," he sneered.

Abaddon sat up and then looked back down at the briars to determine how he could best use this situation to his advantage. "OH! I KNOW! This is going to be grand!" He then slipped off the ledge down the hill to the collection of bushes just on the edge of where the community would roam.

He lowered himself, crawled silently into the bushes, and found a flat area that was obviously the spot where the big goat would bed down. "Oh, this is almost too perfect!" he hissed. Abaddon turned in circles a couple of times, flopped down, and lightly dozed, waiting for the sun to come up over the valley.

Lucas, the oldest kid, woke up early and rubbed the sleep from his eyes. He stretched and bounced into a half hop, looking around. The community was just beginning to stir, and so he set off to gather all his other little troublemakers. There was no point in making a scene if no one was around to watch it.

Once Lucas had them all just out of earshot of the family, he spoke up. "Look, it's early, and I think we need to pay Gruff back for pushing us into those bushes. I still have a thorn in my backside, and he is going to pay for that!"

A little goat, Remi, with barely a whisker on his chin, spoke up. "But he saved our lives yesterday. Don't you think that may…" and before he could get his thoughts out, Lucas stepped into him and shoved him to the ground.

Lucas hissed angrily, "You will do as you are told and not question me. I am in charge here, and you will shut your mouth and listen to me!" He pumped out his chest in an attempt to make himself even bigger.

"We never would have been in those bushes if Gruff had not pushed us into them, and that eagle only saw us because Gruff made us follow him." Lucas tossed his snout in the direction of Gruff's home. "If he just would have stayed where he was, NONE of this would have happened! He is going to pay for what he did to us!" Lucas began pushing and shoving all his followers into a tighter group.

"But didn't the elders beat him? Our own father beat him. I saw them beating him. It took all of them, but I saw it." Remi spoke up and then quickly backed up and kept quiet.

Lucas spun his head around, glared angrily at the little one, and then sneered. "What did I just tell you not more than a moment ago? Now, get in line, and let's go before the parents get up."

He then headed out and started for the hill and the bushes where Gruff liked to sleep, with all the other kids following along behind at a short distance. They all approached the bushes where Gruff would sleep, but only Lucas was brave enough to approach the den.

"I can hear him sleeping!" Lucas snickered, looking back at his entourage. His little band all perked up their ears and stared wide-eyed. "YOU, come here!" he whispered harshly, summoning little Remi, who had the flappy mouth just a bit ago.

"Ye...yes?" The tiny goat approached with his head hung low.

"Listen to me," Lucas said, pushing on Remi. I want you to charge and bash Gruff in those bushes! You remember from yesterday our games and how to do that, right?" Lucas towered over the scared little one to intimidate him.

"Ye...yes, I remember, but I don't want..." the little goat started to mumble.

"I didn't ask what YOU wanted!" Lucas whispered even more harshly now. "I told you that YOU will listen to me! Now, go BASH him!"

The little goat closed his eyes, raised up, and charged the bush, giving it a good shove and smashing into the object hidden by the limbs and leaves.

"Perfect! Now, how about this time you open your stupid eyes and do it again until I tell you to stop!" commanded Lucas.

Working up his courage the best he could, little Remi dashed at the bush and smashed into whatever was hidden behind the vegetation. The bush shook, and the little kid cocked his head, reared up, and started to walk forward to take another charge. He ran full force and smashed once again into the bush.

The other kids were standing back at a distance, acting like fools as usual, but that didn't stop them from noticing and suddenly voicing their approval of little Remi. "Get him, Remi! give him another bash!" They all yelled and laughed hysterically.

Lucas turned around, crossed his eyes, stuck his tongue out at the other kids, and jeered. This only caused the entire group to go into even more antics, shouting all the more.

Finally, Lucas turned back around and looked at the tiny goat. "Ok, Remi! Now, you stick your head into those bushes and yell at Gruff and tell him what a big, blasted..." Lucas taught the little goat new vile words to use to curse things with.

Remi, who was now crying, looked up again at Lucas and managed to squeak out, "I...I don't want..."

"I SAID, DO IT!" Lucas demanded. "NOW!" He stepped forward and shoved the scared little goat to the ground.

Remi slowly picked himself off the ground. He then turned and looked at the other kids and then back to the bushes. He slowly walked back to the briars and sticker bushes and then looked over his shoulder at the gang, who were all now yelling, "DO IT!"

Remi took a deep breath, shoving his head all the way up to his shoulders into the depths of the bushes, and began to shout, "Gru...GRUFF, YOU'RE A BIG..."

And, just as quickly as the words started to come out of little Remi's mouth, he was gone, his blood sprayed across Lucas' face. Pieces of fleece drifted into the air and fell at the hooves of the now terrified kids.

Lucas froze in terror and proceeded to completely wet and soil himself. The other kids shrieked in a panic and tried to run but only ended up in a half-crazed stampede that went in chaotic circles as they tripped and fell over each other.

After just a brief moment of their caterwauling, their mothers began to debate with each other as to who would have to go and find out what was going on this time. Nannie grumbled and complained loudly, cursing about her lazy friends and how if anything needed to be done, she had to do it. She slowly strolled up the small hill, still cursing angrily at having to stop doing nothing at all to go and do something.

Once Nannie reached the top and slowly strolled over to the kids, she noticed Abaddon disappearing up and over the crest of the larger hill and back into the mountains. She took a moment to compose herself and then started bleating at the top of her lungs at the kids. It took her several more minutes to finally get them under control and calm. She brought the little gang all back together. They now stood huddled around a bloody Lucas, ALL of them still terrified, trembling, and crying.

Nannie then looked at the lot of them and cleared her throat. "Listen up!" she bleated. She continued eyeballing them, slowly chewing on her food. Finally, she spoke up again. "You will do well to remember that this is why you travel in groups with smaller goats." She then lowered her head to get another mouthful of grass and smacked it loudly.

Then Nannie belched and, speaking with her mouth full of fresh regurgitation, said, "When you are in a group, it is less likely for one of you to get eaten, BUT if one of you does," she paused, yet again, and swallowed her food. Then she yawned nonchalantly, belched, and regurgitated again. Somewhere in the process, she completely forgot what it was she was going to say.

Nannie stood chewing a little bit of whatever came back up from her stomach, still smacking loudly. "Oh yeah, then there are still plenty of other little kids running around to be annoying." She stomped her hoof. "Now, how about you all get back to the rest of the community and shut your mouths for the day, or I will call that wolf back for the lot of you!" She yawned again and began shoving the kids back down the small hill, causing some of the snot-sobbing youngsters to toss and tumble to the bottom.

Lucas, however, remained on the hill alone, crying and looking at where tiny Remi had just been moments before. He then looked up and into the mountains before bleating the most sorrowful sound he could muster. Then, he lay down and continued crying as he watched the family below through blurry eyes.

11. KATE AND THE WILDMAN

The long, hard winter months were now practically upon Honolulu, and the freezing precipitation warnings across all available broadcasts were nearly a daily occurrence. The last of the summer blooms were fading, and other creatures had long since bedded down someplace that would keep them warm for the next six months of sleep.

Kate once again found herself at the old homestead, huddled by the old fireplace she had come to love. She took out her journal and began to write:

This is probably going to be my last trip up here before winter sets in.

She tossed another log into the fireplace and poked at it.

They are expecting a massive change in the weather within the next twenty-four hours, and it would be wise for me to be off the mountain or at least back to the substation before it gets here.

Kate watched her breath leave her mouth and drift off into the night sky.

As morning broke, Kate poked her face out of her extreme weather sleeping bag. She thought she must resemble a caterpillar and chuckled. She then looked over at her boots, noticing the laces had become frozen to each other. She said to herself, "Journal entry: Looks like we have had our first freeze overnight. Time to get packed up and back down to Granite Lodge."

She broke camp, got her gear loaded onto the ATV, and began looking around. "It will be really great to have a full station up here." She climbed aboard the ATV, gave everything one last look, and started it.

A long moan and shrieks broke through the trees and echoed all around her. Kate held her breath and then slowly exhaled. "Ok, Kate. You said that if you were up here on the last day and this happened, you would go investigate."

She paused and listened again, trying to get a direction. She turned off the ATV. "Ok, if you are going to do this, let's get your backpack loaded with JUST what's needed. I don't want to be lugging around things that are just going to slow me down."

Kate hoped off and started packing her riggings, ropes, enough freeze-dried food for a day trip, her hiking poles, emergency blanket, a few large trash bags, water, knife, journal, compass, GPS tracker, satellite phone, extra socks, thermal undershirt, and drawers.

"Well, I am certainly glad that I decided to bring my cold-weather jacket and pants. Don't need them right now, but the weather could change on a dime, and your tail end will certainly thank you." Kate shoved them into her day pack.

Finally, Kate reached into her equipment case to retrieve her holster and proceeded to strap it to her waist. "I've never had to use this, and hopefully, I will not have to in this case." She pulled and checked the cylinder of her Ruger Redhawk, then slid it back into the holster and secured it.

She grabbed her satellite phone. "This is Ranger 1. I'm packing up to leave primary site. Should be back to substation in four or five hours."

The moans and shrieks drifted across the mountain again. She keyed the phone and said, "I need to take a small detour to investigate something that seems to be close by in Sector 3. It should not take long."

"Come back, Ranger 1? Did you say you are headed into Sector 3?" One of the rangers at the substation keyed the phone again. "Confirm Ranger 1?" They sat listening but did not receive a response.

"Well, how do we handle that one?" said Lara Collingsworth, one of the new ranger hires.

Ed Franks, the senior ranger, spoke up, "We forward the message and the relay to Granite Lodge and Spotted Bear Station as we have been directed to do. We will also go with pre-designated check-in times. She has four hours before next check-in."

Kate drove the ATV up to a trailhead that led into Sector 3. She turned off the machine and sat looking at the shape of the trees and the undergrowth that seemed as if they would close behind her. They certainly offered no ideas as to what could possibly lie beyond.

Whatever was up there seemed to be shrouded in mystery and had no plans of being revealed. Kate blew the hair out of her eyes and adjusted her wide-brim campaign hat.

"Well, let's get this show on the road. Whatever is up there has been calling out to me. Lord, I pray you guide my feet, strengthen my heart, and grant me the courage to do your will. Send me your protector." Kate hopped off the ATV, grabbed her pack and gear, then disappeared into the woods of Sector 3.

Kate found herself sliding down several slopes before finding proper footing and traveling deeper into Sector 3. "Pete, darn it, I am NOT going to fall off this mountain!"

She sat down after finding some fallen trees and took out her journal.

Sector 3 is tough but not impassable. I am confident that we can blaze a trail through this section as well, just as we have with Sector 2.

Once again, Kate could hear the groans and shrieks from somewhere further up the mountain. She looked down at her watch and then keyed up her phone. "Ranger I checking in. Will be delayed in returning to station."

"Copy that, Ranger I. Can you give coordinates and purpose for being in 3?" There was once again silence in response.

"Ok, Kate, all checked in. Four more hours to find the source of this nonsense!" Kate nibbled at some form of prepacked meal and shoved a granola bar into her pocket.

"I pray the weather holds off for at least one more day. Please, Lord, one more day!" Kate closed her eyes and then opened them again to look further up the mountain.

Kate traveled further up some ridges, crossed a small field holding on to the last of a few flowers, and climbed higher into Granite Mountain. By then, it was reaching noon, but Kate could finally smell the signs of a campfire that was not, or at least seemed to be, not too much further. She dodged and weaved between trees and shrubs and finally spied a clearing that was backed by large old-growth trees. The clearing was the size of an oversized backyard but seemed to jut out into the open air to the front, indicating one of Pete's sheer drop-offs.

Toward the back of the clearing by the old trees, a little figure sat poking at a fire. At random times, he would whoop and holler at the top of his lungs. Kate squatted down to observe just out of his sight.

The little figure sat, poking silently at the fire and looking solemn, for that to be completely disrupted by his occasional moments of what could only be described as pure insanity as he fought with imaginary objects and cursed at them.

He finally grew mostly quiet. "I know you are there. No point in trying to hide yourself."

Kate sat motionless, not sure if he was referring to her or some other unseen thing. So, she sat as still as possible.

"I don't know who you are, what you want, or what you are doing up on my mountain…but you may as well get off your duff and come over here." The little man was rolling a cigarette in his mouth but not actually lighting it.

Kate finally stepped out of the woods and into the clearing, approaching the little man. "My name is Ranger Kate Bradigan," she said as she got closer.

"Look, darlin', don't really care who you are," the little man grunted and poked at the fire again. "But how about you tell me what you are doing here on my mountain?" He looked up at her and then pointed to where he wanted her to sit.

Kate obliged and took a seat after putting her gear down. "Who are you?" Kate began to ask before he interrupted.

"I will ask the questions to start with, princess, and then I will decide if you deserve my responses." He rolled the old cigarette around his mouth again, smelled it, and then put it away. "What are you doing up here on my mountain?" He stared at Kate.

"I am the new ranger for this area. I have been hearing things about this mountain, and when I heard screams and groans, it became my responsibility to investigate it." Kate never broke her gaze from the man.

"A ranger. Great. Just what we need up here." The man snorted, then spat into the fire.

"Is that some sort of problem?" Kate shifted and casually leaned over to one side to allow a faster draw of her weapon if the situation escalated.

"I don't know. Maybe." the man grumbled.

"I see. So, until you do know, how about I ask your name?" Kate took a drink of water.

"Not that you need to know my name," the man said and spat again, looking back at her, "but my name is Felix Shaw. You may simply refer to me as Shaw. He took a moment and spat again into the fire. "Matter of fact, I just prefer you to call me Shaw. No one warrants the right to call me by my first name," he said.

"I traveled up to this entire area years ago. Me and…" Shaw paused and took out his old cigarette, then quickly put it back into his pocket and looked at Kate. "I claimed this mountain as mine! Regardless of what some old snot face with a fat bank account and his snot-face imbecilic buddy had to say!" Shaw spouted, clearly agitated.

Kate sat quietly, listening to his ranting.

"And up till now, it's been relatively quiet. I probably traveled more miles up on this mountain than anyone, and it's been as quiet as it should be." Shaw glared at Kete.

"But now, between you and some huge, crazy mountain goat that came bugging me a month or so back. This area was once pleasantly empty and a Shangri-La to the mind. Well, that sure as fire seems over." Shaw spat in Kate's direction.

"Looks like I'm going to have to look into packing up and moving again." He shook his head in disgust. "This was a peaceful location, and you have gone and turned it into a stupid metropolis." Shaw jumped up and stomped his feet in anger. He then glared back at Kate and pointed a bony finger. "Let me guess. You are surveying the area to install a laser train and ski lodges and lifts. Then, you're going to slap out a bunch of don't feed the bear signs, all in the name of corporate greed." He spat on the ground.

"I'm telling you, it's the total rape of the environment. Can't get enough out of raping and cheating each other. May as well do it to the environment!" Shaw shouted as the corners of his mouth were bubbled with saliva.

Kate calmly watched the strange man carrying on but made no move to stand up. She didn't need him feeling threatened on top of his other issues.

"No. I'm not up here to..." Kate tried to get a word in before he launched into another rant.

"Just lovely. I got it all on my mountain. Giant goats, giant wolves, and now a teeny tiny little ranger that thinks she is going to come up here and bring social rights and justice and pet all the plants, so their feelings don't get hurt..." Shaw paused mid-thought.

"OH! And establish some stupid hamburger-flipping joint over on that ridge that doesn't use meat 'cause the people want a salad in the shape of a patty, but only if it comes on a gluten-free bun made out of kale." Shaw rubbed his forehead and rolled his eyes.

"No, I'm not up here to..." Kate once again tried to weasel in a word or two.

"You know, any other time or place, this would be the funniest thing ever." Shaw finally sat back down and crossed his legs. "I'm going to tell you this, ranger. You are definitely out of place, outsized, and well, quite frankly, out-manned, compared to all us beasts up here!" Shaw winked at Kate.

"You think so, do you?" Kate adjusted her hat and took another drink of water.

"One thing is for certain in comparing you, the goat, and the giant wolf." Shaw let out a cackle that drifted down in the mountain and echoed. "You look like you are still in diapers. Maybe you can understand what I'm going to say?"

Shaw hummed an invisible harmonica to get his pitch and then sang a song from an old children's show about something not belonging. Shaw laughed so hard he let out a fart, then scrambled around as if chasing invisible rabbits.

"Those two creatures are bigger than that little squeaker, I can tell you that! But all three can be deadly!" Shaw added, not wanting to miss the opportunity for more inappropriately gross humor.

Kate rolled her eyes. "Lovely." She then shushed the man by putting up her hand. "Giant wolf, you say?"

"Yeah, you heard me, sweat pea. Don't get me wrong. The goat is just as huge." Shaw used his arms to attempt to display size. "But, indeed, what you have to watch out for up here is that huge, mean, hellfire, blasted timber wolf!" Shaw pointed his finger out into the woods behind him.

"He must be pushing 250 plus pounds, easy, and he is black as midnight, paws the size of..." Shaw paused and looked around to think of a good comparison, "paws as big as your head, and he has huge yellow eyes. You could almost say that you were looking at Satan's very own purse pet. So, I gave him the name Abaddon." Shaw paused again.

"I guess that makes him a PIT bull. Get it?" Shaw emphasized the word "pit" and tilted his head towards Kate with one eyebrow raised. He was pleased with himself and let out his toothless, boisterous cackle.

"Well, this certainly explains the noises that echo across the mountain." Kate took out her journal and made some notes.

Shaw quickly composed himself, looked around at the trees, and spied one of interest. "But I don't go into his territory, and so far, thank god, he doesn't come into mine."

Shaw rocked forward into a standing position and walked over to one large tree that had huge scratch marks on it. "You see these?" Shaw pointed, allowing his fingers to trace the marks. "THIS is Abaddon!" He turned to conceal himself, dropped his fake buckskins, and urinated on the side of the tree. "And this, this is MY mark," he said, mumbling, apparently trying to write his name on the tree.

Kate turned her face and cupped a partial fist over her mouth, then cleared her throat to speak. "Uh, so, you are a praying man, are you?"

Shaw turned back around from the tree to look at Kate. "How do you figure that? Oh, don't get me wrong, I've at least read the Bible. It's fairly entertaining in places, but…" Shaw said while hopping up and down to get his fake buckskin pants twisted back correctly.

"Entertaining?" Kate looked over at him.

"Oh, sure. Bible has everything in it: lust, greed, rape, sex, murder. It's a real who-done-it sort of page-turner. But you know the funny thing about it?" Shaw talked while wandering around the small open area.

"What? What is the funny thing about the Bible?" Kate said, looking down at her watch. Her eyes got big as she realized she had missed her check-in, and the sun had begun to move into evening.

"What's funny is, when you look at the Bible as a who-done-it mystery, you realize that we are all just the butler and, according to the Bible, we all did it!" Shaw walked calmly over to another tree and urinated on it.

"Well, you said you thank God that Abaddon has stayed out of your area. So, I just assumed." Kate got up, looked around the opening, and then walked over to the ledge to watch the sun setting.

"Yeah, don't assume anything, ranger. I certainly don't know this god fellow you seem to worship." Shaw paused. "And, quite frankly, don't care to know him. But I will say this. IF he exists, well, he is a great writer and author. Maybe he can try writing some children's books?" Shaw once again started laughing.

Kate turned and looked at him, then back over the edge as she watched some rocks she had pushed off with her boot smack and tumble down the cliff.

"Hey, you don't get too close to that edge, missy. That's a good 40' drop to the bottom of that particular ravine." Shaw paused and then laughed. "And before you even suggest it, I'm not the one that can just come scaling on down there to rescue you, IF I even wanted to!" He once again spat in Kate's direction.

Kate glanced back over the edge as the last bits of sunlight highlighted the floor below and the jagged rocks on the way down, then looked back over to Shaw.

Shaw sat down with his back against the tree and legs stretched out in front, then resumed poking at the fire. He thought for a moment and then looked back up at Kate, who was now putting on her cold-weather pants and jacket. "And as far as believing in god, ranger, well, IF he exists, he certainly hasn't done me OR society, for that matter, any favors."

Scratching at his patchwork beard, Shaw spoke up again. "Believe it or not, I used to be all wrapped up in society." He looked down and poked again at the fire. "I worked the sixty-hour week, watched men come, watched them go. I watched both the young and the old die the same way: wasteful, useless, and just as broke and stupid as when they first came into life."

Almost as if pleading for help, Shaw looked up into the sky. "If there is a god, Kate, why doesn't he try to impress me by trying to clean up all of this mess that's going on, you know?" Pausing, he took a drink from his canteen, his anger returning. "If such a being wants me to worship him, he is going to have to step out and step up."

"I grew up in the church, my mother hauling me to the local religious school. And for what, KATE? Just so I can hear them tell me I'm going to hell because I don't tithe ten percent of MY wages, or that my clothes aren't black enough or colorful enough, or hair is too, I don't know, short and green?!"

"Let me ask you this rhetorical question, Ranger KATE," Shaw sarcastically said her name. "Look at how many have died over the centuries, no, millennia, all in the name of religion. One thing they all have in common is they tell you god won't forgive you unless you pony up some cash for their collection plates, or kill this type of people, or some glorious cause that puts the preacher into a Bentley every other month." Shaw tossed a couple of dirt clods in Kate's direction, hitting her boots with one and watching the other shatter and spread across the ground.

Kate pulled her coat tightly around herself and did a small hop to reseat her backpack back onto her hips. She could tell that a winter storm was approaching, and the chill of the air was beginning to set in. She was certainly not going to get another day of good weather.

Shifting her attention from the ledge, Kate turned to face Shaw. "The issue is man has always been self-serving. Yes, thousands upon thousands have died in the name of religion. Whether you are Christian, Muslim, Hindu, or Buddhist." She took a few steps towards Shaw.

"But I tell you, only ONE man came and told us HOW to actually make ourselves right with God, then offered Himself up as the proof. You have to separate what you think you know, separate yourself from what the world has told you religion is. I know that goes against everything you have built up in your mind." Kate stood facing him.

Kate looked into Shaw's face. "All of society, ALL of the world, is in a fallen state. It doesn't matter how you paint it, what color, what design, or what you may build on top of it to make it appear pretty. ALL of it is corrupted, polluted by sin."

Shaw looked up at Kate. He grunted, spat on the ground, and kicked the results around in the dirt.

Kate looked out across the mountainside and then back to Shaw. "You think that you have left all of society behind you, that you are some sort of sentient being? That you have become smarter and are above it all?" Kate waved her hand in the air like a genie. "I tell you, Mr. Shaw, YOU are STILL just as corrupted by sin as I am."

Shaw drew his lips back into a sneer, kicked his spit-covered dirt clods at her, and continued to glare and scowl.

Kate pointed her hiking pole back at Shaw. "I'm telling you, no matter how you try to run, no matter how you try to paint it or dismiss it, or ignore it, you are guilty. You will be found guilty, and whether you believe in Jesus Christ or not, YOU ARE responsible for your actions, for your doings, for your sins. You WILL stand before the Judge and give an account of your life."

"I'm telling you…" Shaw started to speak.

Kate quickly cut him off. "and I'm telling YOU!"

Using her hiking stick like a foil and jabbing the air in Shaw's direction with each word, Kate said, "Whether you choose to accept Christ as your Savior, or how about this, as your LAWYER, to represent you before God the Judge, or you choose to dismiss it all as you have everything else, there IS still coming a time, a day when the payment for your deeds comes due. You cannot run from it, and the sentence is utterly terrifying."

Shaw shook his head. "Well, my, my; aren't you just a little spitfire." He scratched at his chin. "You know, Kate, you sure are a great *argumentor*." He spat on the ground again. "Yep, a great *argumentor* and a typical woman. I barely can get a word in."

Kate raised her hand to stop and quickly correct him, her patience running very thin. "I don't believe that's an actual word. You mean debater, right? The fact that I'm a woman has nothing to do with this."

Shaw scowled and continued talking. "I can see where you are coming from, but let me tell you this: I don't need a fairytale to help me. Look around you. I get up each morning. I'm the master of my own life. I have no wants, no needs. I've made amends for things in my life that I may have done." He slowly drew the old cigarette back out of his pocket, looked at it, and then shoved it back down deep.

He looked down and held his hand across his pocket, having become melancholic. He then quickly looked back up at Kate and started to yell. "I have no cares, and I live the way I want to, ranger! I represent myself! There is no grand old man up in the clouds! We are here for a spell, and then into nothing, having done nothing, being remembered for nothing, nothing begat NOTHING!" Shaw sneered.

Kate frowned. "Well, it's awfully easy to be cynical, isn't it? When you spend your entire life running from duties and responsibilities and thinking there are no consequences for yourself while pointing out the action or inaction of others." She poked the ground with her hiking stick and squatted down. "Maybe one of the reasons I am also out here is because of you?"

Shaw stroked his beard, then scratched his head while looking at Kate. "How do you figure that? I sure didn't invite you here, and to be honest, I will definitely celebrate the moment you leave."

Kate continued poking at the ground and made little doodles with her hiking pole,. "God wants to make sure that everyone…and that certainly includes YOU…has had a chance to hear the TRUTH of His love for you and accept His Son as their personal Lord and Savior.

"That through faith and belief in HIM and His sacrifice, we can wipe our past clean and once again commune with God and have the righteous life that He so longs for us to have."

Kate paused for a moment. "Without Him, we are lost for eternity." She brought her conversation to a close, looked up at Shaw, and said, "Without Him, you are lost. WE are ALL lost."

Shaw started to cackle and ended up hitting the back of his head against the tree he was resting against. His laugh quickly changed, sounding more like an injured beast's groan. After a minute of vigorously rubbing the spot on his head, he looked up, the look on his face becoming saturated with evil. "LISTEN," he said angrily, thrusting his bony finger into his own chest and then flinging it back into the mountain," I have been out here for years! Do I LOOK lost to you? I know every INCH of this mountain.

"I am responsible only to myself! I make the rules out here. I decide what lives and what dies. I have conquered the idiocy of society. I have overcome the stupidity of people such as yourself!" The foam in the corner of Shaw's mouth began to spill over onto his clothes.

"Now hear me out on this, RANGER, because not only have I grown tired of this entire interrogation of yours, and what I'm going to say, I will only say this ONCE!" Shaw paused and looked at Kate to make sure she was listening.

He slowly crossed his outstretched legs, took the old cigarette from his pocket, rolled it into his lips, and raised his chin to the air as if breathing in all the aromas the world had to offer. He got as comfortable as he could, then spread his arms out wide, clasping them behind his head to act as a pillow, resting his entire body against the large tree.

He calmly opened his eyes, looked at Kate, and spoke slowly, emphasizing each word, "Hear ME, out here, RANGER KATE BRADIGAN, I am NEVER wrong in this reality OR in the print of your little journal!"

Shaw then spat into the air as hard as he possibly could in an attempt to reach the heavens. "Out here, I am the judge. Only I can and will judge myself. Oh, and my life sentence," he said with his eyes still closed as if he was dreaming, "and MY eternity is peace and contentment!"

He once again closed his eyes, then opened them and glared defiantly at Kate. "Out here, KATE, I AM...GOD!"

Kate slowly dropped her head and then stood up, tapping the loose dirt off her hiking poles and smacking the dirt off her boots. She then turned her back and looked out over the mountain toward the late-day sun. Reaching into her pack, Kate took out the satellite phone and called back to the station. "This is Ranger 1, doing my four-hour check-in. Sorry for the delay."

"Rodger that, Ranger 1. Please be advised your GPS does not appear to be working. Need grid coordinates," Lara Collingsworth timidly peeped back.

Taking out her map, Kate watched the late afternoon sun as it set into the evening. "I am NOT at the planned coordinates. I am currently in grid... Hmm, hold on a moment. Let me check this again. Will call you back in a couple minutes."

Kate took out a grease pencil, a protractor, and her compass, then made some marks on her map. She looked over the mountain and then back down at the map. "Woops, um, you are a little far off the beaten path, girl. This spot is not only hard to get to but would be nearly impossible to find."

Looking out over the ridge, Kate tried to check back to the station, but her phone only gave back a "no service" error. "Well, how in blazes does that happen? All the satellites out of orbit? Paging Mr. Elon Musk." Kate tapped the phone to her head and laughed for just a moment.

Kate connected her phone back to her pack, once again doing a little hop to put the weight of her backpack onto her hips. She took a deep breath, scooted close to the edge of the outcrop, and looked again at the drop below.

With her back still to Shaw, Kate said, "Well, I need to make it back to what resembles a trailhead within the next couple hours. There is a winter storm coming up pretty fast, and I sure don't want to have to sleep on this mountain." She continued looking down at the small ravine below. "You should really get back to wherever it is you call home, Shaw."

She paused and tilted her head, having heard some random rustling. She then chuckled, imagining Mr. Shaw getting his britches caught on a tree, unable to free himself. Now, with the rustling came some weird, gargled noises. Kate thought, *Oh Lord, please tell me he is just stuck and isn't using the bathroom again.*

Kate called out, "Mr. Shaw, would you please stop doing whatever it is you are doing? A little bit of common courtesy can go a long way." She coughed loudly. "You do realize that I could give you a fine or even arrest you and haul you into jail, right?"

Kate paused and listened. "I have been very lenient with you, Shaw. A lot of people back in town really want me to haul you down there for some questions. I'm willing to overlook things for now, but I will certainly haul you off this mountain if I have to."

Of course, Kate knew she wouldn't have pulled him into jail. She was too far off the trails to have to deal with a detainee. She stood there listening for his response, but only the rustling and gargling noises continued.

Then, as quickly as the noises came, there was complete silence: no birds, no insects, not even the wind across the trees. The entire canyon below made not a single solitary sound.

Kate's expression changed from annoyed to worried, then to pure terror as she slowly turned her head. Kate's blood turned ice cold, the color leaving her face as the hair on the back of her neck bristled.

She spun completely around, and there, within fifteen feet, stood Abaddon, whose teeth were now firmly lodged around Shaw's neck. Shaw's eyes were open and showed pure terror as he could only blink. The rest of his body involuntarily twitched but had mostly gone limp.

Kate gasped and then yelled frantically. "GET AWAY FROM HIM!" She swung her hiking pole. Then, she looked around for anything that she could possibly throw.

Abaddon glared back at Kate and stepped forward defiantly. He lowered his head slowly, clenching down his mouth to finish cracking Shaw's neck. He then pulled Shaw's body further out into the open, the little man's lifeless legs and arms now dragging along underneath like a dishtowel.

Kate slowly reached down and attempted to unsnap the holster to draw her service pistol, but with every move she made, Abaddon glared at her, almost daring her to draw it. The more she moved, the faster he closed the distance between them.

Even though he was still eight feet away, Kate could feel the heat of Abaddon's breath and see his eyes piercing deep into her body. Abaddon paused, keeping his glaring eyes on her. She grew very quiet and still, her hand ever so close to her holster.

After a few moments, Abaddon snorted and dug his massive claws into the earth. Growling, he opened his mouth and proceeded to spit the small man out onto the ground.

Kate stared at what was once Felix Shaw. He lay in a crumpled heap, resembling an old chew toy that had been bounced across the ground, collected every particle of dirt and grime, and then came to rest in a pile of dog scat.

Abaddon walked across Shaw, now within a good arm's reach. Kate continued to inch backwards, knowing that if she tried to pull her weapon, Abaddon would be on her before she could clear the holster, let alone pull the trigger. Her only option was to stay calm and not move.

Kate was very well aware that she was now on the very edge of the drop. Abaddon suddenly raised his head as he caught the noise of something from a little way off, forcing his eyes into a different direction. He sniffed and snorted into the air in several directions.

She tried to make the most of the distraction and Abaddon's loss of interest in her. She shifted slightly and unlatched the cover to her holster, quickly bringing Abaddon's attention back to her. His eyes grew into yellow slits, and the pupils all but disappeared. His lips furled, showing his fangs, and his fury fell from his mouth in large pools of drool. Abaddon bristled and snapped his jaws, flinging foamy saliva onto Kate's face and jacket. Then, he quickly moved forward and simply gave her a slight push with his snout.

Kate lost her footing, sending her over the edge. Abaddon laid down where Kate once stood so he could watch her bounce off the rocky cliff face, which was sharp enough to slash her backpack, sending the contents across the mountainside.

Her head slammed hard as she approached the bottom. The assortment of falling rocks, dirt, and boulders assisted in dislocating her shoulder and breaking both legs. The sharp edges of rocks ripping her protective winter clothing and opening her flesh.

As she reached the bottom of the cliff, Kate screamed beyond imagination as the pain reached her brain. She lay looking up into the darkening sky as blood started flowing from her nose and a gash in her leg. She tried to look to where she once was, which now seemed miles away.

Kate took as deep a breath as possible, realizing she also had several broken ribs. Each breath felt like a frozen knife slicing through her lungs. Looking around, she tried to take a quick assessment of her physical condition as well as the resources and equipment within reach.

She looked around. "Ok, ok... I'm in a clearing. Ground is soft. Trees... almost like a little glade. Almost? No, come on, Kate. Focus! I think I'm in a glade, and I'm in seriously, SERIOUSLY bad shape. And my weapon, satellite phone, and GPS tracker are scattered somewhere across the mountain."

Kate groaned again. Each beat of her heart forced pain across her entire body. Kate glanced back up and saw a small, distant black figure disappear from her view.

"Oh, Lord, HELP ME!" Kate cried out, knowing that Abaddon was more than likely on his way and would eventually find her. She sat as quietly as possible in pain, praying until the world around her spun faster and faster and then turned black.

12. INTO THE VALLEY

Gruff could feel the sudden changes in temperature and knew a freezing cold was coming soon. He walked around, casually looking at everything. He knew that he would soon need to find somewhere to bundle down for the winter and make sure he had access to water and food.

Some of these things I remember from the bees, he thought to himself, *not to mention that half-crazed toothless man who told me about them.*

Gruff looked around and then walked over to a large tree. He scrubbed his head on the bark. "Yeah, that's the stuff right there!" He scratched from his snout to the tip of his horns and grunted. "Ok, tree, we are certainly not done yet," Gruff slowly turned sideways and ran his scruff to his hind quarters along the tree, which was now starting to bend and protest the assault. He then turned a bit more, dropped his head, and proceeded to give his rear end a big, long scratch.

The tree continued to bend under Gruff's strength until it finally gave way. A loud, splintering crack echoed across the mountain as the tree broke. Gruff chuckled to himself and said, "That Shaw fella would have laughed like he was insane and say I was barking up the wrong tree!" Gruff let out a loud, proud grunt of approval at his joke.

Suddenly, Gruff's eye caught something moving from a little way off up on a ridge. He looked up in time to watch it fall to the ground while pieces of whatever it was scattered into the wind and onto the side of the mountain.

Well, what on the mountain was that? Gruff shook the bark from his fleece. He gave his rump one more good scratch and stood very still to look around and listen.

Hmm, well, it's not like I'm doing anything else right now. Let's see if we can go take a closer look and see if there is anything that we can help with. Gruff then cautiously headed in the direction where he saw the object fall.

Kate woke up and was now in considerable pain. Every fiber in her body screamed with each movement she made. Even breathing was painful. She worked to gather up any supplies that were within reach. She reached her hand up to her nose and head, and it came away bloody. "Well, that's just lovely. Broken legs, a head that is banged up, and no way to contact anyone."

She looked up and could just make out her GPS tracker stuck a little further up the cliff face. It was obviously broken. "Lovely, just lovely." Laying her head back against some of the larger rocks that used to be part of the cliff face, she noticed a small pouch off to her side. "Well, that might as well be ten miles away." She let out an intense moan of pain when she attempted to move toward it.

"Ok…ok! What…oh wait. Let's do this," Kate mumbled to herself, grabbing for a large branch she had broken during her descent. She took the limb and scooted it out from her side. The immediate pain ravaged every nerve in her body, causing her to vomit on herself. She coughed, gasping and fighting for each breath, and then, with one arm, inched the branch toward the pouch just as things went black again.

"Number Forty! Get in the game!" Kate looked around at the defense and offense. "Kate, get going! You are needed in center midfield!" The voice shouted.

Kate looked and saw the coach pointing at her and then back onto the field. "I know these are all boy teams, but DON'T let them get away with anything. You are just as tough!"

Nodding, Kate ran onto the field and assumed her position. The ball was passed to Kate, and she headed downfield, moving and weaving between the defending players.

She was moving well until she got close to the goal. As she prepared to take the shot, she ended up being tackled from behind. The referee refused to toss up a yellow card, and the ball was moving in the wrong direction.

Kate picked herself off the ground and charged back. After a skirmish with the other player, Kate began moving the ball back downfield. Once again, Kate was tackled from behind. This time, Kate glared at the referee and tossed her hands in the air, yelling for him to call the foul, but once again, he didn't.

Getting up from the ground, Kate charged back up the field to wrestle the ball away from the player. She began weaving back towards the goal. Kate could feel the player coming. She stopped short, grabbed him by the shirt, and smashed his body face-first into the ground, causing him to slide into his teammates.

The referee blew his whistle, ran up to Kate, and flashed his red card.

Kate flew at the referee. "Are you blind? Maybe if you would open your eyes a little more, ref, you could see what's going on here!"

The referee held the red card high and blew his whistle again before looking at Kate. Then, he said, "He's coming, Kate. He will be there soon. You must WAKE UP!"

Her eyes opened, and once again, her mind was flooded with all the pain her body was in. She grabbed for her branch and started pawing again for the small bag that lay ever so close but just out of reach. Her head was spinning so badly that she thought she would vomit again. She took a deep breath that felt like wild cats trying to escape from her lungs and tossed out the branch, leaning as much as she could in the direction of the bag. She let out another grimace of pain.

"This is it," she muttered. "If I don't reach it this time, I just simply will not have anything left in me." She once again turned her head as much as she could and tossed the branch, feeling all her muscles and nerves scream in protest. The tip of the branch landed in the loop of the drawstring. Kate exhaled slowly. She began to inch the branch and the sack back toward her.

Kate wrestled with the branch and finally had the item within reach. She laid the branch down next to her. "Not exactly sure what I will do with that, but it's at least something." She could hear movement coming from far away. "I guess it won't be long now before Abaddon is here. Just hope he gets it over quickly."

She tilted her head back toward the cliff face, grabbed the small sack, and opened it. She examined the contents and managed a small laugh. "Well, these are certainly useful but not exactly a deterrent to Abaddon." She laid her head back against the cliff, and her eyes closed again, falling into spinning darkness.

"All right, where is my point guard?"The voice shouted. "Forty! Kate? Get in there!" Kate glanced at the coach and the other players, then started to dash onto the court.

"We are down by ten, Kate!" Shouted the couch. "Be vigilant, and don't let them run all over you!"

"Got it, coach!" Kate glanced at him and took her position at point.

The opposite team came charging down the court. Their small forward ran, purposely tripping Kate to the ground. Kate jumped up and looked at the ref for a whistle. "HEY, how about you pay attention, ref!" Kate screamed and tossed her hands in the air.

"Let's go, Kate! Shake it off!" her coach said, clapping from the sideline.

Once again, Kate lined up to face the other team. Their players charged at her, and once again, one of them purposely slammed her to the floor. Blood flowed from her nose and arms as the coach waved her off the court. Kate looked up at the coach when he took her by her shoulders. "Kate, you need to wake up. He is coming and is going to help you, but you must wake up!"

"Who is coming?" Kate looked into the face of her coach, who she seemed to know but just couldn't recognize.

The coach held Kate by the shoulders. "He has been prepared for you from his birth and for this moment.

Now, WAKE UP!"

Kate's eyes shot open, and she looked around, disoriented, for the voice and a coach who was now gone.

Gruff came up on the small clearing and peered at the figure lying at the base of the cliff. He sniffed the air in all directions, and his eyes focused, once again, on what he could now tell was a human lying on the ground.

He longed to move forward, to take a closer look. His very spirit cried, demanding that he go to this human.

Gruff moved slowly into the clearing. Then, his ears picked up on movements that echoed down to his location, and he froze, looking and smelling in all directions.

Kate opened her eyes and blinked several times, not quite able to tell what she was looking at. She then closed them again and bit her lip to focus on denying that she was in pain.

"If you are here to finish the job, let's just get on with it, shall we?" she said wearily.

Gruff took several more cautious steps toward the human, pausing with each hoof placement to sniff the air. Kate once again opened her eyes, and now a massive beast of a mountain goat within arm's reach. Gruff paused and stood still, lowering his head so he could take a little closer look.

"Oh, hey! Yeah, hey there, beautiful," Kate groggily said while attempting to smile. "I know you are probably looking for salt, but unfortunately, my friend, all I have is this granola bar and a couple of heavy-duty green trash bags."

Kate did her best to feel in her pockets for anything else. "Everything else has been broken, ruined, or blown away. But I'm willing to give you this granola bar." Kate unwrapped the bar and sniffed at it. "In my condition, fella, I certainly will not be needing much of it."

Kate opened the granola bar completely, slowly took a small bite, and sniffed at it again. Gruff stood watching curiously, snorting and sniffing the air. Kate then took the granola bar and held it out the best she could toward Gruff.

"Here you go. It's all I have, and it's for you." Gruff stepped forward, touched his nose to the granola bar, then looked into Kate's eyes. "Go ahead. I promise you it's not going to hurt you. I'm not going to hurt you, either." Kate moved the treat up and down on Gruff's snout to try and entice him.

Gruff stepped forward. His immense size now completely shadowed Kate. "You are absolutely beautiful," she whispered, reaching up to touch his velvety snout. "You remind me of someone that I've only seen in dreams," Kate said, giving a little chuckle that hurt every inch of her body.

Gruff lowered his head a little more and moved his face even closer to Kate. "Yes, I do know you, don't I?" Kate whispered, staring hard back into Gruff's eyes. Kate dropped the granola bar, reached out her hand, and touched Gruff's face. Gruff inched forward, stuck his muzzle into Kate's hair, and breathed deep, allowing her to run her palm over his nose and chin.

Gruff closed his eyes and continued to breathe. Her hair smelled like jasmine and wild berry blooms. His mind flashed back to everything he had seen and done and the smell of the earth when it was in full bloom. He breathed in deeply again and pressed his cheek to her cheek, feeling the warmth and smelling the slight aroma of honey on her skin.

This is who he had been looking and waiting for all this time. Gruff realized the TRUTH. His mind flashed, and he seemingly heard voices echoing in his head. He saw images of Zeki and heard his voice talking to him. "You don't have to live a life of abuse, servitude. Life is precious. Life is worth defending.

"You do not have to perpetuate the cruelty that has been done to you. YOU ARE MORE than just yourself, worth MORE than what others would sell you for. You have been created and designed for a unique purpose by the Creator and for the Creator; A purpose that only you can do through faith IN the Creator." Gruff opened his eyes and was brought back into the moment.

Kate closed her eyes and held on to the sides of Gruff's face, her broken body screaming out with each movement. She then whispered, "Thank you, Lord, Christ Jesus, my Savior, my Creator, for sending me a friend to be with me during my final hours."

Gruff's head jerked slightly as he listened to her. "Did she just say 'Creator?' This human knows the Creator?" Gruff buried his face into Kate's hair again.

"My Creator, thank you for bringing me here and opening my eyes. I plead with you, strengthen me, help me to protect and serve her according to your will." Gruff continued to keep his face buried in Kate's hair, praying for them both.

Kate held on to Gruff with what strength she had and continued praying. "May my last thoughts be on You, Lord, for you are my all in all. I pray that you forgive my sins against you and bless this beautiful creature to Your everlasting care."

Gruff snorted, looked at Kate, and then stared off into the distance. "Yeah, I know what's coming, fella. I suppose you have seen him as well?" Gruff just snorted and pawed at the ground with one of his hooves, continuing to look off into the distance.

"Well, I think we missed a couple things of importance." Kate looked into Gruff's eyes. "Introductions, I suppose, are in order?" Kate shifted a bit, crying under the pain it generated.

"My name is Kate, but what should we call you?" Kate thought the best she could. "Hmm... Well, I remember a story that my mother would tell me long ago about a family of goats, a bridge, and a nasty creature that lived underneath." Kate found herself giving up a small laugh. Kate looked at him again the best she could. "How about I just call you Gruff?"

Upon hearing that, Gruff tossed up his head and pawed at the ground, sticking his nose back into her hair and snorting. "Ok, Gruff, it is! I'm afraid, though, my friend, that this is going to be a short relationship." Kate patted his nose.

"I'm out in the middle of nowhere. There is a winter storm getting ready to break loose any moment. My legs are broken, my head is broken, and my leg is bleeding pretty bad." Kate let out a breath and rested her head against Gruff.

Kate paused and looked down at her leg. She ripped some of her t-shirt out from underneath her work shirt and coat and tied it around the wound as best she could. "I really need something to stop this bleeding. I don't suppose you have an extra hand, a roll of gauze, or some sort of magical dust in that fleece?" Kate chuckled again.

Gruff looked back into the forest in the direction he knew Abaddon would be coming from. He snorted, turned, and headed in the opposite direction, walking quickly at first and then breaking into a full dash as he went up the other side of the mountain.

"I don't blame you, Gruff. If I could high-tail it out of here, I certainly would!" Kate lifted herself the best she could. "Love having met you!" She tried to call out, but that only made her head swim and her lungs burn. Kate sat, again alone with her thoughts and pain, waiting for Abaddon as the darkness continued to creep in.

13. THE CONVERGENCE

Kate woke up from a doze, or maybe it was a nap. She could no longer tell what was reality or a dream, nor could she tell exactly how long she had been unconscious. All she knew was that when she was awake, she was in severe pain, and there was only just enough light left in the day to see the tree line that was only fifteen feet away.

Kate shifted, causing more painful spasms. "Well, if Abaddon doesn't kill me, my injuries certainly will soon enough. If not the injuries, then the coming storm." Kate closed her eyes.

"My Lord, I pray that you forgive me…receive me." She had no sooner said "amen" than Gruff returned from the forest with a large collection of something in his mouth.

Gruff walked over to Kate and dropped all the contents of his mouth into her lap.

"What's this?" She looked up at him. "Ok, um," Kate looked back down at the gifts he brought her. Gruff just snorted and used his hoof to paw at the ground. "Well, if you insist. Let's see what all of these goodies are and why you think they are so important." Kate reached out and touched his nose.

She looked down and opened a huge green leaf that was hiding other items. She began to sift through the contents that surprisingly were not covered in mouth slime, drool, dirt, or, well, whatever else these things were picked up from.

Kate's eyes grew wide. "How in the world…, what...?" She continued looking down at everything. "Gruff, how did you know to get these things?" Kate stammered while looking at all the things that were in her lap.

Gruff stepped up close and stuck his nose again into her hair, wanting to be as close to her as he possibly could.

"Well, I don't know how, but LOOK! A huge mullein leaf, and how in the world did you come up with honeycomb?" Kate looked up at him.

Gruff stepped closer, looked down at the mullein leaf, and began to heave and hack.

Kate looked up at Gruff. "Uh, are you ok?"

At that very moment, Gruff vomited up a mouthful of various flowers, or at least what was left of them, with their leaves onto the large mullein leaf.

Kate looked up and Gruff and then back down at the pile. She knew she wanted to vomit, but doing so would only bring more pain. She finally looked down. "Ok, Gruff, this is just a little gross, don't you think?"

Gruff pawed at the ground. Kate looked at Gruff and then back at the pile. She then took her finger and poked around in the pile of vomit. "Well, fortunately, it has not been in one of those stomachs of yours for too terribly long!" She paused and looked closer into the goop. "What in the world!? We have some arnica! OH, my goodness! We have some yarrow!

Kate continued to think about what he brought back for her. "Ok, so we have some beautiful mullein, and I'm not even going to ASK how you came up with some honeycomb!"

Immediately going to work, Kate crushed the mullein leaf into the shape of a small bag. Then she scooped up the gelatinous flower concoction into the mullein and tied it closed as best she could. She looked up at Gruff and smiled, exhaled slowly, and then let out a high-pitched yell as she quickly shoved the herbal poultice deep into her leg wound.

"Believe it or not, Gruff," Kate said, looking up at him, "all the things you brought me will help stop the bleeding and act as a little bit of a pain reliever, and all of it can be antimicrobial, not that you really wanted to know that. I know you don't understand me, but this stuff is gold when you are in a bad situation like I am right now."

Kate popped a small piece of the honeycomb into her mouth. She then ran a little over her leg wound and smeared what was left into the various cuts and gashes on her head and face. "I know raw honey for an open wound is risky, and it could get infected. But again, the situation I'm in right now, do you think I'm really worried about that? Honey is magical." Kate looked up at Gruff and waved her fingers in the air like a magician.

She then pulled the laces from one of her boots and tore one of the trash bags into wide, flat strips. She wrapped the strips several times around her leg as a makeshift trauma bandage and tied it with her bootlaces. "Let's keep that at least covered, shall we?" Then, she used the rest of the bag to fashion a sling for her dislocated shoulder.

Gruff looked up and sniffed the air. His ears stood stiff and pointed in the direction of movements. "He is close by, isn't he, Gruff? He has just been laying there watching us, studying us all this time," Kate whispered.

The entire area fell silent, and the only thing that could be heard was Kate's breathing. Gruff slowly turned away from her, so all she could see was his rear end. He stood in front of her, looking into the forest, which was now motionless.

"I tell you; you just don't know when to mind your own business, do you?" A low, raw, and raspy voice flooded in from the woods, and the hair on Kate's arms stood on end as she heard the low growls, powerful enough for her to feel in the pit of her stomach.

"I suppose some old fool of a crow put you up to all this? All because he can't manage to do it himself." Abaddon continued to growl. "And just where is he now? I will tell you where. Sitting his old feathered rear end on some cozy nest, while you, well, you are out here in, quite frankly, a very serious situation." Abaddon gave a little sickening laugh.

"It doesn't matter where Zeki is," Gruff grunted back. "THIS IS my business, and I highly advise you to just go away, Abaddon. She belongs to me." Gruff snorted and pawed his hooves into the ground.

Abaddon laughed. "Oh, I don't think you fully understand the predicament we have here. You seem to think you are more important than what you really are." Abaddon let out another huge growl. "I can assure you; you are not that important."

"I don't think YOU understand, Abaddon!" Gruff snapped back. "I just happen to be friends with a man that lives on this mountain, and he will be coming to help me if I call out for him." Gruff snorted. "Shaw is his name, and he is more than able to take care of you!"

Abaddon stayed just inside the wood line, watching the sun slowly disappear into the mountains. "Oh, I'm sorry," he sneered, "but I think Shaw is a little, um, how shall we say…unreachable for this particular situation, well, any further situation, really."

Abaddon then let out a huge blood-curdling howl followed by growls and teeth gnashing. Kate closed her eyes, and she prayed. Her head was now swirling, and she began to shake with fear, which only caused more pain to ripple through her body.

"I have to say, you certainly are a sizable goat. I've only seen you from a distance up until now, but don't think that your size alone will save you," Abaddon sneered from the shadows. "I've seen what a big pushover you are, and I suspect things have not changed."

He huffed and slowly emerged from the forest and then casually flopped onto the ground, his voice changing from a frothy sneer to nearly sugary sweet. "However,..." Abaddon said and began to roll over onto his back to paw playfully at imaginary creatures.

Abaddon continued to paw at the air for a while, then slowly twisted his head to look at Gruff upside down. "Look here, my friend, I'm mostly honest, and I'm sure that you and I could come to some understanding, an agreement if you will."

He rolled upright and sat like he was guarding pyramids. "That is, we can both get something mutually beneficial out of this in case your little brain can't comprehend what I'm saying."

Gruff stiffened his footing, his stance as solid as the mountain he stood on. "I understand you perfectly well, Abaddon. What exactly did you have in mind?"

Abaddon got up off the ground and slowly stepped further out into the little clearing toward Gruff. His yellow eyes flashed at Kate. Kate gasped at the sheer size of these two squaring off at each other.

"I see you know my name, not that it really matters. It's the only name you really need to know, anyway. However, it must have been that little loudmouth, half-crazy human Shaw who told you." Abaddon started to pace back and forth. "He liked to think he came up with that name but let me tell you something...goat. I'm older than these mountains, and I whispered my name to him while he slept."

Abaddon sneered again, "I whispered it to him until he went completely insane." He started a snarly laugh. "You would be very surprised to know what I got that human to do." He stopped and looked Gruff in the eyes. "You see, goat… out here, I'm god. I decide who lives, who dies, and, for that matter, when and HOW they are going to die. Why, you may not believe it, but I'm really just as honest and fair as I can be, and I'm giving you the chance for a great opportunity. A favor for a gift in return, if you will…goat."

Gruff stood his ground, not taking his eyes off Abaddon. "And just what gift would that be?"

Abaddon howled with a sneering foamy laugh. "You have to ask? Ok, let me see if I can make this simple. I'm giving you your life, stupid. How absolutely fantastic is that…goat? All I ask in return for your life is that you do me a little favor."

There was a moment of silence between the two juggernauts. "This is so simple, even YOU should be able to comprehend it!" Abaddon's eyes shimmered. "Your good buddy Korvus certainly understood it."

Abaddon paused in thought, then said, "That little, tiny brain of yours surely can understand and take this favor. Then you can go back to wandering around sniffing flowers or whatever it is that you do…goat."

Gruff stiffened a bit more and glared at Abaddon. "Not that I care to talk with you or that I really want to know, but what exactly is this favor... Abaddon?"

Abaddon paced a little and then returned, stopping again to face Gruff. "Just take a step to the side, a little to the left or a little to the right, your choice. That's all you need to do.

Abaddon casually scratched at his hind leg, then turned his head back to Gruff and produced a toothy smile. "You've been doing that your whole life, haven't you…goat? Why should you bother standing up now?

Gruff's posture changed slightly. Abaddon spotted Gruff's self-doubt and quickly seized the moment. He continued, "Yes. . .goat, I know you. I know where you come from. I've looked out over your meadow. I've looked down from the ledges and watched them beat you, abuse you. YOU are an outcast, yet unable to leave, held as a prisoner for their enjoyment!"

"You've seen my home?" Gruff stomped at Abaddon.

"OH, my friend, I've seen what they did to you!" Abaddon looked at Gruff, feigning concern as best he could. "What would you say if you and I go back there a little later together? We could really shake things up, don't you think?" Abaddon stifled a laugh.

"Could you just imagine the look on all their stupid faces!" The great wolf howled with laughter. "Well, you take a moment to think on that, but I advise you not to think too long. You need to know that my mercy only goes so far and is only offered for so long."

"You stay away from my family," Gruff said, holding back his rage.

"Oh, my dear friend, with all they did, you would STILL defend them?" Abaddon looked surprised. "Well, it's far too late for that sort of thinking. You should know I have even taken some of your family members from time to time; well, the ones that were offered up willingly." He sneered more than laughed.

Abaddon finally rose to his feet. "But YOU need to remember. No, YOU need to understand, I AM the strength of this mountain, and I decide who. . . or what comes and goes." He looked over Gruff as Kate. "Yes. Yes, indeed, I decide, and you just might decide that having me as your friend can be a good thing. We could do quite a bit together! You just take a step to the side. . .goat, and we will ALL be somewhere else by the time this storm starts."

Gruff shifted the weight on his hooves but refused to budge from his spot. Abaddon took that as an agreement and began to move forward, trying to walk past. Gruff quickly adjusted and lowered his head. He gave Abaddon a shove and pushed the wolf back to the tree line.

"I'm warning you! BACK OFF, Abaddon! This human is mine!"

Sneering at Gruff, Abaddon slowly paced back and forth, snarling and showing his teeth. "You are a blasted fool, GOAT! There is no point in both of you dying and me wasting energy on the likes of either of you."

Abaddon looked at Gruff and then over to Kate and bristled. "Just give me the human, and you can leave. She is weak and going to die anyway. Just LOOK at her! There is no point in sticking your nose into things that are absolutely none of your concern! Isn't your life worth more than hers!?"

Spit and foam began to form and flow from Abaddon's mouth as his rage grew. He continued his lecture, saying, "Let me point this out to you. You owe her no loyalty, no commitment. In fact, you have no duties to this human. It's because of THEM that everything is stained!"

"Our ancestors once walked with them, Abaddon. If the Creator calls on me to watch over and protect them, then so be it, regardless of what may happen to me!" Gruff angrily replied.

"The creator? Don't be so stupid! That is just that old bird you think is your friend playing you for a fool." Abaddon chuckled, the drool and spit flying from his mouth.

Once again, Abaddon paced back and forth. "How do these humans treat you? They couldn't care less about you! You could stumble and fall from this very mountain, and they would just point at your dead body, laugh, stuff your corpse like a trophy with the fluff from your own backside!"

Abaddon stopped in his tracks and looked Gruff in the eyes, "I tell you… goat, don't you know they kill you just for SPORT of it?! They stand over your dead body and gloat to one another about how mighty they are. Does that sound like creatures who deserve your respect? That deserves your protection?"

As he began pacing again, Abaddon glared at Kate and Gruff. "You know...goat, I've already told you I know where you have traveled from. I'm not lying. I've seen your valley, I've looked out over your meadow, and I've watched and seen these very humans kill some of your very own!" He paused and slowly turned his eyes back to Kate before snarling at Gruff, "Just for the pure pleasure of it. This is MY mountain, and there will be consequences. There will be retribution, payment, especially from the likes of these humans!"

Abaddon suddenly stopped and looked back to Gruff. He said in a soft, almost calming voice, "I'm telling you...goat. They will never be anything more than what they are: dirty, filthy, idiotic, and self-absorbed. They are certainly not worth OUR time or compassion."

In a new fit of rage, Abaddon let out a blood-curdling howl. "And if that is not enough...GOAT, I declare by this very mountain that if you don't step aside, I will not ONLY kill you, oh no, YOU will be the last, but I will hunt your family to the ends of the earth and kill them in front of you just so you know MY power and MY word is law!"

Gruff lowered his head and turned slightly. He then very slowly looked back at Kate. Kate looked into Gruff's eyes, and the grave look on his face told her that things were looking very hopeless.

Kate shifted her body, letting out a screech of pain. She then refocused on the two titans squaring off. Her pain caused her to weep openly. She was growing weak and taking deep breaths, slowly exhaling, knowing that time was short.

"And now, finally, my friend, here is the truth about YOU. You have been wandering around looking for it, listening to stupid old crows," Abaddon said, watching Gruff lower his guard and turn to look at Kate. Abaddon snarled low and long in anger, baring his long white teeth that were now just barely visible through the foam and drool. "YOU will never be anything more than a miserable, stupid, worthless GOAT!"

At that very moment, Abaddon lunged at Gruff, tearing at his face with his claws and clenching Gruff's ear in his mouth, ripping half of it from his head.

Gruff twisted and rammed his head into Abaddon's side, pushing him back to the trees. Abaddon charged again and cleared the top of Gruff, landing in front of Kate. He grabbed her by her shin and dragged her a couple of feet from the cliff face, where she came to rest after she fell, her lower leg almost entirely in Abaddon's mouth.

Kate screamed in agony as she could feel her leg slowly snapping. She writhed and tried her best to punch and slap Abaddon's face and body, but that only caused him to bite down slower. She could see from the look in Abaddon's eyes that he seemed to be enjoying this moment, inflicting as much pain as slowly as he possibly could.

Gruff spun around and quickly countered, once again ramming Abaddon's side, causing him to drop Kate. Gruff continued pushing Abaddon sideways into the trees. Then, Abaddon snapped his jaws on Gruff's face and clawed at his body. Gruff gave a mighty shove that picked Abaddon off the ground and smashed him against one of the large trees. Slowly, Gruff returned to Kate and stood between her and Abaddon.

Abaddon picked himself off the ground and glared at Gruff while he slowly approached. "Know this, goat. Take it as my PROMISE. I'm most certainly going to kill your family. That was my plan, regardless of what you chose to do! You will remember and KNOW that I decide who lives and who dies. You will come to respect me and do what I tell you to do… GOAT! I am the God of the mountain!"

Abaddon suddenly leapt again toward Gruff, dragging his massive claws across Gruff's face and body before snapping his teeth on Gruff's neck.

Gruff stumbled and fell to the ground, bleeding from his face and down the entire length of his body. Abaddon finally let go of Gruff, then walked back around and circled before finally standing in front of Gruff to square off again.

"Well, now, look at how mighty you are! Look at the great protector!" Abaddon gloated. He threw his paw and knocked Gruff to his side. "Look at your stupid self. I won't break your neck. No, I want you to hear and see what I do to this human you apparently love so much," snarled the great wolf.

He walked around and casually slapped his paw at Kate's broken body, causing her to shriek again in pain. He then turned back to Gruff and laughed. "Here you are, the great protector sent by the creator, now in no better shape than this human!

Abaddon stood over Gruff and looked down at him before turning to look at Kate. "Both about to bleed to death. Well, at least one of you. The other, well...let's just say she will be slowly parting ways. One small piece at a time." Abaddon snapped his jaws at Kate. He laughed in his low, raspy growl and started to approach Gruff.

Then, Abaddon crouched down to Gruff's partial ear and whispered,"Shhh, listen to what's coming, Gruff. I want you to hear every moan, every groan, every shriek until she begs me for death. And you, well, there is NOTHING you can do to prevent this."

Abaddon began to back up and prepare himself for the final attack. "Korvus has failed you as a teacher, you have failed this human as a protector, and your god and creator has failed you at his big plan of redemption. And now, you know this truth. I AM GOD," Abaddon snarled.

Gruff looked up at Abaddon and snorted, trying to get back up off the ground. His legs collapsed underneath him. Abaddon snarled as he watched

Gruff collapse back to the earth. Abaddon then suddenly crouched and leapt with all of his strength, energy, and fury over Gruff toward Kate.

Gruff closed his eyes, and, for a split second, he seemed to doze. He whispered silently, "It's not whether I live or die, but that with my last breath, I will have lived faithfully to the Creator…I live and die for my Creator!"

Gruff opened his eyes. He could see Abaddon coming in the air over him to get to Kate, and two words suddenly resonated in his head. The words seemed to shake the mountain they stood on and were carried into the valley by the storm winds. Kate's eyes grew wide as she screamed and covered her ears from the sheer volume and power that blasted over them all.

"GET UP!"

Gruff suddenly jumped up and tossed his head forward, catching Abaddon under his neck and chest. Gruff raised up and drove his horns further into the wolf's neck and then deep into Abaddon's head through his chest.

With one final twist, Gruff's horns broke, shattering from the sheer force, and disappeared fully into Abaddon's body. With a sickening thud, the great wolf fell to the ground just at Kate's feet. The look of shock in his eyes was the same Kate had seen on Shaw's face.

Gruff slowly turned and approached Kate. He nuzzled her hair, still loving the sweet smell of jasmine and berries. "Thank you for being with me, Gruff, and for saving my life, even if it will only be for a few minutes. I glorify God, Christ Redeemer, our Creator, for sending you."

Kate held on to Gruff's face the best she could and looked at him. "I guess this will be how we both die, but at least it will be with a friend," she said, holding her hand over Gruff's wounds. "It could be a day or more before we are found…IF we are found," Kate said, looking up at Gruff.

He looked around for just a moment and then stepped to the side. He began digging and scraping down into the earth with what strength he had left, remembering what he had learned from his time spent with Stephen and Zeki and his various little adventures.

"And just what are you going to do with that?" Kate said, trying to keep her head as still as possible so she wouldn't pass out again.

Gruff continued to dig and scrape out an indent that was just about as long as Kate and maybe a couple of feet or so deep. He then gathered up broken tree limbs, brush, and leaves and tossed them into the hole. Then, turning back to Kate, he lowered his head and snorted.

"Are you being serious?" Kate groaned and then groaned again. "You cannot possibly be serious. This isn't a science fiction movie!" exclaimed Kate, but Gruff just snorted and began to nudge and push her into the somewhat shallow grave as the freezing winter rain and snow began to fall on them.

Kate let out screams of pain as the movement shook her broken legs back to life, but Gruff was relentless. He kept nudging and pushing until she was now lying face up on a bed of pine limbs in the trench.

Kate lay there, looking up at Gruff. "Ok, now what?"

The freezing rain now began sticking to her hair and freezing to her cheeks. Gruff looked back up at the mountain for a moment and wandered off before returning just as quickly. Gruff stood over the trench and looked down at Kate, and she looked up at him.

Gruff let out groans of pain as he lowered himself and covered the trench and Kate with his own body, sealing it. Kate ran her frozen hand up and across Gruff's face, looking him in the eyes, then buried her hand and face deep in the wool of his neck, soaking up whatever warmth was left in him.

Gruff twisted his neck and face and lay next to Kate. He then covered her face in such a way he looked like a swan keeping its young warm. As the sky grew dark and what was once day continued to fade away, they both closed their eyes and drifted off into uncertain darkness; the stinging cold set in, leaving only the wind to call out to them.

14. PAIN OF THE UNKNOWN

The phone broke the silence and lit up the bedroom. "*You have an incoming call from. . . Jaxon.*" James Bradigan stirred, cracked open an eye, and glanced at the phone that once again lit up the bedroom.

"James, who is it? What time is it?" Hannah asked, rubbing her eyes and trying to disappear back into her pillow.

James picked up the phone and looked. "It's just after 2 am, go back to sleep, babes," he spoke softly. The phone rang again.

"Well, who is it on the phone?" Hannah said, now reaching over to turn on a small table lamp.

"It's Jaxon," James replied, taking a deep breath and answering. "Hello? Jaxon? What's going on?" By this time, both James and Hannah were sitting fully upright in the bed, Hannah hanging onto James' shoulder to try and hear.

"Dad, I need to talk to you and Mom about something that is going on. Put me on speaker." Jaxon paused long and tried to control the emotions he was feeling, but they showed in the cracking of his voice.

By this time, Hannah was nearly frantic and pawed at James. "What's going on? What's happened? JAMES talk to me!"

James held Hannah's hand to keep her from pawing at him and turned the phone speaker on. He took another deep breath. "Ok, Jaxon, what's going on?"

Jaxon spoke slowly. "Mom, Dad, about eight hours ago, the Honolulu Station that Kate is working from lost contact with her." Hannah gasped and started to sob.

Jaxon coughed and then continued, "She checked in at her scheduled time, but then they lost phone contact with her. She never checked in after that, and two hours later, her GPS apparently had failed. She had left her proposed scheduled coordinates for reasons we don't know, and she is in a very rugged, difficult area to reach. At that time, they weren't sure where she might have been. It's a VERY large area." Jaxon paused, still fighting back his own emotions.

Hannah was now crying loudly and beating on James' shoulder, repeating over and over again, "Why!? WHY?!"

James was fighting back his own tears. "Jaxon, you said, '*AT THAT TIME they weren't sure.*' What does that mean?" James took the phone off speaker and held it to his ear.

"Well, Dad, it's odd, but about an hour or so ago, her GPS turned back on. So, we have pinpointed WHERE she is, but we do not know anything else other than that."

"I see, so…" James paused and swallowed.

"Dad," Jaxon continued, "it's approaching ten below zero in that location, and I don't want to give any false hope. If she was hurt, she may not have survived, much less survive these temperatures, even if she isn't injured."

James wiped tears from his cheek. "I understand. When will there be a rescue attempt?" Hannah paused her sobs when she heard the words *rescue attempt.*

"Dad, I'm getting ready to board a flight now and will be on the ground and mobilizing at the Granite Lodge in time to work with the crew that's being organized. Dad, I just never realized that my advanced mountain rescue training would need to be used to find Kate."

James mumbled, "Shhh," as he tried to quieten Hannah as she progressed from sobs to full-on wails.

"Dad, we cannot go until first light. It's too dangerous for EVERYONE to attempt a rescue, let alone just being able to find her up there in the dark." Jaxon then continued, "Mom, Dad, I have to go! The plane is boarding and is going to be taxiing soon. I will call you once I get up there. Dad, it's going to take God's intervention to get us up there to get her." Jaxon then hung up the phone.

James whispered, "His will be done…" He then hung up his phone and clung to Hannah.

Jaxon closed his eyes and tried to settle into his assigned seat. He was fortunate to get an exit aisle so that he could at least stretch out his legs. With his size, any other row of seats would have made it look like he was squeezed into a clown car.

He shuffled various topography and aerial maps across his drop-down table and looked them all over. He glanced over several reports that Kate had filed with the station in hopes of finding SOMETHING that would help in the search. He then closed his eyes and dozed.

"You may be taller than me, but I can still whip you," Kate laughed and pushed Jaxon out into the backyard, then hit him in the back with a well-placed throw of a frosted cereal box.

"Bring it on, squirt." Jaxon placed a large palm on the top of her head, pretending to control her like a marionette. "I don't think you have it in you to take me down!" Jaxon said, once again treating her like a little puppet.

Kate quickly smacked the side of his leg with a well-placed kick that caused the muscle in his leg to contract with spasms, bringing him to the ground in a heap. She then put her palm on the top of Jaxon's head. "I'm still your big sister, punk. Last one to the river gets a mouthful of it!" Kate shrieked and took off, dashing across the yard and into the field, Jaxon limping and running the best he could.

"*Please put your trays and seats in the upright position,*" came the announcement over the intercom. Jaxon wiped the crud out of his eyes, blinked a few times, and then quickly put the maps and reports back into his pack before adjusting the seat and tray per instructions.

He checked his watch. "Four hours? I've slept four hours?!" He glanced out the window and saw the colors of the sky announcing the coming sunrise.

"Jaxon, welcome to Great Falls International Airport. I'm Senior Ranger Ed Franks. I wish it was under better circumstances but let us get you into gear and transported to the area."

The men dashed for an Airbus AS365 helicopter that was preparing for lift-off. "Dr. Marcus sent this to pick you up!

Jaxon and Franks climbed aboard the Airbus, and it quickly rose and headed toward the distant mountains. "We have a CH-47 helicopter waiting in Honolulu, and a Bell is over the terrain now where we picked up Ranger Kate…er, where we picked up Chief Bradigan's GPS."

The Granite Lodge was fully lit like it was its own small city. The Airbus circled several times before finally coming to rest next to the Chinook helicopter, whose rotors began to spin.

Franks looked at Jaxon and pointed in the direction of the chinook. "You still remember how to repel, right?

Jaxon nodded. "Yes, still current and certified for mountain rescue operations!"

"I hear you are definitely one of the best qualified! The rest of the team is already on board!" Franks smiled wearily, and then they grabbed Jaxon's carry-on gear and ran for the heavy transport.

The ten search and rescue team crew members did a quick round-robin of introductions. They quickly strapped into their jump seats and set their headset microphones so they could discuss the mission and get updates from the Bell, which was already in the search area.

Thirty seconds after boarding, the huge craft lifted into the air, dipped, and hurried away from the Granite Lodge and Honolulu to begin its climb, charging headfast into the unknown.

"She is pretty far up in a remote spot of Sector 3," Franks said, his voice crackling across the headset, just loud enough to be heard over the roar of the engines.

Franks continued, "Jaxon, this is Dr. Phillips. He is a retired military emergency surgeon. He ran with the Green Berets back in the day and now runs the clinic in Honolulu. He is certainly no stranger to difficult situations."

Jaxon looked over the maps, before peering out the small windows and nodded. "When we get on site, I'm going need to be on the line with Dr. Phillips. We need to go down the line first when we get there. If I'm looking at this right," Jaxon looked up, "and understanding the information coming from the Bell, there will only be enough room for just us two initially. Once we get on the ground, we will be able to quickly assess the situation better."

Phillips looked across to Jaxon and pumped a fist into his chest a few times and then turned it into a pointing finger at Jaxon with a head nod. His face was stone, blank of emotion. Then he spoke, or rather shouted, into the headset. "We got this, Jaxon, you and me!" He then leaned forward, slapped Jaxon's helmet, and smiled.

"It's the only way to get to the swing!" Jaxon said to Kate. "Swim over to the ledge wall we jumped off of, grab the rope, and climb!" Jaxon splashed water into her eyes and started swimming towards the stone wall.

The length of Jaxon's body already put him at a huge advantage. Poor Kate looked like a little raft getting pulled along by a battleship. Even so, Kate managed to keep up, just a half-length behind.

"Get up that rope, Kate." Jaxon flipped the rope at Kate, who was now busy treading water.

Kate reached but couldn't quite grab the end. "Oh, haha, funny, Jax," she said as she splashed water in his face.

"Come on, get a hold of my shoulders." Kate put her arms around Jaxon, and he reached up, grabbed the rope, and started climbing up the rope and out of the river with Kate dangling off his neck. Halfway up the rope, Kate proceeded to shimmy up Jaxon's back, grabbed the rope, and finished climbing on her own.

Once she and Jaxon reached the top, Kate quickly took the rope again and ran, swinging wide away from the ledge and flying back down into the water. Jaxon looked down at her tiny face in the water and laughed.

"Yeah, that's real cute, Kate, but now let's see you get back up the rope!" Jaxon peered down at Kate and waved.

Phillips suddenly spoke up, "Jaxon! HEY, Jaxon, we are over the target area. Get into the harness and clip in!"

"How…how long was I out?" Jaxon grabbed at his harness.

"Not long, Sleeping Beauty," Phillips said sarcastically. "Now, would you like a hot washcloth for your face? Or for me to fluff your pillow?" Phillips smiled like a waiter in a 4-star restaurant, then shouted, "HOW ABOUT YOU GET IN THE GAME AND GET CLIPPED IN!" Phillips barked, his military training hitting Jaxon like a steel fist.

Jaxon suddenly popped back into reality and shook his head at Phillips, giving him a thumbs up, then snapping his carabiner into the straps and tightening his harness. The huge helicopter hovered over the reported target zone, kicking up ice particles, shaking the trees, and turning the area into a frozen fog.

The pilot chimed in, "Colonel Phillips, you have a green. If you are going to go, you need to do it now before the winds pick up again!"

Jaxon looked at Phillips. "You and I go down first. The rest of the team will follow shortly, once we get things cleared."

"Not my first rodeo, junior," Phillips laughed and looked at Jaxon. He then gave a thumbs-up to the pilot and shouted into the headset. "THANKS, Smitty!" He then looked back to Jaxon and said, "It's too small of an area to set down, and just the two of us can cover it. Ready? On one!"

Smitty and the chopper crew chief lowered the ramp of the chinook, allowing Phillips and Jaxon to walk out and look down as the huge helicopter hovered. Then, they both jumped and disappeared into the frozen fog and the whiteout caused by the helicopter's rotors. Finally, their feet touched down on a small outcropping. The two-man team pulled the line, cleared themselves from the helicopter, and waved it off.

Once the ice particles settled, Phillips lowered his mask and spoke. "Jaxon, we are right on top of the last GPS signal. She HAS to be close!" They started walking in a circle, moving outwards. After just a couple of moments, they happened upon a mound of snow and ice. "NO!" Jaxon shouted and immediately dove onto the pile to clear it.

"EASY, easy! We don't know her condition. You don't need to make it worse!" Phillips and Jaxon carefully removed the snowpack to reveal the seemingly lifeless, frozen form hidden underneath.

Jaxon stopped clearing and looked up at Phillips. "Uh...well, who in the world is that?!"

Jaxon took a step backward as Phillips jumped in to check for signs of any life. After a few minutes, Phillips got up and stood next to Jaxon, looking down at Shaw's face, now staring hollowly back at them.

"I have NO idea who this person is, but that was certainly not caused by falling." Phillips pointed at Shaw's neck. "By the looks of that, whatever got at him was certainly enraged and HUGE!"

Jaxon looked at Phillips. "You don't think that Kate and whatever that was. . . .?"

Phillips put his goggles and mask back on. "Stay focused, Jaxon! We have got to keep looking!"

The two began to make small sweeping searches, and Jaxon came to the ledge and looked over. His eyes strained to see the area that lay below. The sun bounced off every surface, causing glares and false images. Jaxon stood there for a couple more minutes, just looking down.

"Phillips! Look at this!" Jaxon pointed over the edge. Phillips quickly walked over and looked over the edge. Jaxon said, still pointing, "You may call me stupid, but I could almost..." Jaxon paused, cleared his goggles, and looked back down. "I am telling you, I am seeing a backpack, or at least part of a backpack, stuck on that set of rocks right there!" Phillips looked over the ledge to where Jaxon was pointing.

Phillips grabbed his gear and started pulling out the repelling rope. "Good eyes, Jax. I see it too! Let's get tied off and get down there!"

Jaxon grabbed the rope and ran back to find a tie-off point. He quickly tied off the rope to a large tree with huge scratch marks on it. Jaxon paused for a moment, his eyes getting big as he ran his fingers into the marks and traced them. "Lord, have mercy!" He then quickly returned to the ledge and threw the lines over to proceed down.

As they descended, they saw remnants of what was once a ranger's backpack, now ripped and torn, the contents long since blown away or buried by the storm. Jaxon's heart, once racing, now sat low and sad in his chest. After a few minutes, the pair put their feet back on the ground.

Phillips pointed, "You go that way. It's a very small clearing, and we should be able to cover this entire spot in five minutes. Check every possible inch she may be able to fit into!"

Jaxon walked a few feet and came across another figure covered in snow. He knelt down and frantically started clearing the snow and ice yet again, calling Phillips to come help.

After a moment, they sprang from the ground and backed away from the form. Abaddon lay still, just as frozen as the form they left in the area forty feet above them.

Jaxon exclaimed yet again, "Christ Lord, have mercy!" He looked over Abaddon's body again, noting that this beast would easily be as tall as he was on its hind legs and probably weighed as much, if not more, to boot.

Not a moment after the shock of seeing Abaddon, Phillips's eyes were drawn to another huge mound nearly up against the cliff face. Had they hugged the mountain any closer, they would have repelled and landed practically on top of it. Phillips looked down at Abaddon, then over to the other form, and quickly dashed over to it.

Phillips shouted out to Jaxon, "She is over here! She over here!" Jaxon sprinted to the location in four leaps and dropped to his knees to help clear the area. It did not take long to find what was buried under the snow.

"I don't understand what I'm seeing," Jaxon said. pulling down his face mask.

"KEEP CLEARING!" Screamed Phillips.

The two worked quickly and completely uncovered Gruff. Kate's face was buried in his neck, and Gruff's head was curled and wrapped around hers like a massive pillow, preventing her head from being able to move. Her hand was still buried deep in his fleece, but it was apparent that a couple of exposed fingers had become frozen.

Phillips went into action and quickly checked the best he could. Taking off a glove, he shoved his hand down into Gruff's fleece to reach Kate's neck. He paused, looked around, adjusted his hand, and then looked back down at Kate, pausing again.

"Jaxon, she is still alive! Get into my bag and get that IV for me! I've got a single vein in her neck that I can reach." Phillips took the IV and ran the tubing down to Kate. He popped the cap off the needle and slid the IV needle into Kate's jugular.

Phillips mumbled to himself, "There we go. Yeah, that's it. CVC is done, and these lactated ringers are going to start to warm her up and hopefully give us a more stable blood pressure. Let's just keep an eye on her and make sure she doesn't go into shock." Phillips continued evaluating. He started looking over the entire situation and gasped.

Jaxon looked up and over to Phillips, who reached out and took a partially exposed GPS tracking unit out of Gruff's mouth. They looked at each other and then back down at Kate.

Jaxon stammered, "I don't under..." but before he could finish, Phillips' facial expression changed again.

Philips looked at Kate and then at Gruff. "Look. It's a good thing that we got here when we did. But we do have an issue. This beast is the only thing keeping her from going into shock and possibly throwing a blood clot."

Jaxon removed his goggles and stared at Phillips, who finally looked up at Jaxon. "Come on, Jax, you have heard of crush wounds. Well, this is pretty similar to that. We have a very large object resting on top of a person, and that can be constricting the blood flow to areas of her body, which actually COULD be saving her life. If we move this beast, well, we could cause a massive hemorrhage, stroke, you name it." Phillips looked back at Gruff.

"I want to take BOTH of them back down the mountain together. We can barrel roll this thing off her when we get down off the mountain and have emergency medical transport and," Phillips paused, "quite frankly, access to more equipment, not to mention better conditions.

Jaxon looked at Kate and then at Gruff. He noticed the bloody scars across his face and body and the place where his two horns should have been. He took off his glove and ran his hand across Gruff's head, resting his palm on his forehead. "What happens if this thing wakes up in the middle of transport?"

Phillips was practically face-deep in Gruff's fleece, trying to get a better assessment of Kate. "Well, then we will have a serious…SERIOUS…issue for everyone that is helping transport!"

Phillips continued to mumble from within the fleece, "I'm not a veterinarian, but I'm not entirely sure this poor creature is even alive. I do know an animal doc a few towns over. I will give you his information. Get Dr. Marcus on the phone to call him."

Phillips emerged from Gruff's fleece. "For now, the plan is to have paramedic crews and equipment waiting once we get down the mountain. We can see about doing a barrel roll with this monster and get her to the hospital as quickly as possible via medivac air." Looking back up at the top of the cliff, Phillips said, "She was just short of the LD50 measurements by the looks of things, but it looks to me like she took a terrible beating down the entire cliff face."

"LD50? That was dealing with fall and injury ratios, right?" Jaxon looked back up to the ridge as well.

"Yes, LD50 is, well, basically a way to determine the fatality risks of falling from a certain height. LD50 is about 48 feet. She would have a fifty-fifty chance of surviving." Phillips raised his hands to his mouth and exhaled into them to warm them.

"Look, enough of this. Get on that radio, and let's get this moving. We don't have time for questions!" Phillips patted Jaxon's shoulder.

Jaxon looked down and momentarily fumbled for his radio. "This is Jaxon. We have her, but we are going to need the rest of the team down here. And, uh," Jaxon paused, looked at Gruff and Kate, and continued, "we are going to need at least a four-man basket lift. The bigger, the better. It's going to need some sort of lower platform that can be used as a…well, sort of like a spatula." Jaxon and Phillips looked at each other and then back to the forms they had uncovered.

Jaxon then keyed his radio again. "Oh, um, and get on the phone with Dr. Marcus and tell him I need to talk to him immediately."

"Could you repeat that last?" came the chatter over the radio.

Jaxon barked back into the radio. "YOU HEARD ME! GET IT DONE!"

"We are going to have to dig down just a bit to where she is laying and shove a board, a big board, underneath them both to transport," Phillips said, looking at the patients and thinking. "Let's start getting some thermal coverings on both of them as best we can."

"What do you think that thing weighs?" Jaxon said, looking at them.

Phillips answered, "Well, I don't know, easily 350 pounds or more. One thing is for sure: she is pretty well covered by the goat. Fortunately, it is laying in such a way that his weight is fully supported on his tucked-in legs."

Phillips started speaking into a handheld recorder. "We have no idea of Kate's injuries until we get back down to base." He leaned on Gruff's side and peered back down at Kate.

"G...gr...gruff." A frozen word came up from Kate's lips, causing both men to stop working and look at each other.

"G...gr...gruff." The word drifted up again from underneath the mound, causing both Jaxon and Phillips to drop their faces toward Kate to listen and peer into Gruff's fleece.

Kate looked like she was just sleeping, and with Gruff's fleece all around her head, it looked like she wore a huge parka. The two men were still, listening, but the small voice had gone silent. Phillips looked at Jaxon, "I'm telling you. She spoke!"

The radio crackled to life, causing both men to jump. "We have everything set and ready, Dr. Phillips. Heavy is on its way back up to you with team and equipment. We are standing by..."

Phillips stood up and stretched his back for a moment. He then walked to the edge where the tree line was. "It is a miracle she landed there! There's another 500-foot drop just beyond these few trees!" He paused again in thought. "Hmm, it really is just a few trees, honestly." Then, he looked at Jaxon and shouted into the radio, "HEY, Smitty! Send me down a few more men and a couple large chainsaws!"

Jaxon walked over to Phillips. "Chainsaws, what are you thinking?"

"Copy that, Colonel. Enroute," Smitty shot back.

"I'm thinking of a much safer way to transport us all off this mountain." Phillips scratched at his lip.

"Smitty, I'm going to need a pinnacle landing. Will clear and mark," Phillips shouted into the radio.

The radio crackled back, "You clear it. I will build the bridge, Colonel Phillips."

15. PREPARE YOURSELF

Kate lay motionless, her brain still engaged in a massive headache, and her eyes made everything look as if she was in a dense fog. As she lay there, she could hear voices and her name being softly called out.

She knew one of the voices was Jaxon's. That was certain, and maybe Peter's voice? Over the past several days, Kate had drifted in and out of being in a dream and being in what she thought was reality.

"When did she wake up?" she heard Jaxon say, grabbing her hand into his.

"Just a few hours ago. Everything is looking very promising, Jaxon." Ok, now she definitely knew Peter's voice.

"You think we can take the bandage off?" Jaxon said, inquiring.

"Yeah, I think we can do that," the attending physician spoke up.

"Kate, if you are awake, you are in St. Patrick's Hospital in Missoula. We have had to bandage your eyes to help them heal. We are going to take those off now. Will that be ok?" Kate moved her hand to indicate that would be fine.

Jaxon slowly came into view. He was once again towering over her. Kate smiled the best she could. "You may as well take your chance, Jax. This is the only time you are going to be able to beat me." He laughed and scooped her up into a sobbing hug.

"Uh, easy there, mongo. We don't need to be breaking her again, at least until after she leaves the hospital." Pete was now tapping Jaxon on the shoulders.

"I really thought we had lost you, Kate," Jaxon said, pulling up a chair next to her bed. Peter walked over and stood in a corner, pinching his lip and looking at her. He then asked the rest of the hospital staff to give them all some time alone.

"How long have I been in bed?" Kate looked for technology that would offer any indication of time and date.

Jaxon lowered his head, holding on to her hand even tighter. Then, Peter stepped forward and spoke, "Kate, you have been in a coma for four months."

"FOUR MONTHS!?" Kate managed to shout, "But everything feels like it was just a few hours ago!" Kate closed her eyes and tossed her head back into the pillow, hot tears now pouring from the corners of her eyes and down her temples onto the pillow.

"How is…where is Gruff?" Kate's voice crackled. Opening her eyes, she stared back at the ceiling.

"Let's talk about you right now, Kate. Mom and Dad are off having breakfast and will be back shortly. I want you to know what's going on with YOU before they get here." Jaxon squeezed Kate's hand again.

"Ok, so talk to me, Jax," Kate said, sitting up in the bed.

"Well, first off, you had suffered a bad concussion. You probably still have a headache. And even if you don't, you may have migraines off and on for maybe the rest of your life." Jaxon looked up from the bed to look at Peter and then back down to Kate.

"Ok, so I will have bigger headaches than the two of you to contend with. I can deal with that." They both chuckled. "Ok, what else?" Kate said, patting Jaxon's hand and reaching out for Pete's.

"Kate, um, due to the intense cold temperatures that you were in, they um..." Jaxon paused and looked up at Peter.

"OH, OUT WITH IT! Quit yammering and tell me. I'm not eight years old anymore!" Kate said angrily.

"Kate," Peter stepped forward, taking her hand. He paused and looked down, his voice now crackling. "Due to the nature of your injuries and exposure to the elements, they had to amputate two fingers and your left leg below the knee." Jaxon was now sobbing again while he listened to Peter, forming both of his hands into clenched fists on the bed.

Kate looked suddenly down at her hands, which were still bandaged, and then laid her head back into the pillows and cried softly. She then raised her hands to look again. Sure enough, she was missing her left index finger and part of her ring finger.

Kate raised up in bed the best she could. She dropped her hands and then slowly reached for her legs. "Peter, my brain is telling me that it's there, but my hand is telling me that it most certainly is not." Kate flopped back into the bed and wiped her eyes.

"Well, Jaxon, I'm sure you told them to do the amputations because you are tired of always losing to me." Kate managed to let out a small chuckle. "How is Gruff?"

Jaxon got up from the chair and glanced at Peter. He wiped off his face, walked over to the window, and looked out. "Tell me about him."

Kate propped herself back up. "I was sent into Sector 3 because I was told to go. Oh, I can't explain it all, but only that there was someone who needed to hear God's truth, and I was up there to deliver it. God then sent me a protector when I needed one when my moment was darkest." Kate started to cry again. "He came out of nowhere and actually ministered to me.

"I cannot explain it by human thoughts. Only God could have provided such a thing. Gruff brought me some food and herbs, kept me warm, and he stood between me..." Kate let out a sobbing wail, "and a wolf that was beyond description."

Jaxon continued looking out the window, his fists now wrapped up in the curtains, remembering the deep gashes he had seen on the tree, the dead man they first found, and the huge wolf that was so very close to where she was finally found.

Kate continued, "I was talking with this fellow. His name was Felix Shaw."

"The scraggly little fellow?" Peter asked.

"Yes, that was his name! Felix Shaw. Well, I looked over the edge that I was standing on, and suddenly he was, well. . .he was gone!"

Kate closed her eyes and put her hands to her head in an attempt to fight the visions. "He was gone, Jax! And he was looking at me, his eyes, those eyes pleading for help, and there was absolutely nothing I could do!"

Kate was in full-on sobs. "Abaddon..." Kate stopped.

"Abaddon?" Jaxon said, turning around and sitting back down in the chair.

Kate lowered her head back into the pillow. "Yeah, that was the name of the wolf. At least, that is what Shaw said its name was. If anyone else ever asks, I would say that it is a very fitting name. He certainly brought death and destruction."

Kate looked up at the ceiling and then back to Peter. "He was just gone, Peter, dragged along like a chew toy. I tried to get Abaddon to let go, but if you ever saw the size of this beast, you might understand."

Peter reached down and wiped Kate's face with a warm cloth as she stared blankly into space. "Abaddon literally pushed me out into the open, and I only had two options: to go over the ledge or face the same fate Shaw did.

For a moment, I thought it would just be a faster death to resign myself to Abaddon than it would be to jump."

Kate paused. "Then, a distant noise came from the woods, and Abaddon paused and took his eyes off me to look around for it. I thought I could skirt around him to draw my weapon, then make a run for the tree line." Kate wiped tears from her eyes again.

"Jax, Peter," Kate paused, looking back and forth at them, "I'm telling you; I really think Abaddon pushed me off that ledge on purpose just to watch me fall." Kate looked into Jaxon's eyes. "I just can't explain it."

"Take your time, Kate. You don't have to do this right now if you…" Peter started to say.

"I hit the bottom of that ledge, and all the wind was knocked out of me. I remember the pain in my legs and head, and then Gruff showed up out of nowhere!" Kate's eyes began to well up.

"He was nearly as big as Abaddon! Oh, he was so beautiful, his white fleece, those dark eyes. He was so calm and gentle with me." Kate started sobbing again, reaching up her hand to touch a muzzle that wasn't there. She dropped her hand. "I offered him my only food, a single granola bar. He just snorted and stuck his nose in my hair. Then, he wandered off briefly and brought back, of all things, a large piece of honeycomb. I don't have to tell you about the healing abilities of honey and propolis. Anyway..."

Kate fully sat up in the bed. "I don't understand, but Gruff dropped the honey and all the other items he collected for me. I formed a poultice out of it and used his honey for the wounds on my leg and the one on my head."

Kate paused and looked up. "What animal does that for another? Jax, I had dreams while I was out there that Gruff was my protector and was sent by God to take care of me!"

Peter and Jaxon looked at each other.

"You may think I'm totally crazy, but that is the truth." Kate looked at Peter and then back to Jaxon. Then, she finally took a sip of some coffee that had been brought in, and she looked up at Peter.

"Look…" Kate furrowed her brow at Jaxon and Peter, "God sent me up that mountain, and it was on my last trip up that He sent me further into the unknown to bring the Truth to Shaw. Because I was up there, He also knew I would need a protector…and sent me Gruff!"

Jaxon looked thoughtfully at Kate and at Pete and poured himself some coffee. "Let me tell you something, Kate, I KNOW what I saw out there. There were things that I could not explain." He took a sip of coffee.

"Like what?" Kate asked while flapping a packet of sugar to pour into her cup, trying to calm back down.

"Well, for one, did you put your GPS tracker into Gruff's mouth?" Jaxon put his cup on the table and leaned forward.

"GPS tracker? Kate looked at Jaxon, puzzled. "Jax, I lost all of that when I went over the ledge. My packs were all destroyed and scattered all across that mountain." Kate looked at Jaxon and Peter.

"Kate, the only reason we found you was because the GPS tracker was in Gruff's mouth and being held together to keep it activated." Pete turned around and ran his hands through his hair before bringing them to rest as a teepee in front of his mouth. He then spun around again to look at Kate, who was now staring back at her brother.

Peter was the first to speak up, breaking the silence. "Kate, let me say something. Are we not told that we entertain angels unaware?"

Kate nodded her head.

Peter stood up and looked over to Jaxon. "Also, who are WE to question God's methods for intervening for our benefit."

"God had David use a simple sling and a stone, Elijah got ravens, Elisha had bears, Daniel had lions. It took a whale to convince Jonah and a donkey to shake Balaam!" Peter held Kate's hand.

"The way I see it, Kate," Peter said, putting his arm around Jaxon's shoulder and holding Kate's hand, "the Lord gave you one HUGE mountain goat!"

"What is the one thing about David, Elijah, and Daniel? What did all three have in common, Kate?" Peter let go of her hand and leaned over to touch her cheek. "Faith! They had faith in God and that, in doing God's will, HE would provide."

Kate burst into tears. She wiped her face and then became irritated. "But you still haven't told me! HOW IS GRUFF?!" Kate slammed her cup down, sending coffee onto the tray.

Jaxon looked Kate in the eyes. "He..." Just then, the door slowly opened. James and Hannah poked their heads into the room like slapstick characters and then flooded into the room like a pair of cartoon magpies.

James whispered to Jaxon, "We were told she is awake? You want one of our egg sandwiches?" By this time, Hannah had pushed past James, tossed her purse onto the visitor chairs, and snatched Kate up in her arms.

"EASY!" Pete said, scorning Hannah, who only gave a defiant glare in return.

"Why didn't you call me back?" Hannah said while squeezing Kate in her arms.

"Mom, seriously? You still going on about that?" Kate looked at Jaxon and rolled her eyes.

"I am so thankful you are now safe!" Hannah said while grabbing a chair with her foot and scootching it up underneath her bottom. Kate looked at James and rolled her eyes again.

"If you want, I can make her go sit in the car." James winked.

James turned to Pete and gave him a big hug. "Dr. Marcus, it is nice to see you again. Of course, I think you have spent more time in this room than anyone other than Kate! Thank you so much for all you have done for us and Kate over the past several months." James finally made his way over to Jaxon. "So, I hear the new station is just about ready to be manned?"

"Um, don't say the word 'MANNED.'" Jaxon glanced over to Kate and winked, remembering their last encounter. "But yes. It's ready to be occupied." Jaxon looked at James. "It will be a minimum of a 5-ranger team. From what I understand, they are just waiting for the new District Ranger to arrive and officially accept the position."

Jaxon raised his coffee and talked in between sips. "Then, I will be on my way to my new station."

James turned to Jaxon. "Shh! Don't tell your mother! We will talk about it later."

Kate looked over to Jaxon. "Huh? What? Just who is the District Ranger going to be? You know I had been working with Todd McMillan and hoping for that position." Jaxon frowned and looked at James, Hannah, and Peter.

Kate then looked at Jaxon "What…? What's the word? What am I NOW not being told?"

"Well, we have someone here who may be able to explain things a little better." Jaxon walked over to the door and motioned to someone to come in.

Todd McMillan rolled into the room, forcing a couple of nurses back out into the hallway with his size. "Kate, glad to see you are finally awake! If you don't mind, we need to have some discussion about Honolulu Station." Todd glanced around for a chair to sit on but settled for a physician's stool.

Todd scootched up to Kate's bed in little forward shuffles, the stool's wheels screeching with each of Todd's efforts. Kate almost burst into laughter watching him, as he resembled a bullfrog trying to perch on a toothpick.

"I'm in serious trouble, aren't I," Kate paused, "for being up in Sector 3?"

"Normally, yes. You would be in serious trouble, and your position, not to mention your job in general, would be in jeopardy." Todd wiped his forehead. Kate lay quietly, just staring down at her hands.

"However, seeing as the land that you were on was still technically privately owned, and when we reached out and asked the owner of the land, they indicated that you had their full permission to be up there."

Kate looked up at Todd, puzzled. "I don't remember..."

"Before you finish that statement, Kate, "Todd raised his palm to hush her, "the owner indicated that you had full permission to be up there; therefore, as far as the Bureau is concerned, that last trip up there was on your own vacation time."

Kate looked around the room at everyone and then back to Todd. "But what about..."

"Look, all the equipment, resources, ALL of that has been covered." Todd also looking around the room. "We are classifying it, technically, as Honolulu's first mountain rescue training exercise."

Kate continued to lie there, looking bewildered. Todd patted her hand and said, "I trust that we will be keeping those to a minimum from today forward, yes?" Todd wiped his forehead again. "Now for the formalities. Congress, as well as the Representatives of Montana, finally approved the transfer of the private lands, and there was quite a bit of it, into our care last month." Todd paused. "So, everything is all official except for one detail. Jaxon, if you would, please," Todd said, waving his hand in the air.

Jaxon opened his case and took out some paperwork. "I know you are tired, and this is all a LOT to take in, but as soon as you sign these papers, we can get started."

Kate looked down at the paperwork offering her the position of the District Ranger for Honolulu. Kate flopped her head back into her pillows and reflected on all that had happened.

"My Lord, thank you for my life and the directions you have safely taken me. Guide us, strengthen us, and encourage us to abide by your will." Kate sat back up, signed the papers, and handed them back to Jaxon.

"So, who is my Honolulu team?" Kate looked at Jaxon.

"Well, there is me, but I'm only temporary until you are up and running," Jaxon said with a stupid grin, causing Kate to roll her eyes once again. "Hey, there are some big things going on in that little town. I want to be a part of it before I move on to my next station!" Jaxon said as James held Hannah down in her chair and put his hand over her mouth.

Jaxon then walked over to the door. "Ok, come on in, rangers." Three other rangers entered the room and stood at the end of her bed.

"This is Dr. Lee Phillips. He was actually with me when we first found you. BUT I think you already know him, since he runs the emergency clinic in town."

"Dr. Phillips! I'm so glad to see you. Thank you so much for everything you have done for me!" Kate reached out for his hand.

"This is your senior ranger, Ed Franks. He was the one to begin the rescue mobilizations. He was our eyes in the sky and relay, so to speak." Kate shook his hand. "And, of course, you know Lara's little voice from the radio. They are both transferring from another station." Jaxon continued talking.

Franks spoke up. "Oh, and I'm sorry, our fifth ranger, Ranger Smith, is fresh from training and still wet behind the ears. He is at the fire tower for the main station way up in Sector 4. We must always have someone there."

"Main station? You got the station built?" Kate said, looking around the room.

Franks looked at Jaxon, then over to Kate. "Well, not quite yet. It's in progress, but once again, thanks to Dr. Marcus, we at least have a new substation in place, and construction is ongoing at the site you laid out for the main."

Kate looked around the room again. "I don't think there could be any finer group of friends and family than what is in this room right now."

"I agree, and I don't think ANY district in the United States is as blessed as Honolulu to have such a huge benefactor and believer in what is going to be accomplished here. That just doesn't happen anymore. Todd said while eating the congealed fruit cup from Kate's breakfast plate.

16. A FOUR LETTER WORD

"We sure appreciate the time you have spent with us, Ms. Bradigan," an extremely thin-set nurse, who, according to her badge, was named Dottie, said, helping Kate into a wheelchair.

"You have most definitely been a model patient if there is such a thing?" The nurse began pushing Kate down the long hallways with half-opened patient room doors. "I hear that they are going to move you to a smaller rehabilitation facility where they will work with you to get you back up on your feet."

No sooner had she finished that sentence than Dottie was profusely apologizing. "Oh! Ms. Bradigan, I didn't mean to sound uncaring or…"

Kate tossed her head backward and looked at the nurse upside down. "Look, it's quite alright. I'm still not used to being a foot shorter than I was." Kate smirked.

"I hear that the facility is in Honolulu! That's going to be an amazing change to this place!" Dottie practically danced around Kate's wheelchair. "The sun, the beaches, tropical drinks, tanned cabana boys, ahhhh-mazing!" Dottie tossed her head back like she could just feel the tropical breezes. Then she beamed with delight, feeling like she successfully changed the topic.

"Oh, I do hear that it's fantastic." Kate smiled.

Dottie pushed Kate up to the elevator. "Oh! It's a shame you will not be completing your rehab in Montana."

"Really? Why is that?" Kate asked, looking up again at her.

"Well, did you ever see that Dr. Marcus?" Dottie cocked her hip into the air and casually bent down to whisper in Kate's ear. Dottie's reflection in the elevator door made her look rather like some sort of circus contortionist. "I hear he is a really hot Physical Med doc somewhere further up north." Dottie looked up at her reflection and teased her hair for a moment.

"I can certainly say, mmmm, without a doubt, he is definitely one that I could see helping me with a few adjustments." Dottie smiled without shame and nodded with a sly wink. She then slowly stood up and straightened her scrubs, making sure that anyone within eye distance could catch the show.

Kate looked back at Dottie with raised eyebrows and then back toward the elevator door at Dottie's warped reflection before they both started laughing for very different reasons.

Kate and Dottie finally made it out into the lobby and out the front door for pickup without much further ado. "Is your family? Husband? Coming to pick you up?" Dottie stood on her tiptoes to scan for Kate's ride.

"No, I think an Uber is coming for me." Kate looked down at her paperwork from the hospital and then at the crutch she was given.

Finally, a Dodge Caravan pulled up to the curb and out popped Pete with his stupid grin from the driver's side. He opened the numerous doors and began loading the van with Kate's belongings.

When all the loading was finished, Peter turned to Kate. "Well, Ms. Bradigan, shall we?"

Dottie's eyes and desires got the better of her, and she stepped forward quickly, practically trampling Kate, as she chimed in, "Do you need any help, Mr.? Um…Mr.…"

Peter braced Kate's wheelchair, and Kate raised her arms and clung to his neck as he lifted her out and into the passenger seat, then placed her crutch alongside her. He then placed a basket of pastries he made for her on her lap. Pete closed the door like a matador doing a final ole'.

He then turned to Dottie and shook her hand. "Well, hey there. Aren't you helpful, Ms. uh?" Peter lowered himself and leaned forward to read her name tag.

"My name is Dottie," she quickly interjected, wiping her palm off on her scrubs and throwing out her hand.

"Well, Dottie, it has been nice to meet you, but I think I have it from here. Thanks, though. I'm Dr. Peter Marcus. I really appreciate you bringing her down. I hope you have a fantastic day."

Peter disappeared around the van and hopped back into the driver's seat. Kate turned and looked out the car window at Dottie, who had turned a lovely shade of red.

Kate rolled the window down and held back the laughter. "Dottie," said Kate.

Dottie looked a little bewildered as she stepped closer to the door and squatted down at Kate's window.

Kate whispered, "I've not met that doctor you are talking about, but he certainly sounds fabulous." She then took a bite of a muffin and patted Dottie's hand as they began to leave the pickup zone.

The Caravan began the long journey back to Honolulu. Kate sat quietly, looking out the window. She reflected on everything and fought back hard against newly forming tears. Even though she was in mental and physical pain, she found great comfort being back in that stupid beat-up Caravan passenger seat next to Pete, listening to him broadcasting the next pothole and the duration it would be in play like a sports announcer.

Peter broke the silence that had lasted for the past hour. "I've got you moved into my bedroom downstairs. The room is larger, along with the bathroom and small sitting room. It will be easier for you to initially get around, until we can complete your rehabilitation."

Kate looked over to Peter and smiled, then turned her attention back to the mountains that were getting larger.

"I will move upstairs to one of the other rooms." Peter glanced over to Kate and gave her a small smile.

Kate still looked out the window. "Thanks, Peter. You certainly don't have to do that." Kate used her finger to draw figures in the condensation that was forming on the window.

"I've moved all the other guests out of Granite Lodge, with the exception of that rather large brother of yours." Peter made a gesture like he was a gorilla, but it didn't seem to faze Kate. "He is in the room across from me. This way, you don't have to worry about the townsfolk talking or your parents getting a little mad about you staying in a house alone with some dude, no matter how awesome he may be." Pete once again looked at Kate to spark a laugh, but she just sat quietly, looking out the window.

Peter quickly glanced again at Kate and then back to the potholes. "I've also converted the common room into our little makeshift clinic. We should be able to complete everything right at Granite Lodge." He quickly glanced and smiled at Kate.

Kate finally broke her silence. "I wish I knew what happened to Gruff, Peter. I've never seen ANYBODY be so tight-lipped about something." Kate went back to running her finger over the condensation on the window.

"You know I tried to get information, as well. You would have thought I was trying to get glimpses of Roswell aliens." Peter rubbed his chin. "Things people don't understand tend to scare them."

Kate started crying again. "He saw ME, Peter. I don't know how or what sort of animal he truly was, but when he looked at me with his eyes, I felt like he could see my soul, Peter... I can't explain it."

Kate wiped her face. "I was terrified of all the things going on around me. That man being killed, a creature that surely was from hell, and then Gruff came on the scene, and it was like for those moments when I was convinced I was going to die, it…" Kate closed her eyes and tried to collect her thoughts.

"It was like Gruff and I were walking with Christ, and it was just the three of us. That was the only thing that mattered. NOTHING else on earth mattered." Kate turned back to the window.

"This past year, certainly, as well as losing my parents several years back, has taught me many things." Pete reached over and put his hand on Kate's. "I've learned not to take things for granted: things that I've ran from, things that are important, and people who are important…things that I now pray to have in my life." Kate turned in her seat and looked at Peter.

Peter slowed the caravan down and finally came to a stop on the shoulder of a long, lonely road out in the middle of nowhere. Peter sat for a few minutes and then shifted in his seat to look at Kate. "I don't know what you went through in those mountains, Kate. I can't even begin to understand," Peter desperately searched Kate's face for some kind of answer, "but I do know how I felt when I got the word that you were missing and that things were not looking very good, and I can tell you that I by NO means liked it one bit!"

He looked back out the window and then rubbed his face. "You are going to be the District Ranger for this entire area, and if you don't think you were busy before?! I have told myself over the past month that maybe it's time for me to move on from Honolulu."

Kate looked up at Peter and started to cry again.

"My father started something out here, Kate, something that I only fully realized over the past few years, thanks to Dr. Phillips." Peter grew quiet and fidgeted with his hands. He raised his hands to his mouth like a teepee and blew into them in frustration. "Dr. Phillips and my father were really good friends, and they discussed HUGE plans for this area, one of which was to turn the mountain over to the National Parks Service so it could be protected for all people to enjoy one day."

Kate looked at Pete, confused. "You are saying that YOU were the one all this t…"

"No, I'm not saying that. I only acted and completed what my father wanted done, what he had envisioned." Peter looked at Kate again.

"Dr. Phillips came looking for me after my dad died. Apparently, it was in their agreement that Dr. Phillips would make sure that I was gainfully employed at something other than partying," Peter said, managing a small grin.

"But when he found out I was also a doctor, what better way to get me up here? I don't think my parents even expected that one." Peter grew quiet. "I failed them on so many levels. I was NOT going to fail at this!"

Peter closed his eyes. "I still wish there were times that I had paid more attention to which Honolulu was being presented in that job offer." He then opened his eyes and chuckled a bit.

"All of this, Kate, was initially my desire to complete my father's wishes. Something he dreamed of doing. I had every intention of selling the lodge and moving on from Honolulu once I had completed the land transfer." Peter took Kate's hand and gave it a small squeeze.

Kate closed her eyes for a moment, forcing the restrained tears she was holding on to down her face off her cheeks and onto Peter's hand.

"But then you showed up and threw a wrench into everything." Peter squeezed her hand again.

"Me? What do you mean, Peter?" Kate wiped her cheeks again and looked up at him. Her voice trembled. "I've been through so much, Peter, and I could really use some honest, direct answers. You aren't the only one who has been given the run-around or lost someone close."

Peter's voice cracked. "All the planning, the prep work, the meetings, the paperwork, my clinic with Dr. Phillips. I thought that maybe it would be best that we part ways once we complete your rehab process so you wouldn't... So that I don't have to face the prospect of..." He looked at Kate as she watched his face. He then took his hand and wiped the tears off her cheeks. "Of losing something and someone so special to me."

He then shifted in his seat, grabbing the steering wheel with both hands and growling back the emotions in his throat. "I just don't think that I..."

Kate continued to search Peter's face for some answer as to what was going to come next, and she felt her heart breaking even more as she watched Peter's face drop, the shine seemingly disappearing from his eyes.

"Just say it, Peter. If we need to pull off the band-aid, just do it in one quick motion." Kate's voice cracked under the turmoil she felt.

Peter looked up from the steering wheel. He finally turned to Kate and took her hand. "You know, you travel through life cruising down an interstate at eighty miles per hour. Every ten miles, there is a huge sign lit up to entice you with the next greatest thing, but you have to stay on that road for another ten miles to get to it."

Kate sat quietly, watching and listening to Peter through her tears.

"You finally get further down the road, and what happens? You are presented with yet another sign, 'Oh, you are just about there! Keep going!'"

Peter's emotions started to pick up steam, and his hands bounced from one part of the van to the other. "So, you keep going, waiting, expecting to have that great reward for your dedication in doing what the sign says!"

He paused and once again gave Kate's hand a squeeze, and she began to speak. "Peter I…"

He lowered his head, then looked back out the front windshield. "But then you slowly start to realize that you have driven yourself mad, completely into the ground chasing after the next great thing that's promised, yet it's never delivered."

Looking at Kate with what appeared to be desperation in his eyes, Peter continued, "And so, you start to take a look at yourself and truly examine, inwardly, that busy road you have been on for all those years, and all the traffic, all the rage, all the disappointments, the frustrations, and you think, 'ENOUGH! I wonder where that exit ramp goes?'"

Peter let go of Kate's hand and brushed the hair out of her eyes. "So, you finally dig deep and take that exit, leaving behind what you have always known, what you have always done, what was always expected, ignoring the empty promises…to discover just what that road less traveled has on it, the road called faith." He ran his hand down her cheek and wiped off the tears."Then, you discover a new life, a new way to see things, and you are rewarded not for how hard you work, but for merely having faith in the Lord that this road would be the one that leads you home."

As Kate reached up and touched his cheek, Peter grew quiet and then looked at her. "I have traveled this small road with faith in Christ that He would not only lead me home but build me a home in Him. Looking back on it all now, I just think that all this has been a part of His plan for me from the beginning. He set us all on a journey that would bring us all together, at one time, in one point, and in one place."

"Peter..." Kate said, sobbing, "I understand if you need to go your own way. I certainly will not hold you back, but what you are putting me through is definitely more painful than what I have already been through."

"Kate, listen to me. I know I have been rambling on and not making much sense." Peter wiped her cheeks again. "Kate," said Peter softly, "the Lord has helped me realize that I needed direction and guidance, and I can no longer live a happy and fulfilled life without having you in it. I'm not sure where we go from here. I just know how I feel when I'm not with you and how I feel when you are close."

Pete grew quiet and looked again at Kate. He gently lifted her chin so he could look her in the eye. "I have come to love you, Ms. Kate Bradigan. From the moment I saw you sitting at my kitchen table watching the sun come up, I knew that I really...REALLY wanted you to totally complicate my life, and I cannot spend another moment with the thoughts of you not being in it." Kate lowered her head and again wiped the tears off her eyes and cheeks.

Kate finally looked up, breathed deeply, and then slowly exhaled. The complete silence in the van was now deafening. "Kate, I know that when we first met, we really had no intention..." Pete fidgeted with the Caravan's dashboard buttons.

Kate dropped her head, trying to stifle back the tears and failing miserably. "Shh, Peter." Kate placed her finger on Pete's lips. "You have said what you needed to say. Now you need to hush, quit fidgeting, and listen to me." Kate squeezed his hands to keep them still.

Peter looked out the front windshield and then out his side window before bringing himself to the point of looking Kate in the eyes.

"Peter, I agree. Neither of us really planned for this. Now that we have gotten to know each other in the beginning and especially over the last several months, it's very clear that the Lord has been moving us in a certain direction. All things happened for His will and not our own," Kate said as Peter just sat quietly, his head slowly bobbing up and down like it was on a spring.

Kate reached up and took his face into her hands. "Peter, there is something that I have wanted to do since we first met...and also something that I need to say."

Peter closed his eyes, took a deep breath, and waited for her to speak again.

"Open your eyes, Peter, and look at me," she whispered.

He opened his eyes, and Kate was now a nose distance away from him, and he could feel her breath brushing across his cheeks. Kate sat holding his face and stared back into his eyes for what seemed like hours.

She smiled through her tears and then quickly smashed a cupcake into his forehead and dragged it down his nose. "You talk way too much!"

"Oh, Monsieur Pierre, I really want you to complicate my life, and I really...REALLY love you!" Kate quickly closed the distance between them and kissed him.

Kate stepped in front of the mirror in her uniform and lifted the campaign cover to her head. She then quickly snapped to attention and smiled. "Looking good, lady. Time to get this show on the road!"

She then wandered into the kitchen and took her favorite seat so that she could watch the sun come up over the mountains and waited for Peter to show up and make her some breakfast or at least a good cup of coffee.

She chuckled at the thought of her having a culinary degree but not having told him about it. *It's nice to be waited on sometimes. Well, if it is making Peter do the cooking, then it's nice to be waited on all the time.* She laughed and then grinned when Peter finally came around the corner and into the kitchen.

"What's so funny?" Peter stood looking at her.

"Oh, nothing. Will there be breakfast this morning at Granite Lodge?" Kate smirked.

He wasted no time in preparing coffee and placing it in front of her. He bowed profusely and slowly backed away. Kate burst out laughing. She softly clicked her wedding ring on the handle of the cup.

"C'est tout à fait magnifique, mademoiselle," Peter said while whipping some eggs and starting some toast. Then, he slid across the floor to kiss her forehead and then her ring.

"You two are really going to make me vomit," said Jaxon as he walked into the kitchen and mockingly stuck his finger in his mouth before sitting down.

"So, what's on the agenda today, District Ranger Kate Marcus?" Peter began setting breakfast on the table and smiling so big that his cheeks disappeared into his ears.

"Well, now that my rehabilitation is pretty much complete, I need to get out to the ranger station in Section 2 and see what sort of nonsense this Ranger Jaxon Bradigan doofus set up." Kate glanced at Jaxon and wrinkled her nose at him.

"I hear that this Ranger Smith is finally out of training and is up on some ridge a little further out. So, I will head out there to finally meet him and make sure he will be an acceptable member of the team." Kate poked at some scrambled eggs while looking through her journal.

"I'm really excited to get up to the substation and see the main lodge! It has been a while." Kate raised her head, looked out the window toward the mountain, and disappeared into thought.

Jaxon picked up a plate and helped himself to half of everything on the table. He poured it into his mouth, wiped his chin twice, and spoke mid-chew," Anyone else find the name of this town awkward?" He stood up and placed his dish in the sink.

Kate shook off her daydream when she heard Jaxon's voice. She and Peter looked at each other, smiled, then in unison said, "Never really thought about it."

"Ok, so this is the deal," Jaxon said while palming a piece of toast off Peter's plate and shoving it into his mouth.

Peter looked at Kate wide-eyed and mouthed, "Wow," before getting up to make another batch.

Jaxon chewed and talked, toast sweat sticking to his fingers and crumbs falling onto the table. "We have at least been able to improve the trail roads a bit. So, we have a two-hour drive to the substation and about a one to two-hour drive up the mountain via Mr. Pibbs.

"Do you normally eat like that?" Peter said as he walked over to Jaxon, poked at his stomach, and listened for the response.

Kate rolled out her maps so Jaxon could point out the trails and road, only to have him dump even more toast crumbs onto her charts. Kate looked up. "Seriously?! You just planning to leave things like that?"

"I honestly think he is picking stuff up off the floor and putting it into his mouth," Peter said while calmly stirring his coffee. Then, he sat down next to Kate to watch.

"Oh, sorry about that, Chief!" Jaxon licked his fingers and used them to brush off her maps. Then, just as quickly, he retreated from the kitchen table to a reasonably safe distance from Kate.

Jaxon took the prep towel off Pete's shoulder and wiped his mouth with it, then put it back. "Anyways, ranger Smith is probably another hour further across the mountain in a remote viewing area in Sector 4."

Jaxon looked at Pete. "It's probably going to be tomorrow or the next day before we are back in Honolulu, Pete," Jaxon said, polishing off the rest of the bacon. "But once you get the permanent station up and running, you will be able to get a proper duty schedule going so that it won't be so taxing on your entire team, Kate." Jaxon paused, looking around for anything else that was edible.

"I have a light day in the clinic, just a couple of patients needing follow-ups and then some work to do around Granite Lodge, like going to the grocery store to restock," Peter said while amusingly watching Jaxon eat anything that wasn't tied down.

"I've honestly never seen such a thing," Peter whispered to Kate. Pete sat, thinking. He then continued, "Well, maybe in a kangaroo or a pit bull with misfiring blobby bits."

Kate suddenly spit her coffee across the table and erupted in laughter. "Oh! I'm sorry, Jax. Please continue." She coughed a few times in between laughing.

Jaxon eyeballed Peter and Kate, then wiped his mouth and sat back down. "Listen, Kate, there really wasn't going to be any good time to touch on this, but..."

Kate looked over to Jaxon and then to Peter before focusing again on Jaxon. "Well, this day started out great, but let's get this over with. What? What could possibly be the issue?"

Peter took a small box out of his pocket and placed it in front of Kate. "I had that made for you." He then stood, backed away from the table, and stood with Jaxon.

Slowly, Kate opened the box to reveal its secret contents. Her face changed from mildly curious to hurt. Then, she appeared seemingly alone in the universe as tears ran down her face. Kate jumped up and turned her back to them both, spilling the contents onto the table.

Peter walked to Kate, put his arms around her, and whispered, "I had this made for you so that you could carry him with you wherever you go." He then kissed the back of her head and walked back to once again stand with Jaxon.

Kate looked down at the table and what now lay across it. She stood there, wiping the tears off her cheeks, and took a deep breath. "Thank you…both of you. Peter, would you please?"

"Jaxon took me along, and we went back up to where they found you. He didn't think it was a good idea, at least not until…?" Pete turned to Jaxon. "What was it you said? Something about timing and unknowns?"

Jaxon quickly turned his back and just shrugged before sticking his mouth into his pot of coffee.

"Well, anyway, when I got up to the area you were at, I found this. I had it turned into a necklace." Peter stepped forward and secured the white gold chain that was fashioned with the top portion of a mountain goat's horn. He also handed her a small leather pouch that contained a large swatch of snow-white fleece. Kate sobbed and clung to both Peter and Jaxon.

"Thank you to both of you. My two guys. I love you both!" Kate took a deep breath and whispered, "May the Lord bless you, my dear friend, and grant us the chance to see each other again one day." She then kissed the broken horn and tucked it down into her shirt.

Kate took a deep breath and rolled up her maps and charts. She then stood up, whacked Jaxon with the rolled-up tubes, and looked at Peter. "Well? Let's get this new adventure started."

17. A NEW DAY

Jaxon put up his hands for a high-five from Kate and Peter, not that either of them could actually reach his hand to perform the customary response.

Jaxon then walked out of the Granite Lodge and hopped into the truck. "Let's go, all you little people, er um…Chief. Team is waiting, and we still have a LOT of wilderness to cover!"

"I should be back at Granite Lodge by tomorrow evening, Peter," Kate said while getting into the truck.

"Don't overwork that leg, Kate. Take breaks! Oh, and…" Peter closed the door to the truck.

Kate clasped her seatbelt, squirmed around to get comfortable, and finally looked back up at Pete. "Yes? You were saying don't overwork, take breaks, and…?"

Pete leaned in and kissed her. "Don't lose your GPS tracker." Jaxon immediately let out a laugh, nearly falling out of the truck.

"And with that, away we go, Chief!" Jaxon turned over the engine and started down the gravel road. He then grabbed the shortwave. "This is Honolulu 1. We are enroute to Substation 1."

Jaxon looked over to Kate. "It's going to take us about two hours to get up there, which is really a big improvement since the last time you were there. So, sit back and try to relax a bit."

Kate closed her eyes and tried to rest, her hand holding onto the seatbelt and her head resting on her hand. After about fifteen minutes, they turned off what paved road there was and then onto a gravel road; at times, even calling it gravel was questionable.

For another ninety minutes, they bounced, rocked, and shook all the way up the trail until, finally, she could make out the little substation that led to another small roughed-out trail of crush-and-run gravel.

"They really got the little station up and running quick, didn't they?" Kate said, squinting to make out the shapes.

Jaxon chuckled. "Yeah, the wonders they are doing these days with shipping containers!"

"There are enough supplies to relay to the main station to be self-sufficient for six months and enough on hand at the main station to go fourteen months if need be. Granted, a lot of that is freeze-dried, canned, and stuff left over from WWII but surprisingly still edible."

As they got closer, Kate became a little irritated as she could see the new station decorated with "Welcome Aboard, Chief Marcus," written in pink and surrounded by large pink balloons. Kate looked over at Jaxon. "I suppose you had nothing to do with that, huh?"

"I have NO idea what you are talking about," Jaxon snorted and laughed out loud.

Jaxon pulled up to the station and said, "Your team assignments, schedules, and where everyone is right now are on your desk. There are also some rather nice fruit pastries provided by yours truly." Jaxon grinned again and said, "Welcome home, Chief Marcus."

After looking over the substation, Kate walked out, got into Mr. Pibbs, and waited for Jaxon. "Sorry, Chief!" Jaxon said, running out of the station five minutes later. "I had to make a quick call."

Kate nodded and yawned. "Whenever you are done fooling around." She waved her hand in the air.

Jaxon hopped into the truck and headed up the trail. "You were in a portion of Sector 3 when we had to come find you. Much of that area is still unknown, but I will make sure to get you the latest topologies and aerials that we have," Jaxon said as they bounced along the trail.

"We named the higher spot that's circled Shaw's Ridge, and the lower area, well, that's Bradigan's Plateau." Jaxon glanced out of the corner of his eye at Kate, but she just pretended not to hear.

"I'm sure that you will eventually want to get back up there, but only when you are ready, of course." Jaxon smiled and poked at Kate's arm.

"Two hands on the wheel, stretch. Or do I need to drive this thing?" Kate adjusted her campaign cover and bumped Jaxon with her shoulder.

"So where is this ranger Smith on the map? Don't think that I didn't notice that he was not at the meetings, nor at the so-called meet and greet." Kate said while making air quotes with her fingers.

"Yeah, he wanted to be there but had to do some pretty intense last-minute training. He couldn't manage to get back in time for all of that." Jaxon looked over to Kate to see if she was listening. "But rest assured, Chief. He is up on the ridges in Sector 4, keeping things tied down at one of our largest fire towers in the state."

Kate glanced out the window and kept jotting down notes in her journal.

Jaxon glanced out the window. "There are some really beautiful spots up there, and that new tower can just about overlook your entire new district and into the horizons."

"Pull over and let me drive," Kate chimed in. "I miss driving my old friend." Jaxon came to a stop and jumped out. Kate just casually slid across the bench seat.

Jaxon piped in without missing a beat, "I will drop you off at the trailhead to 4 once you look over the main station, and you can take the smaller 4x4. But that is going to take you a solid hour to get up there to him."

Kate hit a tree root growing across the path, causing Mr. Pibbs to bounce and making Jaxon hit his head on the roof. She chuckled. "That will work." She laughed and gunned the engine to continue up the path.

"They certainly don't make these for tall people," Jaxon said, rubbing his head and scrunching down in the passenger seat.

"Hey, what exactly is he doing up there on 4?" Kate looked over the massive steering wheel, then quickly down to tap on her GPS tracker that was clipped to her belt.

"He has been doing what we have all been doing, waiting for you to give some directions. We told him you were coming, though I'm not exactly sure if that registered with him." Jaxon glanced at Kate.

"What do you mean it *didn't register with him?* You know we can't have bullheaded foolishness up here. If you are going to be on my team, you are going to have to listen to what I say and do a little obeying." She glanced over at Jaxon.

"Understood, Chief. I can tell you this: Smith is at the top of his class! Instructors say that he is the best thing since sliced bread."

"You've met him?" Kate asked while taking on another root on the trail and bouncing Jaxon into the roof again.

"You have definitely been riding with Pete way too long!" Jaxon laughed, "But, yes, Smith is very impressive. I certainly like him. He will fit in with the team."

They rode in silence for a few moments, then Jaxon spoke up, "One quirk: he always seems to be looking off into the horizon like he is waiting for someone or something." Jaxon shrugged. "We are not exactly sure what. He doesn't talk about it, but maybe you can pull him back to reality? Either way, we will get it taken care of!" Jaxon said quickly and popped a salute as best as he could while being bounced around by Kate and Mr. Pibbs.

"Yeah, I don't like that in a new ranger. You must keep a level head and be focused. You and I are seasoned, Jax," Kate said, looking over at Jaxon, "and look what nearly happened to me, thinking I could go off on my own! Things can change rapidly, and we can't afford a dreamer. Dreamers bring unnecessary risks." Kate looked further up ahead of her and watched the trail they were driving on snake and wind up the mountain. After a couple of hours of loopbacks and various ruts, they finally came to the main ranger station.

"Look at that!" Kate's eyes grew huge. "What in the world…" she said, finding it hard to finish her sentence. "How?"

Jaxon looked out through the windscreen from under the sun visor. "You can thank your husband. He had the entire thing built over the course of the last six months." Jaxon hopped out of the truck.

"You should have seen the contractors and how they got all this in here without damaging the area! Pete said that the new substation he is going to build is going to be a wedding present for you. Don't tell him I told you. But this one, the main station, is in memory of a fallen ranger."

"A fallen ranger?" Kate said, sliding out of the truck and onto solid ground.

"Yes. Pete explained to me that he once met a ranger who was an Assistant District Forester back in the Smokey Mountains of North Carolina." Jaxon took off his hat and scratched his head. "Pete said he was probably the nicest person you could ever hope to meet. Thought the world of him." Jaxon bowed his head. "He unfortunately lost his life in the performance of his duties."

Kate walked up to the entrance and looked at the large brass plaque.

"In memory and honor of Curtis Jessen and to the men and women of the ranger and park services across our great land who have given their lives in that service."

Kate's eyes began to well up, and she sat silently on the steps to gather herself. "It's beautiful, Jaxon. We will be sure to take good care of everything we have been given and honor those who are no longer with us.

Jaxon took Kate by the hand as she stood up and took another look at the station and the grounds. "It's a little smaller than Granite Lodge but even more stunning to look at!" OH! I'm so glad that you saved the fireplace from the old homestead."

"We revamped that fireplace, so it's now an outdoor barbeque area, and yes, I really think this station is just a pinch smaller than Granite Lodge. But man, what a beauty it is," said Jaxon.

Jaxon looked at Kate. "One thing I do know is, your boy must be seriously loaded, which brings up the question as to WHY he drives around in junky old vehicles."

Kate smirked at Jaxon. "You mean the executive limo?"

"Is THAT what he calls that stupid Dodge Caravan?!" Jaxon started laughing.

"They are in the process of running electrical lines up to this area from the substation way back down the mountain, but THAT is going to take a little longer. Until then, we will be running primarily on solar and a diesel/propane generator." Jaxon opened the door and led Kate inside.

Senior Ranger Ed Franks and two other rangers met them in the lobby. "Welcome home, Chief." Franks reached out and shook her hand. "Our communications room is just behind the service desk."

Kate nodded to Franks and then looked at Jaxon.

Jaxon then ushered her on a grand tour. "We also have oil lamps for the evenings when you really want that turn-of-the-century rustic vibe. Most of the lodge areas, like the conference room and the various bunk rooms, are closed up to simply save on resources until we get the power lines ran."

Kate nodded and continued jotting down notes. "Excellent! This is all stunning! Let's grab a quick lunch, and then you can get me up to Trailhead 4." Kate turned and looked at Jaxon and Franks, who were trailing behind her as she looked over everything.

Kate sat quietly but rather restless, checking her watch practically every five minutes. She kept looking out the various windows, knowing that the trailhead into Sector 3 was no more than a mile from where she was sitting.

Jaxon sat watching Kate and finally broke her thoughts. "You sure you want to do this, Chief? You know, I can come with you if you want?"

He then stood up, walked over to a vehicle sign-out board, and grabbed another set of keys for the smaller 4x4.

Kate shook her head and brought her attention back to reality. "No, I got this. I will meet up with Ranger Smith later this afternoon or early evening. I have my gear, my new satellite phone, and, of course, my GPS tracker. Once I meet up with him, we will start moving back over the ridges toward here, our new station..." Kate paused in thought. "But I think we will take a detour and come across and down through Sector 3." Kate looked at her maps, tracing them with her finger.

"Uh, you sure that's a good… You really need to give yourself a little time to..." Jaxon rubbed his chin while he spoke before Kate cut him off mid-sentence.

"Smith does know to stay put, right?" Kate glanced up at Jaxon. "I'm not going to go running all over the mountainside again, and the last thing I need right now is a green, wet-behind-the-ears kid who doesn't know a pine from an oak!"

Kate grabbed her backpack and headed for the 4x4. She tied all of her equipment to the carrier on the back as she started through her checklist. "Extra fuel, water, food, maps, compass, trekking poles, GPS tracker, flashlight and batteries, first aid kits. Yeah, I think that about does it for a short trip."

Jaxon walked over with Kate. "He isn't going anywhere until you get onsite." Jaxon turned the ignition and brought the 4x4 to life. "At least it's early summer. All you will need to be seriously concerned with are the mosquitoes. Look, about three miles up that way there is the small trailhead to Section 4. Most of the brush has been cleared enough for you to make most of the trip on the 4x4, but the last half mile or so, you are going to have to hoof it in." Jaxon chuckled and then slowly started to walk back to the station. Are you going to be able to manage that with that gimpy leg, Chief?" he turned back around and puffed out his chest.

Kate looked up and glared at him. "Ranger Jaxon Bradigan, I guarantee you that I could still outrun you, and this nifty piece of carbon fiber and titanium will fit ever so nicely where my boot would LOVE to go right now."

Kate revved the 4x4 and looked at Jaxon. "Now, I suggest you and a couple of other rangers, when they finally show up, go back and start cleaning the substation! It looked to be infected with some sort of pink mold!" She shouted at him as she drove off for Trailhead 4. "And I don't want my stations looking like some sort of deranged nightmare of a cupcake!"

Kate drove across the compound and up into the woods. "Ok, these trails certainly have been cleared out pretty good. I will give them that one," Kate said while slowing down to look for the entrance to Section 4.

"Ok. . .OK! That's pretty obvious. I must give the Power Rangers another kudos." She slowed down to a wooden sign that simply said "4." She came to a stop and called into the station. "This is Chief Marcus, headed into Section 4. Next check-in will be about an hour."

"Copy that, Honolulu 1," the 2-way responded back. Kate secured the mic and slowly proceeded up the trail. The further in she drove, the more the trees began to block out large swaths of sunlight and cast odd shadows across the forest floor and into her mind.

Kate pressed on, constantly looking over her shoulder and thinking that she could hear something coming up from behind her. It took a large root on the pathway to bounce her mind back into the here and now.

With each turn of the pathway, she saw images of Gruff and Abaddon fighting for the rights to her life and how Abaddon had killed Shaw.

She slowed and came to a stop. Then, she took her necklace out from her shirt and looked down at it. "I know you made this area safe for me, Gruff. God provided you, and you provided for me! I WILL not fear. Fear is NOT of God! Great is our Lord, and Mighty is HIS Hand!" Kate tucked the necklace back into her shirt and headed back up the trail.

"Honolulu Substation 1, this is Chief Marcus. I have finally made it to the top of Trailhead 4. Will be on foot." She chuckled for just a moment at the irony, seeing as she only had one left. "I will be on one foot for the next bit to meet up with Smith. Can you relay a message and let him know."

"Uh, yeah, not sure how to respond to that last transmission, but will do, Chief," came back the response from Lara.

"Ok, first thing they are going to work on is a little radio etiquette. This isn't Snapface or Chatbox!" She then secured the 4x4, took out her hiking poles, rigged up her backpack so that the weight was set right on her hips, and headed up the trail. "Ok, Smith, you better be where you are supposed to be."

As she walked up the trail using her hiking poles for support and stability, Kate thought, *Eh, only one leg; while yes, it can be inconvenient, it certainly hasn't slowed my stride down any.* Kate focused and continued blazing up the trail, whacking some branches out of the way with her poles.

"Ok, let's not push things. I promised Peter I would take breaks." She paused a moment, wiped the sweat off her forehead, and opened her canteen just in time for all the hair on her arms to act like they were stuck in a freezer. Kate lowered the canteen as the hair on the back of her neck stood on end.

Slowly, the entire environment around her came to an abrupt halt as the forest and the very mountain itself became deathly silent, and nothing moved. The only sound she could hear was her own breathing and now her heartbeat, which was beginning to echo in her ears.

Her mind began to float as her eyes slowly searched the forest. She could just make out the end of the trail and the opening that would certainly give way to the clearing and the Section 4 Tower, but she couldn't move... She dared not move.

Kate's eyes and head slowly moved, carefully searching, and always coming back to the opening just a hundred yards or so just ahead of her.

"What did she say that wolf's name was again?" Jaxon whispered to Peter as they stood in the hospital room, looking down at Kate.

"She said its name was Abaddon." Peter looked back at Jaxon.

"Yeah, that's its name," Jaxon said. "You know we never found it again when we went back up there. Completely gone from the area. I will make sure to take you out there in a few weeks when we know she is out of danger, and I will show you where we found them all."

Kate shook her head. "I thought I just dreamed that?! No wonder they didn't want me up here alone. PTSD? NOW is really not the time!"

A cold breeze rushed through the trail and up from behind her, knocking her cover off and onto the ground and blowing her hair forward as if having been passed by a bullet train. Kate gasped and looked around before dropping to the ground to get her hat. Then, as soon as it stopped, the forest erupted with life once again, insects happily returning to their songs.

Kate finally exhaled nervously and started to get to her feet when, suddenly, the entire forest came to a halt again, and a long, deep, guttural noise echoed across what felt like the entire mountain.

Kate covered her ears for a moment to think. "I have to make it to the tower." Then, she began moving inch by inch before picking up her pace, first into a walk and then into a full-out run.

Once again, the sound echoed across what Kate felt was the entire face of the earth. She finally dove through the clearing, backpack and all, into the full glow of sunlight. Kate tossed the backpack off and rolled over onto her back to look up at the sun coming through the scaffolding of a HUGE fire tower.

Kate waited a moment, then looked back into the forest and over her shoulder the best she could to take in what she could of the area. "Where is that blasted Smith?" she grumbled as she slowly stood up.

18. THE NARROW GATE

Gruff opened his eyes, finally feeling the warm sun and breeze across his face as he looked down on the valley. He had left what seemed like a lifetime ago.

He could see the community he was once part of below. The parents stood around, ignoring everything that didn't glorify themselves and taking credit for things that they could then lord over one another.

Gruff looked and watched the unruly kids as they ran around, expecting to see them acting just as obnoxious as they always have been, but…

He shifted his footing and looked up into the sun, loving the smells of the spring and early summer grasses carried by the breezes. Then, he looked back down and out to the horizon.

Closing his eyes, Gruff breathed deeply, knowing that he was now free from the past that he could see below, and a newness in spirit cleansed him. He now saw things with fresh eyes, new perspectives, and a closeness with the Creator.

Gruff opened his eyes, again looking out onto everything. He then tossed his head into the air and let out a loud and very long guttural bellow, which, had he been any bigger, could have caused a small rockslide!

All the valley, and most likely the entire mountain, stood still, got very quiet, and looked up to where Gruff was now standing. His fleece had been washed clean, and he stood tall and proud, holding his chest out with authority and strength.

Gruff whispered to himself, "My Lord, My Creator, thank you for my life. Direct my hooves in your pathways evermore, and may I proclaim your loving kindness all my days."

The noise from Gruff shocked the community below. A great number of them panicked and ran in hopes of being hidden by the rocks in the mountains.

But the kids, all of the kids, stopped their playing, looked up, and squinted. Finally, Lucas stepped forward slightly and whispered to the others, "Is that Gruff? I think that really is Gruff!" The kids looked back and forth at each other in amazement. "I really think that's him, but…but what's happened to him?" Lucas continued to whisper to the others.

Lucas shouted excitedly, "He really looks fantastic! I have got to go see him…I really need to talk to him!"

The small band of kids slipped away from the adults, who were still in various states of confusion, and ran excitedly towards Gruff and up the small hill to the ledge that overlooked the area. They came to an abrupt stop just short of where Gruff was standing.

They all looked up at Gruff and momentarily backed away when they saw the deep scars across his face and the long marks down his body, which his fleece was unable to cover completely.

Lucas slowly emerged from behind the other kids. He hung his head low and walked forward before shamefully saying, "Gruff, some terrible things have happened. I have done some horrible things, and everything was my fault!"

Lucas flew into a sobbing wail and placed his head against Gruff's leg. "I'm so sorry for what I have done, what WE have done to you." All the kids were now beginning to sob.

Gruff looked down. "Lucas, I'm so glad to see you again, my little brother. Come up here, and let's talk for a little bit."

The goat moved forward and leapt up onto the ledge to stand next to Gruff. The rest of the band also moved forward so they could hear.

"Lucas, we cannot undo or change what has already been done," Gruff said, looking out to the others who had gathered. "But let me tell you, you don't have to perpetuate the evilness that you have become accustomed to.

"Oh sure, you can choose to continue living the way you do, or you can put your old self aside and discover the truth of what the Creator really desires for you." Lucas and all the others looked up at Gruff, all of them now in complete tears.

"How DARE you show your face around here!" Gruff's mother, Nannie, burst through the small band of kids and tried to get up on the ledge so she could bleat more profanities at Gruff. However, she failed miserably and slid back into the kids, cursing all the more.

"It's YOUR fault, Gruff, that poor little Remi was killed. He was such a dear thing and never did anything to anyone!" She turned her attention back to the band of kids, who had stopped crying but now also started standing a little more stiff-necked towards her.

Nannie began to quickly head-butt each of them back down the hill. "ALL of you get back to where you belong!" She then angrily turned back to Gruff, and evil flared from her eyes. "Do you really think you are so smart? Do you really think you are better than us?" she bleated and bloviated.

"I am telling you now like I have told you since you were born, you were born an idiot, are an idiot, and will forever be a big idiot. You are nothing more than a worthless, disgusting stain on the earth, goat."

Gruff stood and watched her, quietly listening, and allowed her to catch her breath before she laid into him again.

"I don't care how clean you may make your outside; you are still a filthy, nasty, disgusting, poor excuse for a living thing, and I have hoped since your birth that the Creator would just strike you down." Nannie paused and panted.

Gruff raised his eyebrows and pointed his ear forward. "You have known about the Creator?"

Nannie paused for a moment and then looked at Gruff with even more hatred. "I will not have you corrupting our youth with your stupid ideas!" She screamed, completely hysterical. Turning in circles and stamping on the ground, she said, "It's a shame that you just didn't die out there somewhere across the mountains. Your Creator would have done us all a favor!"

She paused and panted again." I wish William would have listened to me and left you out for Abaddon."

Gruff's ear shot up. "You KNEW about Abaddon?!"

"Oh, don't act so surprised, Gruff. I knew about Abaddon, and I made an agreement with him to let him have one of the kids for dinner from time to time and leave the rest of the community alone." Nannie spat at Gruff.

She looked back at the community and then glared at Gruff. "The only one that ever had a problem with this whole arrangement was William. HE was the only reason why you didn't get fed to that wolf early on. All William ever did after you got a little older was talk about you and worry about YOU."

"But William beat me ruthlessly." Gruff glanced around. "Where is William?" Gruff looked around again and then down into the community.

"Oh, you are such a blithering imbecile. He beat you to placate ME, you blasted fool!" Nannie shrieked, nearly hysterical. "That blasted useless, no good, donkey-tailed father took off into the mountains to look for you when you left. He never came back. So now I HAVE TO DO EVERYTHING AROUND HERE!" Nannie once again launched into a tirade of profanity, spinning around like she was fully crazed.

Nannie stopped spinning and spat onto the ground, her rage and hate brimming as her mouth began to foam. "Hear ME, Gruff! I swear by my own blood, by whatever is above, below, seen, unseen, or by whatever you think you know! I will make sure that these kids and the future kids' kids forget all about you!" She turned to walk away with her snout and her tail stuck in the air.

"Do you really think you can change or do anything now?" Gruff calmly said, looking down at her and then over to the kids gathered just at the base of the small hill.

Nannie turned and looked back at him. In her rage, she had completely forgotten about Lucas, who was standing next to Gruff. She then quickly turned back to the kids she had pushed off the hill.

"Let me tell YOU something, Mother," Gruff paused and looked back down at the kids, "it only takes ONE living in faith, integrity, and humbleness of serving the Creator, and THAT, my mother, can change the course of everything..." Gruff looked down at Lucas, who was watching and listening to every word that was spoken, and smiled at his young brother.

Nannie turned her back, snorted, and stomped dust and gravel back at Gruff. "I'm done talking to you! You just think you are better than us. You will never be anything more than what I said...a goat! And THAT is exactly what I'm going to teach these kids!"

Gruff resumed his stance and looked back out over the horizon. "You will see what you want to see, Mother, totally blinded by your own foolishness." Nannie stopped walking and partly turned her head.

"But let me tell you this: you cannot stop what has now started. Go on. Look at those young kids." Gruff smiled again at Lucas, then turned and walked back off the ledge and further up the hill.

Once he reached the pinnacle, he turned around and looked down over the valley and the community down below and again let out a long guttural bellow that sounded across the mountain face and back down into the valley.

The community once again paused to look up at Gruff. But then, all the kids responded in kind, and they all let out the loudest bleat their tiny bodies could manage.

Zeki suddenly landed on Gruff's head. "Now THAT, my brother, is powerful! May the strength, grace, and peace that only comes from our Creator be with you!" He then flew up into the tower to watch.

Gruff suddenly felt a familiar hand stroking his nose and then scratching behind his ear. "I assume you are Ranger Smith?" Kate wiped tears from her face and jumped, latching onto Gruff and burying her face in his neck. "I've so wanted to see you again, to thank you, to say how much you mean to me." Kate was now engaged in full, heaving sobs.

Gruff bent his neck as much as possible and shoved his nose into Kate's hair. His eyes closed, and he deeply breathed in the smell of fresh jasmine and the wildflowers of the plains that seemed to now pale in comparison to just being close to her.

Gruff made soft sounds with his throat, almost like he was singing to her, as she continued to hug and rock back and forth, causing her to cry even more. This was Gruff's new family. This was what the Creator had prepared him for since birth. He would take care of and protect Kate for as long as he was able to do so.

Zeki flew down from the tower, landed on Gruff's head, and spread his wings out to cover Gruff face and partially envelop Kate. "You were once a prisoner, Gruff, and are now set free."

Kate momentarily looked up at Zeki. "I don't know or understand, but I can only assume you had something to do with all of this." She smiled and dove back into Gruff's neck, gently stroking Zeki's wing with her other hand.

Gruff looked up at Zeki the best he could with a small human wrapped around his neck. "I've had much time to think on your prisoner comment. You always told me that there was more, and indeed there was! I was born in a prison, raised in a prison, lived in a prison, and was prepared to die in a prison."

Gruff paused. "You came and opened the door, told me that there was more than what I could see or what I was told. You have to have courage and a seed of faith to take that first step outside the walls and discover for yourself." Zeki nodded as Gruff spoke.

"And, what then? What would I have wasted if there was nothing to be found outside the cell?" Gruff looked up at Zeki again. "I would have just wasted a little time, which was already passing me by anyway, closed off. But what did I have to gain if what you said was true? OH! Zeki, my beautiful little friend... I had EVERYTHING to gain, and now I see!"

Gruff suddenly let out another long, loud bellow, praising the Creator, and, once again, tiny little voices from down on the plain responded with their answer.

Kate let go of Gruff's neck and wiped the remaining tears off her cheeks. She looked at him, looked quickly at Zeki and then Lucas, who was still in the middle of them. "Something tells me you just needed to do that, didn't you, Gruff?"

Kate sat down to look out over the valley and at the band of goats below. Then, she wrapped her arms around Gruff's neck and held onto him tightly. Gruff immediately shoved his snout back into Kate's hair, snorted the sweet smell of jasmine and wild berries, and grunted happily.

"I've really missed you, Gruff. My heart was broken, and no one would tell me what had happened to you!" Kate said, reaching for her two-way radio. Kate keyed the mic. "This is Chief Marcus checking in. I have found Ranger Smith and I'm with him now."

"Jaxon, why didn't you tell me when I have asked all this time?!" There was a long pause in the answer back.

"Come back, Base. If I have to come off this mountain to get a response, there is going to be someone that gets hurt." Kate keyed the mic again.

Jaxon, Peter, Ed Franks, and Dr. Philips slowly emerged from the small path that led back down the mountain and walked toward Kate. She shook her head at all of them and could feel her irritation and anger reaching a peak. Gruff turned and then stood between her and the fury she was feeling.

"Kate," Jaxon was the first to speak. "I didn't want to say anything until we knew that Smith, er...Gruff was going to survive, let alone even you!" Jaxon said, now scratching on Gruff's ear.

"We didn't want you to have to go through reliving the entire ordeal over again. Once we saw that you both were going to be ok. That's when it became QUITE apparent, he wasn't going anywhere and basically refused to leave."

Franks spoke up. "We could only assume that he had some kind of bond with you and was waiting for you. He is the first ever to go through this training, but he more than excelled, better than most human rangers," Franks laughed. "But he took to his service animal training, and we thought he would then make a darn good member of the team." Franks patted on Gruff's back.

Kate coughed for a moment. "I see." Kate glared at Jaxon. "So. . .remind me to beat you when we get off this mountain, and Gruff isn't here to hold me back."

Kate turned to Peter. "Did YOU know?" Peter quickly darted behind Jaxon.

"Uh, I just want to let you know that behind me is probably the worst place you could possibly choose to hide when Kate is gunning for you," Jaxon said, lifting his arm so he could peer down at Pete.

Pete held around Jaxon's waist, glanced up at him, then over to Kate and said, "Jaxon called me from the substation and told me I was needed at the main station. So, I high-tailed it up there and met with Ed." Peter quickly added, "We both then went up to the main station. Dr. Philips was there, and he told me what had happened. I convinced them that we needed to come up the rest of the way to be with you."

Kate scowled at all of them, then reached down to adjust the gear harness that Gruff was wearing. He leaned into her side and snorted at the valley below. "I don't know if you can understand me, Gruff, but you are certainly more than that bunch of goats down there and SOME of the rangers up here!"

As she looked down into the valley, Kate scratched behind Gruff's ear and said, "You are my protector! I thank my Creator, Lord, and Savior, Christ Jesus, for bringing you to me."

Looking at the group of men standing there, Kate said, "Now, gentlemen, let's say we set up and camp here tonight since I have all my fellows with me. Then, we will get over to Sector 3 tomorrow."

"AND you have two more!" came a wheezing shout from the tree line.

Kate looked over the top of the rangers and saw Todd McMillan roll out of the forest, beet red but with a smile on his face. He was packing two

HUGE fanny packs that had to be linked together to ensure they could wrap his circumference.

"I think this one belongs to you? Found her wandering around, lost in the woods." Todd laughed as Lara peered out from behind him, clearly embarrassed that he had carried her practically the entire way.

"Director McMillan! How did you…?" Kate stammered.

"Oh, hey, it's just Todd now. Retirement is all official." He beamed.

"That's wonderful news, Todd! But how did you?" Kate still stammering.

"Look, my little darlin', I'm hugely fat. I huff, I puff, I wheeze when I walk, AND I'm surprised that Elon Musk doesn't have a Starlink satellite, or two, orbiting me, but given all that, it doesn't make me an invalid!" Todd grinned.

Kate grew a little more embarrassed. "Oh, I certainly didn't mean anything or imply..."

Todd tossed back his head and laughed again. "One thing you are going to have to do, Kate, if I may say, is you are going to have to ease up a bit. Take a joke. You are too high-strung. ENJOY life and these friends that you have; don't waste it. You made it, little lady. You are at the pinnacle of what you had been working towards, for now at least." Todd panted and wiped his forehead.

"Besides, though I look like a giant puffball, I love me, I love people, and I GUARANTEE you that I could beat your entire ranger team back down off this mountain!" Todd glanced back at Lara and gave her a wink, then smiled as everyone laughed.

"Now, move this big gorilla out of my way." Todd gave Jaxon a playful shove. "Because I have graham crackers, chocolate, and marshmallows in these packs that are just begging for a campfire, and man, oh man, do I have some stories for you!" Todd said, patting his oversized accoutrements.

The sun began to drown the area in glorious golds and reds before giving way to an infinitely starry night. Eventually, the rest of the newly hired rangers showed up, and they all sat around the campfire, laughing and reflecting on any topic that happened to come up.

Gruff slipped away and sat just a few yards from the group with a rather large old crow and a couple of younger goats that managed to sneak away from their parents.

The fire slowly burned down over the hours, giving way to a bed of coals that provided just enough light to see each other as they sat quietly and reflected on the events.

Peter sat behind Kate, allowing her to use him as a pillow, and pulled the blanket a little tighter around her while they both quietly watched Jaxon poking at the fire with a long stick.

Ed Franks watched the curious menagerie that had gathered with Gruff. "You know, Chief, I really think you have the beginnings of a couple of new recruits there."

Jaxon looked over to where Gruff was sitting with two of the kids and scratched his head. He then palmed his mouth briefly and watched the old crow hop from one of their heads to the other and then wallow in the dirt before repeating the entire sequence. He marveled for a moment and shook his head. He then shook his head again and said, "I still don't understand." Jaxon looked back at Kate. "I wonder what Gruff and that old crow are talking with them about?"

Peter kissed the back of Kate's head before resting his cheek on it. Kate looked at Jaxon and then over to Gruff and his odd little gathering and smiled.

"Oh, I can assure you, Jaxon, that it's something absolutely wonderful and completely glorious!"